Help us Rate this book...
Put your initials on the
Left side and your rating
on the right side.
1 = Didn't care for
2 = It was O.K.
3 = It was <u>great</u>

_____ 1 2 3
_____ 1 2 3
_____ 1 2 3
_____ 1 2 3
_____ 1 2 3
_____ 1 2 3
_____ 1 2 3
_____ 1 2 3
_____ 1 2 3
_____ 1 2 3
_____ 1 2 3
_____ 1 2 3
_____ 1 2 3
_____ 1 2 3
_____ 1 2 3

DATE DUE

NOV 2 1 2011		
JAN 2 3 2012		
NOV 2 1 2018		
AUG 0 5 2022		

DEMCO 38-296

THE BROTHERHOOD

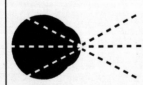

This Large Print Book carries the Seal of Approval of N.A.V.H.

THE BROTHERHOOD

A PRECINCT 11 NOVEL

JERRY B. JENKINS

THORNDIKE PRESS

A part of Gale, Cengage Learning

GALE
CENGAGE Learning™

Detroit • New York • San Francisco • New Haven, Conn • Waterville, Maine • London

GALE
CENGAGE Learning

LIBRARY OF CONGRESS CATALOGING-IN-PUBLICATION DATA

Jenkins, Jerry B.
  The brotherhood : a Precenct 11 novel / by Jerry B. Jenkins.
    p. cm. — (Thorndike Press large print Christian fiction)
  ISBN-13: 978-1-4104-3529-3 (hardcover)
  ISBN-10: 1-4104-3529-6 (hardcover)
  1. Police—Illinois—Chicago—Fiction. 2. Gangs—Fiction. 3. Chicago (Ill.)—Fiction. 4. Large type books. I. Title.
PS3560.E485B76 2011b
813'.54—dc22   2010049954

Published in 2011 by arrangement with Tyndale House Publishers, Inc.

Printed in Mexico
1 2 3 4 5 6 7 15 14 13 12 11

To the police officers in my family:
  Harry Jenkins
  Jim Jenkins
  Jeoff Jenkins
  Tim Jenkins
  Bruce Thompson
  Klaude Thompson
  Harold Sprague
  Rollie Tuttle
  Burt Tuttle

With thanks to John Perrodin for research assistance

It was enough to make anyone want to be a cop. But for the young collegian idly watching the CBS local evening newscast in Chicago one fall evening in 2008, something deep within was stirred anew.

The anchorwoman dispassionately reported horrifying murder statistics the news team had gathered, but the wannabe police officer was taking it personally. Why? He had his ideas.

Maybe it was the similarity between the street gangs doing most of the shootings and the bullies who had terrorized his friends when he was a kid — and who had tried to terrorize him.

More than 120 people had been shot and killed in Chicago that summer. That was almost double the number of American soldiers killed in Iraq during the same time. Beyond that, nearly 250 others had been shot and wounded in Chicago.

If there was anything — even one thing — he could do to thwart these thugs once he earned his badge, he would do it with all that was in him.

1
JUSTICE FREAK

1:58 a.m., Friday, December 16, 2011
"Wanna take this one yourself, Rook?"

Boone Drake shot his partner a double take. The 911 dispatcher had broadcast a domestic disturbance in progress at a seedy apartment building on West Jackson Boulevard in Chicago's most dangerous precinct, Harrison, District 11.

"Myself?"

"I mean take the lead," Jack Keller said, eyes fixed on the pavement as he maneuvered the blue and white Crown Vic squad through icy streets. "I'll have your back."

Boone didn't want to sound too eager, but there was no way he'd turn this down. He had excelled in twenty-three weeks of training at the academy and was just weeks into his eighteen-month period as a probationary police officer. Boone hoped someday he would look as comfortable in his gear as Keller did. The press described his partner

9

as rugged or chiseled, not bad for a man in his late fifties with a short crop of gray hair.

Boone took pride in being in shape and athletic, but there was no hiding his youth. He couldn't let that get in the way if he took the lead on this call. He tightened the Velcro on his bulletproof vest and ran his fingers across his Sam Browne utility belt, including his 9mm Beretta.

"It's put up or shut up time, Boones," Keller said as they neared the address.

"Sure, I'm in."

"Head full of all that training? Planning your approach?"

Boone couldn't stifle a laugh. "All I can think of is the POLICE acronym."

Professionalism, Obligation, Leadership, Integrity, Courage, Excellence.

Keller shook his head. "Big help if this guy comes at you. Remember your moves if he's armed?"

"Hope so."

"You hope so. Well, so do I. I don't want to have to put one in a guy because you can't subdue him."

"Long as I know you're there, I'll be okay. You bringin' in the M4?"

"That's way too much firepower for inside. My 9 will be plenty."

Once Keller skidded to the curb out front,

blue lights dark to avoid attention, Boone grabbed his nightstick and his uniform cap and slid out. As he slipped the stick into the ring on his belt, some druggies on the corner, their breath illuminated by the streetlight, called out, "Five-oh!"

Keller turned on them. "Shut up or you're next!"

The gangbangers cursed the cops and flashed signals but quickly disappeared. As Boone rushed the front door, it occurred to him that those types were the real reason he was a cop. It was about the gangs. It had always been about the gangs.

Keller grabbed his sleeve and slowed him. "Don't get ahead of yourself."

When Boone got inside and mashed the elevator button, Keller passed him on his way to the stairs. "On the other hand, we don't want to be waiting when someone's in danger."

They trotted up the stairs, gear jangling and leather squeaking, Boone aware of Keller panting as they reached the fourth floor. An apartment door was open a couple of inches and an elderly woman in a bathrobe peeked out, hands clasped as if in prayer. She nodded toward the next apartment.

Keller whispered to her to close and lock

her door and back away from it. He unholstered his weapon and fell in behind Boone, who stepped before the next apartment. A man inside shouted; a woman whimpered.

Boone spread his feet, rapped hard, and called out, "Police department! Open the door!"

The couple fell silent.

"Now!" Boone said, laboring to sound authoritative.

The man whispered; the woman whined.

"Open the door, sir!"

"He's got a knife to my throat!"

"And I'll cut her if you try comin' in!"

"You don't want to do that, bro! Now open up and let's talk about it."

The man swore.

"Don't do anything you'll regret, man. Come on now."

The door swept open and there the man stood, reeking of alcohol, the woman locked in the crook of his arm, a six-inch steak knife at her Adam's apple. Boone ran through all his training in an instant. He knew where to grab, where to twist, how to use his weight, the angles, everything.

But when the man threw the woman aside and lunged at him, everything left Boone. He threw an uppercut so vicious that when it caught the bad guy under the chin, Boone

12

feared he might have killed him.

The knife, which dragged a jagged tear under Boone's shirt pocket but had not damaged his vest, went flying. The man's head snapped back, his feet left the floor, and when he landed, he tumbled back and smacked his head against the far wall as he dropped in a heap.

The woman squealed and ran to him, falling to her knees. Boone held her back as Keller radioed for an ambulance.

Two hours later, as Boone banged out his report, the woman had been pronounced healthy and returned home, her boyfriend was in the drunk tank with a concussion, and Keller was still chuckling. "You gonna teach that move at the academy, Boones?"

"Am I in trouble for that?"

"You kiddin'? You were in imminent danger. And so was she. And so was I. You subdue an arrestee any way you need to. Though I got to say, that was creative. Must've felt good, eh?"

Boone nodded. "Can you believe she's refusing to press charges?"

"Predictable. But *you're* going to press. He came at you with a deadly weapon."

It had become Boone's routine at the end

of the first watch every night to change clothes in the downstairs locker room while listening to the veterans swap war stories. Domestic cases were one thing. Standing up to the ultimate playground bullies — that was living. Sometimes he would slowly change out of his uniform, just to hear another story of gangbangers getting theirs. That early morning a heavyset veteran regaled his colleagues with an arrest he and his partner had made at the end of the shift.

"Perps are liars, right? We all know that. We're patrollin' a neighborhood where the Latin Kings been terrorizing people. See a kid, early twenties, cruisin' like he's casing a house. Pull him over. He wants out of the car right now, ya know? I tell him to stay right where he is and show his hands. I call in the plate, and 'course it's stolen.

"When I approach, he's giving me all the is-anything-wrong-Officer bull. Covered with tattoos. We roust him out and cuff him and start asking what he's doing, whose car is it, all that. He says he's just coming from his cousin's. I ask him his cousin's name. Clearly makes one up. I ask him the address, he fumbles with that too. I ask him whose car he's driving, he swears it's his but left the title home. I ask him can we search the car, he says sure.

14

"While my partner is searching the car, I'm quizzing this guy six ways from Sunday, telling him I think he's lying, that he knows nobody around there and I don't believe it's his car. He's swearin' on a stack of Bibles and his mother's life and his baby girl's life that it's his car. Partner turns up a .22 and a little stash of coke.

"I say, 'That's on you, bro.'

"He says, 'Not mine. Never saw it before.'

"I say, 'Found in your car.'

"He says, 'Ain't my car.' "

The locker room resounded with laughter.

On his way home, Boone's amusement at the story turned to a hard resolve. He had learned early that cops embellish their arrest stories to make themselves look good and the gangbangers look like buffoons. And while some of them might be, the sad fact was that the Chicago PD was losing the war with the gangs. They were more organized than ever, growing at unprecedented rates, and gaining ground all over the city.

Boone had never wanted to just work a shift, put in his time, and collect a check. He'd heard all the stories of wide-eyed, idealistic rookies coming in with grand ideas of changing the world, only to become jaded cynics who realized they were never going to make a difference. That's how the gangs won. They were more dedicated to their tasks than the cops were to theirs. Boone simply would not accept that.

Arriving at his apartment, Boone slipped silently into bed with Nikki, his wife of three years. As usual, he remained awake until she rose to tend to the baby, Josh. Then they would rehearse their respective days before Boone went to sleep.

Josh slept in longer than normal that morning, yet not only could Boone not drift off, his excitement also woke Nikki early.

"So what happened, big guy?" she said, rolling to squint at him. "You obviously have something to tell me."

She clearly did not find Boone's first collar as amusing as Jack Keller had. He pushed her long, dark hair away from her face. "C'mon, babe. This is a big deal."

"Well, of course I'm proud, but really, Boone, is every arrest going to be this dangerous?"

"Nah. Well, maybe. Some even more. You know if that guy had caught me with the knife, Keller would've shot him dead."

"How pleasant."

"I'm just saying . . ."

When they heard Josh, Nikki fetched him

and brought him into their bed. Still breast-
feeding, their son was focusing now, able to
lock eyes with his mother and dad and be
coaxed into smiles and coos. Presently she
passed him to Boone, who sat up and
burped him, then held him before his face.
"You know you and your mom are my life,
don't you? Yes, you do."

Nikki laughed. "Is that how you talk on
the job? Is it? Yes, it is."

Soon she darkened the room, took the
baby to the farthest end of the flat, and let
Boone sleep. He dreamed of a house. Nothing spectacular. He and Nikki always said
they wanted just enough grass to mow.
Boone had started as a PPO with a salary
in the midforties, to increase by a thousand
a month after a year and then to nearly sixty
thousand at the end of eighteen months.
That was their timeline, their goal. A house
with a yard before Josh was two.

No one was surprised that Boone Drake
had grown up to be a policeman. From his
days of grade school and Sunday school,
through Little League, Scouting, junior
high, high school, and college, he had been
a better-than-average student and a star
athlete. More importantly, he and his three
younger brothers had been raised in a small

town in central Illinois by an old-school ex-Marine civil servant (who eventually became a city manager) and a mother who sacrificed and pinched pennies so she could stay home until the kids were in high school.

Something in the mix made Boone a black-and-white kid. He actually loved rules. While it had never been beyond him to get into mischief as boys will do, he avoided serious trouble. By fifth grade he became known among friends as Honest Abe and was often called upon to settle disputes. Boone soon earned a reputation as the one kid bullies avoided. Once in junior high, when a half dozen had surrounded him, he looked each in the eye and called him by name. "You cowards do whatever you're going to do with all your buddies around, but when I find you alone — and you know I will — you're going to regret it."

Seeing the fear in their eyes so emboldened Boone that he became known as a protector. A nerd, a dweeb, a geek threatened by a bully would run to Boone, and soon the word was out that anyone who terrorized the weak had to answer to him.

There were no gray areas with Boone Drake.

He met Nikki, the daughter of a military

lawyer who lived in a neighboring town, at church when they were both in elementary school. They were acquaintances, then friends, then ignored each other, grew up to date others, and finally discovered each other again at community college. He was studying criminology, set on being a Chicago police detective so he could do to gangbangers what he had done to bullies. She wanted to teach kindergarten.

Their relationship began with a frank discussion that Nikki always said had come from out of the blue. They found themselves together in line for something or other and cordially brought each other up to date.

"And are you still a justice freak?" she said.

Boone laughed and told her of his major. "And are you still blunt?"

"Guilty."

He asked her to sit with him at lunch, and there he asked if she was seeing anyone.

"Now who's being blunt?"

"I am," he said. "Are you or not?"

She smiled. "Well, I'm dating . . . but no, I'm not committed."

"Anyone you'd like to be committed to?"

She furrowed her brow. "None of your business."

Boone shrugged.

"Fact is," she said, "I've got three guys

interested. One I kinda like more than the other two, but I can't see it going anywhere."

"Tell all three of them the truth."

Nikki sat back. "Boone! We haven't talked for what, two years, and now you play big brother?"

Boone cocked his head. "Maybe I want to be more than your big brother."

She stared at him. "You're not just trying to run my life the way you'd like to run everyone else's?"

"I come off that bad?"

"You come off like you know better. And maybe you do. So let's say I quit playing the field. What's in it for me?"

"I am. I've known since I met you that we were meant for each other."

That made her laugh aloud. "We were kids! If you really felt that way, you had a strange way of showing it. You never even gave me an inkling."

"Making up for lost time."

"You sure are. And it's creeping me out."

"Sorry."

"Well, you have to imagine how this hits me."

"Sure, if you had no idea. You were never interested in me?"

"As a boyfriend?"

"No, as a justice freak. Of course as a

boyfriend."

"Who wasn't? Big, good-lookin' guy. A little rigid, but hey . . ."

"So can we hang out a little and see where it goes?"

That had meant the start of conventionality for Boone. From that day on, he was careful not to overwhelm Nikki but rather to court her. He was chivalrous, deferential, even gallant. And when it came time to propose, he did it right. No assuming. No dancing around the edges. It came on a Christmas-season walk down the Magnificent Mile and ended with him on one knee in front of a high-end jewelry store.

She taught kindergarten during the first two years of their marriage and planned to return to her career when Josh and any more children were school-age.

Something about the way things had turned out confirmed in Boone's mind that an ordered life was rewarded. He owed that to his parents, he guessed. Having a goal, a plan, and following through paid off. He wasn't sure of the precise definition of the American dream. All he knew was that he was living it.

Did he deserve it? Sure, why not? He knew his own mind: he *was* a justice freak, and everything was working out the way he had hoped and planned. He and Nikki even found a great church, Community Life on the Near North Side. It was a large, multi-campus, cross-cultural congregation pastored by a man not Boone's senior by more than ten years, Francisco Sosa. The engaging leader had persuaded Nikki to teach Sunday school while Josh was in the nursery, and Boone to get involved with junior boys' ministries when his schedule allowed.

Boone had to admit he found it disconcerting to hear Pastor Sosa discuss "the Lord" as a constant presence in his life. It wasn't that Boone didn't consider himself devout. He prayed before meals, prayed when he was in danger, went to church, tithed, and served. He just wasn't obsessed with spiritual things or so up-front about them. Of course, he also spent at least eight hours a day around men and women with the worst language on the planet. Most were also closet drinkers and divorced, some many times over. Jack Keller had three ex-wives. No wonder he was that rare old-timer who still loved the job and had not grown disillusioned or jaded, despite being the very definition of a grizzled veteran. The job was all he had.

One Sunday after Boone — in uniform —

had spoken to Sunday school classes about his job, Pastor Sosa told him that he saw something in him that could really be developed. "You've got a gift for communicating. Hone it and use it."

The pastor also said he thought about Boone often and prayed for him when he knew he was on duty. Boone thanked him, but the truth was, that kind of talk made him nervous. He got the impression that Sosa assumed Boone prayed before every shift. Which he did not.

3:10 a.m., Saturday, January 21

Boone and Keller were on patrol when Keller pulled in front of an all-night convenience store for coffee. While Boone sat waiting in the passenger seat, he noticed a pickup truck slowly maneuvering into the alley behind the storefronts on the other side of the street.

He radioed Keller. "Jack, you on your way out? Just spotted a suspicious truck."

"I'm nuking a bagel. Should I come right now?"

"I'll check it out and call if I need you."

Boone got out and jogged around to the driver's side, then pulled the squad down the block, switching off his headlights before turning into the alley about three hundred feet behind the pickup. He gradually gained on the slow-moving truck as it cruised, stopped, started, and repeated the cycle. He suspected the two occupants were casing the area with burglary in mind and radioed in the license plate number.

Finally Boone eased up behind them and turned on his blue lights, calling out over the PA for them to remain in the vehicle. He approached cautiously, pausing by the rear left bumper and watching to see if they were reaching for anything. When he stepped to the window, staying back so the driver had to crane his neck to see him, Boone asked for license and registration.

The driver was a big redheaded man in coveralls. His license appeared in order, but it bore an Arkansas address. The truck had Illinois plates.

"What're you boys doing out here to-night?" Boone said.

"Looking for the Piggly Wiggly store, but we must have the wrong address. We got a friend who works there all night, and some-body told us it was around here."

Boone had never seen a Piggly Wiggly grocery store in Chicago, though he knew of a few in the suburbs. "You find that registration?"

The passenger made a show of digging

through the glove box. "No, the wife must have taken it out. It's usually in here."

"How long have you lived in Illinois, sir?"

" 'Bout six months."

"And what is your current address?"

As the man was hemming and hawing, obviously pretending to try to come up with it, headquarters reported back to Boone's walkie-talkie in code that told him the truck was stolen. He was about to make two serious collars, and he imagined himself herding the men out of the truck and into the back of the squad.

Boone had formulated the orders he would bark and was ready to cuff the men one at a time, but suddenly he couldn't speak. Something inside cautioned him to go by the book, to engage his partner, call for backup, and take no unnecessary risks.

Nothing he had seen scared him about these suspects. They were big, sure, but he hadn't detected alcohol, nor did he suspect they had guns stashed — though of course he would pat them down. The more Boone imagined himself making this double arrest alone, the more he liked the idea of the admiration that would ensue from Jack and their watch commander, not to mention everyone else in the district. Maybe he would even be cited.

He intended to instruct the driver to step out of the vehicle with his hands up and the passenger to stay where he was. But instead he said, "Turn off the engine and hand me the keys." The man slowly handed them out.

Boone radioed Jack, told him where he was, and asked him to call for backup.

"What's the problem, Officer?" Redhead said.

"Just sit tight and we'll straighten this out."

Eventually the pickup was impounded, and the suspects were on their way to central booking, charged with grand theft auto. Boone's shift was long over, but Keller had to stay at headquarters for a morning meeting anyway, so he said he would finish the interrogation and write the report. "Don't worry; you'll still get credit for the collars."

"I appreciate it, Jack, but you know the collars I really want."

"Don't start with this again, kid. You can't force it. You don't take it to the gangs. You wait till they bring it to you."

"That's the problem! We ought to be taking it to them. Wade in there, show 'em we won't be intimidated. This is our city, not theirs."

"Good way to get yourself killed, Boones.

But I'm not saying I don't appreciate the passion."

The middle of the next afternoon, when Nikki allowed Josh to crawl on the bed and wake his dad, Boone roused to see her with a page in her hand. He roughhoused with the giggling Josh, then asked her what it was about.

"Something strange from my mother," she said. "Found it in my e-mail in-box this morning and printed it out."

Josh squirmed into his lap as Boone sat up and studied the paper.

Nikki, maybe this is nothing, but I can't sleep, and I certainly don't want to call and disturb you. Is Boone working tonight?

At twelve fifteen this morning I was awakened from a sound sleep with such an urge to pray for Boone that I had no choice but to slide out of bed and kneel to do just that. Now you know we've never knelt to pray, and I've never had a vision or a dream or any urging like this. But it was so overwhelming that, as I say, I had no choice.

Call me when convenient. Needless to say, I'm dying to know if it was something serious or just something I ate.

Love, Mother

"Hmm," Boone said. "Interesting."

"Well? What can I tell her?"

"Pretty quiet shift, actually. Only two incidents. One was a drugstore owner telling us that a kid ran off with some phone cards just before he closed at midnight. The other was a stolen vehicle, but it turned out to be routine, and that was around three fifteen."

"That's it?"

"Pretty sure. I would have remembered anything dangerous."

"Boone, three fifteen here is twelve fifteen in Anchorage."

"Well, that's true. But like I say, turned out to be a standard GTA, no resistance, no danger."

That night when Boone showed up for his shift, Keller asked him to sign off on the arrest report from the previous night. "You'll get a kick out of the end."

Boone sat and read it through. The last paragraph read:

Offender 1 told reporting officer that arresting officer was "lucky he waited for

28

backup. If he had tried to take us himself, we were going to jump him and shoot him with his own gun."

2
STREET CRED

Within a year after Boone's first collar, he began making a name for himself in District 11. He thoroughly embraced the department's CAPS (Chicago Alternative Policing Strategy) approach, which encouraged officers to work with community leaders and other city agencies to prevent crime rather than just react to it.

As Boone's duties finally grew to include interacting with gangs and drug pushers — as he had always wanted — he found himself also an enthusiastic supporter of PRIDE (Police and Residents in Drug Enforcement). That meant a lot more interaction with the public and a chance to once again stand between the innocents and those who would terrorize them.

It still wasn't enough. Boone obsessed over going on the offensive. Why did the police always have to wait, to react after the fact? With enough intelligence and paid informants, couldn't they get inside these guys' heads and be waiting for them next time? A cop could dream. Boone could see in Keller's eyes that he was tired of hearing about it every day.

By the following summer, when Boone reached his eighteen-month milestone with the Chicago PD, he had become one of the most celebrated PPOs in the history of the infamous 11th district. Any complaints by arrestees were quickly proven false — usually by Jack Keller, who seemed as proud of his young partner as he would have been if he himself had been so frequently feted.

Keller benefited, too, from how visible Boone had become. While they had been mired in the first watch and often had to come in during the early evening for community meetings as well, exuberant public support brought them to the attention of the brass. Now rumor had it that Keller was going to be urged to apply for the recently vacated role of deputy chief in the Organized Crime Division.

"You gonna do it, Jack?" Boone said. "I hate to think of breaking in a new partner."

That made Keller laugh. "The truth? I wouldn't go unless they let me take you."

Meanwhile, Drake and Keller were rewarded with a move to second watch, which put Boone on what Nikki called a schedule meant for a human being, and they celebrated his freedom to sleep at night and spend time with her and Josh from when he got home late in the afternoon until bedtime.

Keller got the biggest kick out of a call that saw Boone wind up on the front pages of newspapers all over the country and even get a spot on one of the network TV morning shows. A 911 call came in from an eight-year-old girl who had taken over steering the car when her mother collapsed at the wheel. Fortunately, the mother's foot had slipped off the gas, so the girl was steering a slow-rolling car with one hand and screaming to dispatch on a cell phone with the other.

The incident happened close to where Keller and Boone were patrolling, and when Keller spotted the vehicle, his plan was to carefully pull the squad ahead of it, allowing it to lightly bump him, and stop it that way.

Boone said, "Hold on. Let me try something first."

He leaped from the squad, raced down the street to overtake the vehicle, opened the door, and was somehow able to reach in and downshift, slowing the car even more. Finally he held on to the frame and, hopping on one foot, got his other leg inside to reach the brake. Boone wound up being interviewed along with the grateful mother, who had suffered an adverse reaction to medication, and her heroic young daughter.

With everything else came Boone's salary increase to nearly sixty thousand dollars a year. While no fortune, it was something to build on, and Boone took advantage of the CPD's home purchase assistance benefit. A Realtor from church helped the Drakes find a cozy Cape Cod in an old-fashioned neighborhood not far from work with, yes, just enough yard to mow.

After church one hot summer Sunday, Pastor Francisco Sosa asked Boone if they could talk sometime, suggesting they meet after a youth activity in the middle of the week. "Sure," Boone said, "as long as you're not going to ask for more of my time. Josh is nearly two now and into everything, and I don't want to miss a minute of it." Sosa assured him it wasn't about that.

That Wednesday night, Boone had finished helping supervise a junior boys' basketball game when he saw the pastor waiting for him. They repaired to the pastor's study, a book-filled chamber surprisingly under-stated for the senior pastor of such a vast inner-city fellowship. For some reason, even before Francisco Sosa got to the point, Boone felt self-conscious, awkward, out of his element. It was almost as if he had been called to the principal's office without knowing what he had done.

During the ice-breaking small talk about his job, his family, and Chicago sports, Sosa seemed to be peering into Boone's soul. Finally the pastor said, "Life could hardly be better for you, could it?"

Boone sat across from him, bouncing one foot. "Can't argue with that. And believe me, I'm grateful."

Truth was — and Boone assumed Sosa somehow knew this — that was something he would have said only to his pastor. When it came down to it, Boone believed he himself had created the life he enjoyed; he had established parameters, guidelines, goals, and practices that resulted in success.

"I need you to know, Boone, that I ap-preciate your faithfulness here and your willingness to work with the boys."

"Sure."

"I'm impressed, too, that you've never ac-ceded to their wishes that you show them your gun."

Boone chuckled. "I'd like to keep my job. We're expected to carry a weapon at all times, even off duty, but it's not a toy to be showing kids."

"You know the boys have come to me, asking me to tell you to show it to them."

"Not going to happen."

"I know, and our treasurer — who works with our insurance company — is thankful too."

"I just hope it gives you a little sense of security to know I'm armed when I'm sitting in services too, with the crazy stuff you hear about happening in churches."

"Let's pray you'll never need it around here," Pastor Sosa said.

"I heard that."

"Well, that's not why I asked to see you. I want to talk to you about something else. Passion. You follow?"

"Not really."

"You're passionate about your job, aren't you?"

"I live for it."

"And Nikki?"

"My life."

"And Josh?"

"I'd die for him."

"I love that about you, Boone. I really do."

"But . . . ?"

"I want to know if you love the Lord with the same kind of intensity."

Boone shifted in his seat and cocked his head. "Well, sure, yeah. 'Course I do. I became a Christian as a child, never doubted, been a churchgoer forever."

"I know. But I've never heard you speak of your faith, or your ministry here for that matter, with the passion you seem to have for the rest of your life."

"Humph. I guess it's true I'm not comfortable talking, you know, like some do. Like you do. I'm not ashamed of my faith or anything, but it's just not me to talk all spiritual. But that doesn't mean I'm not passionate about my faith."

Sosa fell silent and seemed to study Boone, which made Boone all the more uncomfortable. The pastor was smiling and looked like he cared. Why else would he pursue this? It couldn't have been any easier for him to confront Boone than it was for Boone to talk about such things.

The pastor pulled his Bible from the desk and set it in his lap. Boone had seen him do this before, and it amused him, because it was clear that Sosa had memorized the most familiar passages. He didn't open it, but he sure quoted it a lot.

"The Scriptures say that we believers will

be known by our fruit and how we love each other."

"Uh-huh, I know."

"Do you share your faith with people? Coworkers, friends, unsaved relatives?"

"Not as much as I should." *In fact, no.*

"And are you in the Word and praying every day?"

"Well, not every day. Again, not as much as I should, but I'm working on it. Your sermons get to me."

"Do they?"

"Oh yeah."

"You've got a pretty sweet life, Boone. But you know the majority of the people we minister to need God and don't have him. They need Jesus. And even when they come to faith, they will not likely ever enjoy the kind of lives you and I enjoy. Know what I mean? It takes passion to reach them and to persuade them that their eternal destiny is more important than their earthly circumstances."

Boone nodded, wishing Sosa *had* asked only for more of his time. Now he just wanted out. Sosa wanted him to be something he was not, and yet Boone couldn't — wouldn't — admit it. He was perfectly willing to keep coming to church, giving, serving. But the rest of it . . . Yeah, he could be more spiritual. Meanwhile, yes, his life was great, but the truth was, he could take the credit for that.

Suddenly Pastor Sosa stood, his dark eyes alive. "Well, that's all I wanted, Boone. Let me pray for us and I'll let you get back to that beautiful family." He reached for Boone, who stood and moved close so Sosa could throw an arm around his shoulder.

"Father," Sosa began, "thank you for loving us and caring about us. Fill us with your passion for souls, for your Word, for communing with you. Help us love people the way you do. Amen."

"Thank you," Boone said, feigning as much earnestness as he could muster. Sosa seemed to buy it, embraced him, and let him go. Boone had never felt so relieved to be finished with anything.

Boone arrived home to find Nikki dozing on the couch while her favorite TV show droned in the background.

Boone walked her to bed, then peeked in on Josh, who was illuminated by the light from the hall. The toddler lay on his back, arms spread wide. With his pacifier inches from his face and his tiny lips slightly open, he looked cherubic. Boone laid a hand on the boy's rhythmically rising and falling chest, causing the little guy to sigh and straighten his legs.

Boone could have stood there all night.

Suddenly Josh roused. When he saw Boone, he immediately jumped to his feet.

"Oh, no, no, Joshie. Go back to sleep. Your mom will kill me."

But the boy wanted to play. Boone shut the door and tried to shush him, but Josh found his pacifier and fired it across the room, laughing.

"Okay, time to go back to sleep." Boone retrieved the pacifier, wrestled Josh down, and gently held him there until he relaxed, then wished him good night and crept out. As Boone pulled the door shut behind him, he heard Josh rise and bounce, and the pacifier went flying again.

When Boone went to watch the news and wind down before getting his eight hours in anticipation of the next morning's shift, he noticed Nikki's Bible on the couch. Well, Pastor Sosa would have been proud of *her,* anyway. He was about to turn off the TV when he was startled to see Josh padding out, calling, "Da-da!"

"Hey! How'd you get out? Did you wake Mommy?"

But he knew better. Nikki would never allow him out of bed in the middle of the night. As he carried his son back to his room, he peeked in on her. Sound asleep. He shut Josh and himself in the baby's room and allowed the boy to play while he set about lowering the crib mattress to the bottom slots. It would have been a lot easier with help, but he wasn't about to wake Nikki.

By the time he was finished, Josh was sitting on the floor idly watching, droopy-eyed. He didn't squawk when Boone tucked him back in, and his eyes were shut before Boone left the room. He couldn't wait to see Nikki's reaction to the crib adjustment.

Three Mondays later, dawn broke hot and humid and the Drakes' air-conditioning kicked in before seven o'clock. Nikki looked amazing in short shorts and had dressed Josh in a tiny sunsuit he seemed to like. He was animated and talkative as ever at breakfast, sweeping food off his high chair tray, singing, laughing, and trying his best to talk to Boone about something.

"I'm going to take Josh to the pool today," Nikki said as Boone unlocked the gun safe above the refrigerator and snapped the 9mm into his holster. "Then I'll mow the lawn."

"You don't have to do that, babe," Boone said. "I can do it when I get home."

"No, no, I want to. It won't take twenty minutes."

"Do me a favor, will you? Wear something a little less sexy at the pool?"

Nikki laughed. "Boone! The oldest male there will be about five."

"Really? Even the lifeguards?"

"I don't swim in shorts anyway."

"Can I vote for the one-piece suit?"

She was still smiling. "You know I don't wear the bikini unless you're with me. Now stop it."

"Jack and I may find a reason to cruise by."

"Yeah, you'd better keep a lid on that crime-infested kiddie pool. Hey, before you go, I need help with the crib. You know he's been getting out on his own again?"

"You kidding me?"

"Twice last night."

"I put it on the lowest setting weeks ago."

They went to look at it.

"We're going to have to figure out something else," she said. "You think he's ready for a big-boy bed already?"

Boone shrugged. "Maybe if he's not caged in, he won't feel the need to escape." He looked at his watch. "Gotta get going."

Back in the kitchen, Boone enjoyed a passionate good-bye kiss, then chuckled when

Josh wanted a hug and a kiss too. When he left, Josh was saying bye-bye and waving.

3
THE UNSPEAKABLE

Boone had to admit, if only to Keller, that other than the benefit of more family time, he didn't care much for second watch.

"Tell me about it," Keller said. "All the fun stuff happens at night. I didn't get into this racket to coax cats out of trees or check the credentials of door-to-door salesmen."

"The gangbangers pretty much sleep during the day too."

"Oh, I knew you could do it, Boones. You went almost the whole morning without whining about what we oughta do to the gangs. Enjoy day watch while it lasts. We'll either be back on nights or in OCD before you know it."

"Now, Organized Crime is something I could sink my teeth into. How's that process going?"

"Oh, you know. The bureaucracy creeps along. More'n thirteen thousand sworn officers in this city, and I think every one of 'em wants that job. Believe me, if I get it, you'll be the first to know."

By late morning, Boone was getting hungry. It had been a quiet shift. Their only call had been about a man in uniform going door to door, claiming to be an air-conditioning consultant from the city, wanting to make sure homeowners' units were functioning properly. Keller called the power company and was assured no such personnel were making the rounds.

They staked out the area and caught and jailed the impostor, discovering he had a history of theft using the same MO.

Around noon Boone said, "Fast food or deli today?"

Keller shrugged. "I shouldn't have had that Danish on break. Can you wait an hour?"

"Sure. Just pull into a drive-through so I can get a Coke."

Keller pointed the squad toward a fast-food joint a couple of blocks from headquarters, but just before he turned in, his cell phone chirped. He peeked at the readout, scowled, and pulled to the curb.

"What?" Boone said.

"It's the precinct. Our radio not working?"

Boone clicked the transmitter as Keller flipped open his phone. "Working fine,"

44

Boone mouthed.

"This is Keller. . . . Yeah, he's right here. You wanna talk to h — ? . . . Oh, okay. . . . Yeah? Oh no. Serious?" Keller swore and stole a glance at Boone.

"What?"

Keller held up a hand. "Where? . . . And Dr. who? . . . Okay, we're rolling." He flipped on the blue lights and the siren and swung onto Jackson, heading east.

As other motorists gave way, Boone said, "What's happening, Jack? Where we going?"

"Presbyterian St. Luke's."

The hospital was less than two miles east of headquarters, and Keller was flying, braking only to ease through red lights.

"Why the phone call? We got an officer down?"

"No, Boone, we don't. They don't want me to tell you till we get there, but I will if you'll promise me you can keep it together."

" 'Course! What?"

"It's your family."

Suddenly Boone was aware of nothing but the fear in Jack Keller's eyes. He didn't hear the siren, wasn't aware of his body pressing against the seat belt as Jack raced through the streets. He forgot whether it was day or night, and his hunger and thirst were gone.

"What happened?"

"Some kind of accident."

"In the car? Nikki was going to walk Josh to —"

"No, at home. A fire."

"How bad?"

"Bad, Boone. I'm sorry."

"Tell me they survived!"

"I haven't heard otherwise; now please, just let me get there."

"Jack, I'm not going to be able to handle it if they're not all right. . . ."

"Boone! Now, come on! We don't know anything until we find out for ourselves."

As soon as the squad slid into the emergency room entrance, Boone was out and sprinting, leaving his cap and nightstick in the car. He burst through the door and up to a thin black woman at the desk. "Nikki and Josh Drake!" he said.

"She's already in surgery, Officer," the woman said, eyeing the nameplate over his pocket. "Relative?"

"Husband and father," he said as Keller stepped in behind him. "I gotta know —"

Keller interrupted. "I was told to ask for a Dr. Sarang — something. An Indian name?"

The woman nodded. "Dr. Murari Sarangan is waiting for you in the conference room on 2."

"Sarangan?" Boone said. "He goes to our

46

church. But listen, I want to see my family
—"

Keller grabbed Boone's shoulder. "As soon as you can see them, I'm sure this doctor will make it happen. He'll tell you whatever you need to know."

Desperate as Boone was for hard information, his legs wobbled as he and Keller trotted up the stairs to the second-floor conference room. Dr. Sarangan, tall and in his late thirties, stood clutching a metal clipboard and wearing green surgical scrubs under a white lab coat.

No greeting, no small talk, no smile. The doctor opened the door and said, "In here."

The last thing Boone wanted was to sit, but he didn't trust himself to stand. "Just tell me," he said, dropping into a chair.

"Mr. Drake, I'm sorry," Dr. Sarangan began. "I was just going off duty when I realized it was your wife and son in the ER. I asked if I could consult with you."

"Just tell me they're both alive. I can deal with anything else."

The doctor hesitated and glanced up as Pastor Sosa entered.

"Oh no!" Boone said, no longer able to stifle the sobs. "Are they gone?"

"Your son has died, Mr. Drake," the doctor said. "Your wife is in grave condition."

47

"Not Josh! Not Josh! No! I need to see Nikki."

Both the pastor and Jack Keller reached for Boone.

"I'm sorry, sir," Dr. Sarangan said. "It will be at least an hour before you are able to see her. I guarantee I will get you in there as soon as humanly possible. I need to tell you, she does not know about your son."

Boone looked desperately to Pastor Sosa. "I have to tell her?"

The doctor said, "She is in no condition for that kind of news. We'll have to play it by ear, see if she can be stabilized."

Boone turned to his partner. "I've got to know what happened at home. Can you find out?"

"Right now," Keller said, his eyes red. And as he left, he nodded at Pastor Sosa to join him in the hall.

Boone drew a deep, quavery breath and forced himself to speak clearly. "Doctor, tell me how bad it is."

"I want to do that, if you're sure you're ready. Would you rather wait for Pastor S —"

"No, I need to know. Tell me."

Dr. Sarangan flipped through a couple of pages on his clipboard. "Sir —"

"Boone."

"Boone, I need to tell you frankly that I am stalling because there is something I prefer to tell you in front of our pastor."

"You said she was alive!"

"She is. Now please, just give him a few moments, and I will tell you everything."

"But it's bad, isn't it?"

The doctor nodded. "It's bad."

"We'll get through this," Boone whispered. "But I don't think I can tell her about Josh. Can I see him?"

"No."

"No? You're going to keep me from —"

"Boone, I am so sorry, but you must trust me on this. You would not want to see him. You would recognize nothing of him."

Boone laid his head on the table and wept. He looked up when he heard the door, and Pastor Sosa came in with a can of soda for him. Boone drank it in one shot.

"Okay, he's here, so talk to me."

Sosa sat next to Boone, a hand on his shoulder. The doctor spoke softly to the pastor first. "I told him I wanted you here for this because I realize it is unconventional counsel coming from a Christian."

He set the clipboard aside and spoke softly, directly to Boone. "I believe in the sanctity of life. I am pro-life, anti-abortion, anti-euthanasia, everything you can imagine from a doctor like myself. But, sir, I must tell you that if I were in your shoes — and I say this with all the compassion in my heart — I would pray that my wife did not survive her injuries."

"What?"

"Please hear me out. The medical team working on her even as we speak, to a person, has never seen a worse burn case. The only part of her body not virtually destroyed is her upper torso and chest, where she pressed your son to herself. I don't know how much you know about how burns are rated, but your wife suffered what we call fourth-degree, full thickness burns over every exposed surface of her body, reaching to her fascia, muscle, and even bone."

"But she's alive."

"She is barely alive, Boone. But I confess it would not surprise me to hear any moment that she has expired."

"Then why can't I see her?"

"An entire team is doing everything they can, sir. If by some miracle she would survive even twenty-four hours, at the very least her extremities would have to be amputated, possibly even all four entire limbs. Her spinal cord is exposed, her hair and scalp are gone, her face was burned off.

If God should choose to spare her, she would need constant care, and there would be virtually no quality of life as we know it."

"Can she see? speak?"

"She has lost her eyes, Boone. There is some chance that what they are doing now to her throat and larynx would allow you to understand her, if she were lucid. As you can imagine, she is so heavily sedated that communication would be impossible for quite a while. She would not likely be aware you were even there, and of course you would not be able to touch her."

"I just want to be with her before she dies. She's going to die soon, isn't she?"

"That's likely. Now unless you have any other questions, let me go and check on her, and I'll make sure you know as soon as you can see her."

As the doctor left, Keller returned. "I talked to CFD. I'll tell you what they told me, as much as you want to know."

"I want it all, Jack."

Keller looked to the pastor, who shrugged. "It's up to Boone."

"Are you sure, buddy?" Keller said. "It's not pretty."

"I'm about to lose my whole family. I have to know why."

Keller peeked at his notebook. "The garage will have to be rebuilt, but they were able to save the house. . . ."

"I don't care about the stinkin' house. I couldn't live there anyway. What do they think happened?"

"They have a pretty good account, actually, because of an old lady next door."

"Mrs. Gustavson?"

"That's the name. She says Nikki brought Josh home from the pool in the stroller and he was fast asleep. They chatted for a few minutes, and Nikki told her she was going to take him inside and put him down and then mow the lawn. She says Nikki said something about hoping the mower wouldn't wake him.

"Several minutes later, Nikki had the mower out and was having trouble starting it. She went into the garage for a can of gas, but when she went to fill the tank, she said it was already full. She found some switch that had to be flipped to start the thing."

"The gas line release," Boone said.

"Anyway, she put the can back inside the garage and started mowing. This woman, Gustavson, says it wasn't five minutes later that she heard this horrible blast and the whole garage looked like a ball of orange, flames shooting out the utility door."

"How'd it get to Josh?"

"Listen, Mrs. Gustavson said she stood up from her gardening and caught Nikki's eye. As soon as Nikki let go of that mower — it must have an automatic shutoff —"

"It does."

"— they heard screaming from the garage over the roar of the flames. She said Nikki didn't even hesitate. She ran right into that fire, Boone. And then Mrs. Gustavson heard both of them screaming. She said Nikki was in there so long that she never expected to see either of them again. She was about to run in her house and call 911 when Nikki finally came staggering out of there with Josh in her arms."

Boone covered his mouth and the sobs began anew.

"That enough for now?"

Boone shook his head and took his hand away. "Go on."

"Mrs. Gustavson says Nikki and Josh were completely engulfed in flames. Nikki dropped and rolled on the grass, but it was doing no good. The woman hooked up her garden hose. She feels so bad, Boone. She says it took her way longer than it should have because she was shaking and crying and trying so hard to hurry. She dragged that hose through her hedges and into your

53

yard and sprayed water on them until the fire went out. But she says Nikki had stopped rolling and was unconscious before she even got to them. Other neighbors came running and CFD was there in minutes. The EMTs determined that Josh was gone, but they didn't dare try to separate him from Nikki till they got to the hospital. It was all they could do to keep her alive."

Boone buried his face in his hands. "Tell me I'm going to wake up soon."

4

THE GOOD-BYE

Pastor Sosa draped an arm around Boone. "Father," he said, his own voice thick and shaky, "we hate this. We don't understand it. We wish we could go back to before it happened. But we also believe you're sovereign. All we can do is trust you and beg you to help us endure."

Beyond horror and grief, rage began to roil in Boone. What had he ever done to deserve this? He so desperately wanted to see Nikki and try to communicate something to her, anything. But he was also still thoroughly confused.

"CFD still investigating?" he said.

Keller nodded. "Yeah. From what they can piece together, Josh must have gotten to the gas can in the garage and tipped it over, and the gas ran under the water heater closet door. The fumes would have been ignited by the pilot light."

Boone sat shaking his head.

"But wasn't the baby down for his nap?" Keller said. "Isn't he still in a crib?"

"He'd been getting out on his own lately. I should have done something about that."

"Don't do that, Boone," Pastor Sosa said. "We can't control everything in this life."

For much of the next hour, Boone sat in the conference room, lips pressed together, slowly shaking his head. This couldn't be happening, mustn't be happening. How was he to accept such horror? He had so many questions for Pastor Sosa, but he didn't dare start because he knew his venom would spew. Everything he would demand to know would come out as a challenge. How could God do this? And if he didn't do it, as he knew the pastor would say, how could he allow it? It made no sense.

So many people deserved to die, some even to be tortured to death by fire. But why Joshie? And why Nikki?

His knees were bouncing, so eager was he to see her before she slipped away. Would he pray that she died rather than suffer from such ghastly injuries, as Dr. Sarangan had suggested? He'd seen the results when people survived massive burns. Their faces looked rubberized, their extremities stubs if they existed at all. From what he gathered, Nikki would be worse than anything he had ever even imagined. No limbs, no eyes, some rebuilt face and scalp harvested from the little expanse of skin protected by Josh's body.

If her brain was intact and she was able to speak, would that be enough? Was he willing to care for her around the clock for as long as she lived? He had made that vow, and he was one for keeping promises. But would she want to live that way? Would anyone? Boone sure wouldn't.

Part of him wanted to pray, to plead, to beg, to promise. He would pledge to be as devout and passionate about his faith as Pastor Sosa wanted him to be, if only . . . if only what? Nikki survived? It would be selfish, mean even, to expect her to endure such agony just for him. No, he would make such an earnest supplication and promise only if God would restore her. Couldn't he do that? Didn't he still work miracles?

Wasn't it enough that he and Nikki had lost the most precious gift they had ever received? Was there not something in modern medical science that could allow Nikki to grow tissue, get eye transplants, keep her limbs, even her fingers and toes? Boone didn't care if her dramatic beauty never returned. He loved that about her, of course, was proud of her, had never tired of just gazing at her. But what he really loved was her person, her character, who she was.

"You've got to be hungry," Pastor Sosa said. "You didn't get any lunch, did you?"

"We didn't," Keller said. "I'll get us all something, but you know it's gonna be something out of a machine."

"I couldn't eat," Boone said.

"Even if you don't feel hungry, you need nourishment," Sosa said. "Just something to keep you functioning."

"I need to see Nikki. I just know someone's going to come in here with the bad news, and I'll have missed any chance to say good-bye."

"Murari won't let that happen if he can help it, Boone. You know that."

Keller stood to go get the food. "I'll see what I can find out, too."

Boone felt himself beginning to hyperventilate and puffed his cheeks to blow and try to slow his respiration. "What'm I gonna do, Pastor? I can't live without them."

"You're going to find out what the body of Christ is all about, Boone. You will not believe how your brothers and sisters will rally around you, stand by you, minister to you."

It was all Boone could do to keep from slamming both fists on the table and cursing the pastor and God. He knew the man meant well, and he had little doubt that the people of Community Life would do just what Sosa had said. But nothing would be enough to dull this pain, and Boone couldn't imagine attending that church alone.

"I've got to call Nikki's parents. How am I going to tell them?"

"You need me to do that?" Sosa said.

Boone shook his head. "They have to hear it from me." He dialed their home in Alaska, where her father, Steve McNickle, was stationed at the Elmendorf Air Force Base as an attorney with the Area Defense Counsel. Nikki's mother, Pam, was a nurse at the base hospital.

The phone went to voice mail, and Boone panicked. "Uh, yeah, Mom and Dad McNickle, I'll try to call you on your cells or at work. We've got a serious emergency here, so call me on my cell if you get this before I reach you."

Boone tried to reach Steve at his office, only to be told that he was researching a case in the field. He left a message and, while dialing Pam McNickle's cell, got a call from their home.

"This is Boone."

"It's Pam. What's wrong?"

It sounded like such a cliché to urge her to sit down, but he didn't know how else to start. He knew she could tell from his voice that this was no broken arm or ordinary emergency room visit. "Pam, this is the hardest call I've ever had to make."

Boone heard her stop breathing. To spare her even worse agony, he gushed the news of the fire, that Josh had been killed, and that Nikki was not expected to live.

"Oh, God, oh, God," she prayed. "No. Boone, no."

He told her he was at the hospital and gave her the address and phone number.

She sounded hollow and spoke in a monotone. "I've got to reach Steve. We'll get there as soon as we can get a flight. Would I be able to talk to Nikki? Could they put her on the phone?"

"She's in surgery."

"Boone, you tell her we love her and to hold on and that we're coming."

"She doesn't know about Josh."

She hesitated. "Stay strong for her."

Too late.

Keller returned with three perfectly awful plastic-wrapped bologna sandwiches that felt, looked, and tasted three days old. Boone chewed each bite till it was mush and still had trouble swallowing. How could anyone eat at a time like this?

"Okay, listen," Jack said. "Here's what I got from the Indian guy. Nikki's about to be moved from the operating room to ICU, and while he doesn't believe there's any way she can survive the night, she will not be anything close to conscious for at least another half hour. Here's the good part. He asked the attending to concentrate on her larynx and windpipe, just to see if there was any way she might be able to speak at all. He's making no promises and wants me to remind you that even if they somehow succeed, she has very little possibility of being lucid."

"I understand. I appreciate it anyway."

"So, figure about forty minutes from now he wants you to come to the intensive care unit and meet the attending surgeon. Then you can be with her."

"For how long?"

"He said that if you're prepared for whatever might happen, you can stay with her to the end."

Boone felt as if someone had reached into his chest and pulled the cord on the light of his life. How could anything ever be the same? His thoughts were a mess, starting to include foreseeing the funeral, both families coming, everyone trying to help, to advise, and looking at him with pity. His mother would insist on doing things for him; his father would have some sort of plan. Boone wanted none of it. He wasn't sure he wanted to go on at all.

When it finally came time for them to make their way to ICU, Boone started at a rapid pace. On the one hand, he hoped against hope that he would see Nikki before she died. On the other, he was afraid of what he would see. Eventually the stress caught up to him, and his limbs felt like lead. It was hard to put one foot in front of the other, but he was not going to stumble, and he was certainly not going to be helped along by anyone.

Pastor Sosa stayed half a step behind Boone, while Jack Keller hurried on ahead. When they reached ICU, Dr. Sarangan introduced everyone to the attending surgeon, Dr. Catherine O'Connor. She was short and dark with black hair and held her folded surgical cap in one hand.

"Officer Drake, I am so sorry for the loss of your son," she said. "I know Dr. Sarangan has told you everything, so I trust you'll understand if I ask whether Father Sosa would like to administer the last rites to your wife."

"It's Pastor Sosa, and we're not —"

"I would be honored to pray for her, Boone," Sosa said. "It's your call."

"Why don't you do that now," she said, "and I'll join you in a few moments with more information. Oh, you'll both have to wear masks."

The sight of his mummified wife stopped Boone short. A sheet had been tented over most of her body to the neck, her bandaged arms suspended by thin wires from a contraption over the bed. Her arms were thickly wrapped in gauze, as were her hands, which looked like grotesque oven mitts. The white around her head and face was the size of a basketball. Two tubes ran into a tiny hole through the gauze to where her nose and mouth would have been.

"Oh, Nikki," Boone whispered.

Sosa put one hand on the bed rail and the other lightly on Boone's forearm. Boone found himself deeply moved that the pastor's tears were streaming as he prayed with obvious difficulty. "Father, we confess we don't understand you right now, and all we can do is thank you for Nikki and what a precious wife and mother she has been. We love her and we know that you do too. I pray, if it is your will that she leave this earth, that you would welcome her to yourself without further pain or agony. And I pray your merciful, miraculous comfort for Boone. Please, Lord. Please."

The pastor squeezed Boone's arm and said, "I'll be right outside."

It struck Boone that, besides Sosa's admonition that Boone not blame himself, the pastor had not tried to advise or counsel or even comfort him other than by prayer, touch, and tears. Anything else would have been futile anyway, but he did appreciate that the man was there and trying. When he turned at the sound of Dr. O'Connor, he saw Jack Keller weeping openly in the hall.

"Let's sit here for a moment before you try to talk to her, Mr. Drake."

They sat a few feet from the bed, Boone never taking his eyes off Nikki, the tubes, and the quietly humming machines.

"Let me tell you exactly what we're dealing with here, sir. Your wife is in profound shock due to massive shifts of fluid. Her body is fighting a hopeless, losing battle to heal itself. Normally, with a major burn victim, the first thing we do is establish respiration and circulation. Frankly, we couldn't do a tracheotomy because the flesh around her neck was virtually vaporized. We couldn't administer intravenous fluids because her arms and legs were burned to the bone.

"We have oxygen being pumped in directly through her nasal cavity and down her traumatized esophagus and then we've threaded it directly to the lungs. The other tube is carrying the fluids and anesthetic, mostly to her stomach, which seems intact. Dr. Sarangan told us of your wish to try to converse with her, which I trust he told you is not likely. Nevertheless, seeing that there is no chance to save her, we did concentrate our efforts on her mouth and throat. Her tongue is intact, but she has no lips, so if she were to try to speak, you may not be able to understand her. And with the amount of sedation we are administering, there is no telling when or if she would be conscious."

"I understand."

"The machine is breathing for her, but the scar tissue already forming around her chest wall restricts expansion and would be painful if she could feel it. If she had any more skin to work with, we might have performed an escharotomy, searching for healthy tissue. The sad fact is, she has virtually none, except for where she cradled your son. And that's not enough. I don't know how else to say it, but your wife's body was, for all practical purposes, burned to the skeleton. And had your neighbor not doused the flames, her internal organs would have been lost too. As it is, we are not entirely certain what is keeping her alive. And you have to know it won't be long."

"Her parents are coming more than 3,500 miles."

"I can't imagine they will get here in time to see her. I'm sorry."

"So when can I try to talk to her?"

"The hallucinogenic narcoleptic we used for surgery should wear off in a few minutes. We will know when she attempts to move at all. I can assure you she will feel no pain. Whatever nerve tissue remains is being anesthetized by what is commonly referred to as a morphine drip, but which in this case is actually a morphine stream. See that bag there? It is essentially being poured into her. When she passes, it will be without discomfort and probably without even awareness."

"So talking to her is useless?"

"The mind and body are remarkable instruments, Mr. Drake. There is evidence that hearing is sometimes the last sense to go. And we know from people who have come back from the brink of death that they have not only heard their loved ones' good-byes, but they have also comprehended them, beyond all reason.

"I'm not going to sit here and promise that you will get to communicate anything meaningful to your wife, but if there is any chance, it will come within a few minutes after the sedative wears off. And while I don't expect her to try to speak, if she does, you'll need to listen very carefully. She suffered severe damage to her throat, but it is possible she could generate some kind of sound."

Boone sat staring, still finding it hard to take in. How long had it been since he had been looking forward to a little lunch with Jack? Everything in his life had been smashed beyond recognition; nothing would ever again be the same. How could something like this happen without warning?

"Um, I have a question."

"Anything."

"If she's on life support, how will we know when the end has come?"

"When to turn off the oxygen, you mean?"

Boone nodded.

"Those two monitors over there. One shows her pulse — elevated, of course, as her body struggles to stay alive — and the other shows brain activity. While she is clearly not conscious, she is still emitting brain waves. Those two readouts depend on each other. If her heart stops, her brain will soon follow. And vice versa."

"Can't you keep her heart beating artificially too?"

"Almost impossible in her condition, and there really is no benefit to it. It would only prolong the inevitable. The truth is, she should not have survived this trauma at all, and while we did everything we could to preserve her for this final good-bye, we're all surprised she's still with us."

Boone looked down. "I see what Murari meant about not even wanting her to survive."

Dr. O'Connor put a hand on his. "Oh yes, I'm sorry, but none of us wishes that on her. She would remain on the verge of death with every breath and would be unable to move, let alone do anything for herself. Hard as this is, the absolute best thing for your wife now is to pass."

Boone sighed. "I sure appreciate everything you've done."

"I only wish we could have saved them both, Mr. Drake. Now, would you like me to stay with you, or . . ."

"No, I'm fine." He reached for his wallet. "Let me show you what they looked like."

"Oh, my! Beautiful. And he's a doll."

It was hard for Boone to look at the

pictures.

"We're monitoring everything from out-side," the doctor said. "And I'll be close by. Just watch for some attempt to move, then say your good-byes. She is not likely to linger."

Boone pulled his chair next to the bed and began scanning the monitors while also keeping an eye on Nikki. What had he told the doctor? *"I'm fine."* What a laugh.

When there was no movement from Nikki for more than half an hour, Boone pulled the call cord and a nurse hurried in, fol-lowed by Dr. O'Connor. "Sorry," he said. "I was just wondering. You said the anesthetic should have worn off by now."

"Oh, I'm sure it has," the doctor said as the nurse checked all the connections and changed the morphine bag. "I wish I could promise she would exhibit some animation, but I can't. Her system may be protecting whatever reserves she has left by remaining asleep. And of course, there's the mor-phine."

"Could I wake her by talking to her?"

"That's possible, I suppose, but you risk that any disruption might push her past the brink. Your best chance to communicate with her would be to wait."

"But the longer I wait . . ."

"Mr. Drake, I don't know the likelihood that she'll rouse. I don't recommend overt action, but I won't forbid it either. As I've tried to make clear, it's moment to moment, so . . ."

"I'll wait."

And the wait was excruciating. Every half hour until early evening, the nurse stepped in, sometimes accompanied by Dr. O'Connor. It became clear to Boone that people were waiting around long after their shifts were over. He wanted to tell them that he appreciated it but that they should feel free to go home.

At about six he poked his head out into the hall, where Jack was sitting with Pastor Sosa. They both quickly stood.

"Nothing yet," Boone said, and over their shoulders he saw that the pastor's wife and several of the church elders had congregated outside a waiting room down the hall. Boone noticed several uniformed officers from the 11th milling about too.

"I don't know how long this is gonna be, Jack," Boone said. "You should go, really."

"Yeah, that's me," Keller said. "I'd leave my partner at a time like this. Now shut up and get back in there, and keep us posted. Nobody's goin' nowhere."

Just minutes after Boone returned and sat,

70

Nikki moved her head a few inches. He leaped from the chair, and it was all he could do to keep from touching her. He leaned close. "Nikki?"

She stopped moving.

"Nikki, I love you. Thank you for being such a wonderful wife and mother. Thank you for loving me."

He heard something raspy from deep in her throat.

"What is it, Nikki? Talk to me, baby."

She seemed to hum; then came a sound like she was trying to clear her throat. With tubes running down her throat, it was no wonder. He leaned close and put his ear near her mouth.

"Josh," she managed.

"Josh is fine," he said. "You saved him. He's going to be fine."

She was silent a moment. Then, "Truth."

"I wouldn't lie to you, babe. Now *you* have to work on getting better."

"Boone."

"I'm here. I'll never leave you."

"Boone."

"I'm here."

She said two words he didn't understand, and he asked her to repeat them.

"Not deaf."

"I know."

"Heard doctor."

He didn't know what to say. If she had been awake and heard Dr. O'Connor, she knew everything about her own condition.

"Ready," she said.

"Ready?"

"Heaven."

"Oh, honey, no. Your parents are on their way. We'll work together —"

"Boone."

"Yes."

"Love you."

"I love you too," he said. "With all my heart."

"Take care of Josh."

"You know I will."

"Good-bye."

The whole point of this was to say good-bye, but now he couldn't bring himself to say it. All he could say was, "I love you, I love you, I love you."

"Boone."

"I'm here, babe."

"Good-bye."

"Good-bye."

5
THE VALLEY

Boone watched the monitors, which still showed a pulse and brain activity, though Nikki was quiet. There was so much more he wanted to say, but she had plainly worn herself out.

He sat down and watched the numbers on the monitors begin to diminish. He pulled the call cord. Catherine O'Connor quickly entered alone.

"We talked," he whispered. "She heard what you told me."

The doctor grimaced. "Maybe that's for the best."

He nodded and pointed to the monitors. "Is this it?"

"I'm afraid so. I can't say how long it will take. It's up to you if you want to stay."

"Of course I do."

"And I assume you want no heroic measures taken."

"Right."

"Then I'll leave you till it's over. I'll send someone in to replace the morphine again. The end will be painless."

It was anything but painless for Boone, who sat waiting for the inevitable. Two agonizing hours later, Nikki's heart monitor flatlined, and the brain wave machine began to beep. Dr. O'Connor swept in.

"With your permission," she said kindly, "I'll shut off the oxygen feed."

"Will she be aware?"

"Cognition is gone, sir. You want to stay?"

Boone nodded and stood trembling as the doctor shut down the machines. "I'm sorry for your loss," she said. Two nurses entered, one with Nikki's chart. Dr. O'Connor made a few notes, glanced at the clock, and said, "Let's call it. 8:48 p.m."

"What happens to her now?" Boone said.

"She'll be taken to our morgue until she's picked up by a mortuary of your choosing."

"Is that where my son is?"

"Yes, sir."

"I need to see him."

"Oh no, now I thought Dr. Sarangan told you —"

"No, I just mean, I assume he's wrapped."

"Of course."

"I just need to see where he is."

"That can be arranged. Give us a few

minutes and we'll put your wife next to him. I need to know who would be going down there with you."

"Oh, uh, Jack Keller and Francisco Sosa. I'll ask his wife, Maria, but she might not want to come."

"Mr. Drake, you know you can remove your mask now. That was more for her sake than for yours. And you may also touch her now if you wish."

Boone hesitated and Dr. O'Connor motioned to the nurses to follow her out.

And there he stood, before the bandaged, ravaged remains of his wife. He approached slowly and laid a hand softly on the bindings that covered her forearm.

"Nikki. Nikki. By now you know I lied about Josh. Forgive me. Take care of him till I see you again."

Boone's intuition about Maria had been right. She embraced him and asked if he minded if she declined.

"No, no, I understand."

"You need a place to stay tonight?" she said. "We have a guest room and you're more than wel —"

"That won't be necessary, ma'am," Jack Keller said. "Already thought that through. I'll take Boone to his place to get whatever he needs, and then he's gonna stay with me at my apartment for a little while."

Boone could have wept with relief. The last thing he wanted to do was stay with the pastor and his wife and their young family.

At the morgue, Sosa and Keller hung back as Boone peered through a window to where two gurneys had been set side by side. The gurneys were the same size, but of course the bodies were not. A morgue tag had been affixed to one of Nikki's huge, mitted hands, and another was clipped to the tiny bundle next to her. Boone was grateful he had been talked out of looking past the wrapping on both bodies. This was enough. He knew it was them. He didn't need to see the carnage their bodies had become. He would remember them the way they were — healthy, happy, gorgeous.

An attendant stood silently near the door, his head lowered.

"Would I be allowed to touch the baby, sir?" Boone said.

"I've been instructed to leave him wrapped."

"No, I mean, just . . ."

"Certainly."

He held the door open for Boone, who stepped inside and just grazed the tiny wrappings with his fingers. The crater in his soul told him he had lost his every reason for living.

At the hospital exit Boone embraced Sosa and his wife and nodded as they promised to keep in touch, to pray, to accede to his every wish. Then he had to pass through a phalanx of both church elders and uniformed colleagues from District 11, shaking hands and hearing endless expressions of sympathy. Though the condolences were heartfelt and kind, to Boone it seemed like enduring a gauntlet.

Boone paused at the door and called Pam McNickle's cell phone. That it immediately went to voice mail told him they were en route. He recorded the awful news, then told them where he would be and asked them to call anytime.

Finally outside in the humid darkness, it was just him and Jack again, as it had been right before the fateful call to Keller's cell.

"Thanks for taking me in," Boone said as he headed around to the passenger seat. "You didn't have to do that."

" 'Course I did. You think I didn't see the look on your face when that pastor's wife invited you? Anyway, I was plannin' it all day. I knew you wouldn't want to stay at home, regardless."

Keller put the key in the ignition and

hesitated. He sighed heavily and his voice sounded shaky. "I just don't know what to say, Boones. We say 'sorry for your loss' to somebody every few days, but that just doesn't seem to cut it now. Just know I'm here for ya."

"I know, Jack."

Boone shouldn't have been surprised that his little house was still a hub of official activity. Why anyone thought he could make use of the place, despite the annihilation of the garage, was beyond him. All the utilities were centered in the garage, so there was no power, and for all he knew, no water. Forty or so onlookers had gathered to watch CFD investigators still picking through the ashes and debris.

Keller pulled their oversize flashlights from the car to use inside. In a daze, Boone found a couple of suitcases and threw in whatever he thought he might need over the next several days. He hoped he would never have to return to this place, but he had no idea.

The place smelled of smoke and gasoline, and everything he saw that reminded him of Nikki and Josh stabbed him to his core. He noticed Keller scooping up a couple of family pictures for him, but he was too exhausted to even thank him. They were in and out of the place in minutes.

"I wonder if she's still up," he muttered as they headed back to the car. Several firemen approached shyly with sad looks, offering handshakes.

"Sorry, man," many said. "Awful sorry."

Jack threw the suitcases in the backseat. "If who's still up?"

"Mrs. Gustavson." He glanced at his watch. "It's after ten, but her lights are still on."

"You wanna check?"

"Yeah, I do."

The crowd parted silently as he started up her walk and rapped on the door. She pulled back a curtain to peek out, then immediately burst into tears and hurriedly unlocked the door.

"Oh, Mr. Drake!" she said. "I'm so sorry! I did everything I could. I didn't know what else to do!"

"Just wanted to tell you I appreciate it, ma'am. They didn't make it."

Mrs. Gustavson nodded. "I just saw it on the news. I couldn't imagine they would survive that. I'm so sorry."

"Thank you."

"If there's anything I can do —"

"I'll let you know."

■ ■ ■ ■

On the way to Keller's apartment, Jack pulled into a drive-through.

"I can't eat, Jack, really."

"You mind if I do? Sorry, but I'm starvin' and I don't keep much at home."

"No, sure, go ahead."

Keller ordered for both of them and Boone gave him a look.

"So sue me," Jack said. "You gotta eat whether you feel like it or not."

Boone nibbled at a burger and sipped a Coke as Keller pulled out. Boone's cell phone rang. "Oh no," he said. "My parents."

"Gotta talk to 'em, pal. It's all part of the deal."

His mother and father cried with him, expressed their love and grief, and insisted on meeting him at the district station house the next morning. "We'll walk you through all the funeral stuff," his father said, and Boone had to admit he could use the help.

"I'm not working tomorrow. You want to just meet me where I'm staying?"

"Officer Keller told us someone from downtown was going to be meeting with you at headquarters tomorrow," his dad said. "No?"

"Just a sec." Boone covered the phone. "You talked to my parents already?"

"Yeah, they heard it on the news and called the station."

"What's this about a meeting tomorrow with somebody from downtown?"

"Yeah, sorry, I was gonna tell ya. Somebody from HR or benefits or something wants to go over a bunch of stuff with you. And you know bereavement counseling is mandatory. Time off too. All that."

"This has to be tomorrow already?"

"None of this is gonna be easy, pal."

6
In Limbo

Jack told Boone to go on in and that he would carry the stuff from the car, but Boone would have none of it. He was glad to have something to do. Bone weary as he was, activity was the only antidote to the devastation in his mind. He was grateful he had not seen the destroyed bodies of his loved ones, but his imagining of their terrible deaths was just as bad. If this had to happen — and for the life of him he couldn't think of a reason — could they not have been spared such torture?

He was surprised to see the size and quality of Keller's apartment. All the man had done for the last year was complain about his various alimony payments. And while he had enough years on the job to enjoy a decent salary, Boone had not expected him to have such a nice, big place. The guest room even had its own bathroom.

As Boone busied himself unpacking his

suitcases, Jack stepped in with the family pictures he had taken from the house. "I figured you'd want these eventually. I mean, I can only imagine how hard it would be for you now."

"No, you can't, but thanks. Yeah, if you could just store 'em somewhere for me. Someday I'm going to want to have them."

"You need anything from me, Boones? Anything at all? I can leave you alone. I can order you some food. The fridge is full, but it's nothing much."

Boone shook his head. "Unless you can turn back the clock twenty-four hours, there's nothing else I want. Thanks for staying close today."

" 'Course. My advice? Turn your phone off or even put a message on your voice mail that it might be a while before you call people back. Everybody's gonna be, you know . . . calling."

Boone sat on the edge of the bed, suddenly realizing he was still in full uniform, bulletproof vest and all. "You're right, I know, but I'm just not up to it. I'll turn it off."

"Want me to put a message on there for ya?"

Boone shrugged and tossed it to him, telling him his voice mail pass code. Jack recorded, "Yeah, thanks for callin'. This is Boone's phone, but this isn't Boone; it's his partner. Boone appreciates your call, but I'm sure you understand he may not be able to get back to you right away. Don't leave a message unless it's urgent, because his mailbox will just fill up right away. Watch your e-mail for funeral arrangements and all. If you need anything immediately, you can call me at the following number . . ."

Boone thanked him, stood, and began peeling off his uniform. "I feel like I've been run over by a truck," he said, "but I don't know if I'll be able to sleep."

"Too tired? Been there."

"Just too much firing through my brain. I'm not going to be able to shut it off."

"Take a shower, whatever you need. You want to stay up and talk, I'm game for that."

"Think I'd rather be alone, Jack, but thanks."

"I understand. You know, if you really have trouble falling asleep, I'll bet that Indian doctor guy from your church would prescribe something."

"Ah, I've never used that kind of stuff, and I wouldn't want to bother him."

"Bet he'd be glad to help."

"I'll keep it in mind, but I'll tell you the truth, Jack: I can finally see why people overdose. Put a bottle of sleeping pills in front of me right now, and I wouldn't trust myself not to scarf it down to try to join Nikki and Josh."

"Nobody could blame you, Boones, but you know I don't wanna hear that kind of talk. No sense making a tragedy even worse. Listen, if you get desperate for some shut-eye, I got some cheap wine in the fridge — oh, that's right, you don't drink. Well, I won't tell anybody if you do. 'Least that won't kill ya."

Boone threw on a bathrobe as he heard Jack opening and closing cabinet doors in the kitchen. Part of him wanted to collapse and sleep for days. Yet he had an idea there would not be any sleeping this night.

"Boones," Keller said, knocking softly, "I'm happy to stay up if you want me to."

"No, please. I'll see you in the morning."

"Listen, you need a thing, just knock and don't give it a second thought. Promise?"

"Sure."

Boone had no intention of bothering Jack, but being left alone for the first time since driving to work that morning was not something he relished. That kind of solitude used to be something to look forward to. Usually, after interacting with Jack and the public and other cops and staff all day, he enjoyed just listening to some tunes and anticipating the welcome waiting for him at home.

Boone turned the shower as hot as he could stand it and tried to stifle his loud sobs, hoping Jack couldn't hear. When the water ran so long it began to grow lukewarm, he shut it off, toweled down, and pulled on sweatshorts. He sank down on the edge of the bed and hung his head.

Another light knock on the door.

"Yeah."

"Your in-laws called. They're at the hospital, and he wants you to call. I can tell 'em you're asleep."

"No, I'll call. G'night, Jack."

Boone had never heard the buttoned-down Air Force lawyer sound so shaken. Though there was nothing he wanted less, Boone offered to meet the McNickles somewhere.

"No, no. You try to get some sleep."

"I can't imagine."

"I know, me either, but we're all going to need it. Pam is having a pretty hard time. So am I, of course, but one of the doctors here prescribed a sedative."

They agreed to get together the following evening with his parents. Boone did not look forward to that but could think of no way to get out of it.

When he hung up with his father-in-law, he had to wonder what it was like for a man to lose his only daughter and grandson. Boone wished he could transfer some of his grief and empathize with the man. Steve McNickle had known and lived with Nikki for eighteen years. Boone felt cheated of a lifetime with her.

Did it make sense to be alone with his thoughts? They were jumbled, and his emotions made them worse. Mixed with his horror and grief and loss was that rage over the unfairness of it all. He knew what all the church platitudes would be, and they were no help to him now. People would fall all over themselves to try to help, and while he knew they would mean well — as he would in reversed circumstances — the fact was that there was absolutely nothing anyone could ever say or do to make this better. And right then it seemed nothing could even dull a pain so sharp it threatened to slice him in two.

How long had it been since he had told Francisco Sosa that his wife was his life and that he would die for his son? He meant it then and doubly now. Without Nikki he didn't want any kind of a life. And he would have given everything he would ever own if

God would have allowed him to trade places with Joshie and let Boone suffer such a horrible death so the baby could live.

His hands and feet felt weighed down from exhaustion, yet Boone could not sit still. He paced the bedroom, then the living room, peeking out onto the street and idly watching the occasional car, cab, or truck pass.

If he could talk with anyone, anyone at all, who would it be? Pastor Sosa? Maybe someday, but not soon. His parents? That would come too soon as it was. Jack was a great partner and friend, but he had nothing to offer. Oh, how he longed to talk with Nikki. She knew him, understood him, would grieve with him, stand by him, love him unconditionally, allow him to rage, to question God, to weep, to despair over his very life.

What did other people do in this situation? The devout talked to God, but the sad fact was, that wasn't Boone. Though he'd been a Christian since childhood and a churchgoer his whole life, his prayers were limited to grace at mealtime and pleading with God for something he really wanted or needed — like safety in a life-threatening situation. He had not, as he had heard Pastor Sosa put it so succinctly, maintained his spiritual disciplines.

Sosa had also often warned in his sermons that sometimes God has to allow a person to come to the end of himself before he realizes his deep need. Well, Boone couldn't imagine being more at the end of himself, but right now he and God were not on speaking terms — and he wasn't sure they ever would be.

Everyone who knew and loved him would say something about God being his strength and comfort, his rock in this time of need. But Boone had too many questions, too many challenges, too much of a grudge against a supposedly all-powerful, loving being who could allow such a thing to happen to Nikki and Josh . . . and him.

Boone felt guilty that his stomach was growling. It seemed wrong to worry about physical needs when what was left of his wife and baby was wrapped in gauze and plastic and lying on steel gurneys in a basement morgue. But he was hungry, and Jack was right that it would do him no good to quit eating altogether. With everything he was going to have to endure, he didn't need malnutrition.

The refrigerator was full, as Jack had said, but his hope for a cold piece of beef or chicken or ham was not to be satisfied. The only thing that appealed was a block of cheese. He hauled it out and rummaged through the cupboards, looking for crackers. Boone found a box, hoping they weren't stale, but he also came upon Jack's clumsy hiding place for the family photos he had swept off Nikki's end table. And what was that? It couldn't be. Why would Jack think to bring Nikki's Bible?

Boone couldn't bring himself to peek at the pictures. He also let the Bible lie. It was Nikki who could be found reading it most every day, as casually as the way he leafed through *Sports Illustrated* or *American Police Beat*. He kept his own Bible on the shelf next to his gun safe above the refrigerator. He hauled it out for church each weekend, even though Pastor Sosa projected the passages on huge screens. Few people brought their Bibles to church, but to Boone it seemed like part of the Sunday uniform. And it was the one time he wasn't embarrassed to be seen with it.

It was strangely thoughtful of Jack to have brought it, along with the photos. What must he have been thinking? Keller was about the furthest thing from a man of faith or even a church attender. Maybe he thought Boone would find some sentimental value in Nikki's Bible. And perhaps he would. For the moment, it held nothing else for him. Even if it did, he wasn't about to give it the chance.

Boone hadn't really tasted the bits of food he had forced down earlier in the day, but he did taste the sharp cheese and salty crackers. In a strange way, it felt good to have something hit his senses other than abject grief and revulsion. And now he was thirsty.

Should he try the wine? Would it help him sleep? He'd never had any specific conviction against alcohol. His high school and college buddies had enjoyed beer, especially during and after pickup games and of course at Wrigley, Cellular (still called Comiskey back then), and Soldier Field. Boone had tried it and just didn't care for it. He had tried wine years ago too. To him it smelled like rotten fruit, and in a way that's what it was. He'd never had enough to get any kind of a buzz.

What would be the harm now? It could only help. He desperately needed sleep, if for no other reason than to allow his brain to idle. He found a large drinking glass and filled it half-full of the red. That was the extent of his knowledge of wines. Red and white. Oh, he knew that the older a wine was, the better it was supposed to be, but it seemed to him, the fresher the better. Why not? That line had always made his friends laugh. Well, Jack Keller said this was cheap stuff, and it bore the name of a grocery store chain, so he sure didn't have to feel any guilt about sipping away something valuable.

Boone didn't even have to remove a cork. How convenient, a screw cap. The familiar fermented smell hit him first. He had no idea why people swished wine around in the glass or sniffed it. He would just sip at first, because he did not expect to like it.

And he didn't. Too strong. Tasty after a fashion, but a little went a long way. He reminded himself that this was medicine, anesthesia, and while his curiosity over the wine and his talking himself into imbibing had for a few seconds channeled his mind elsewhere, there was no hiding what he needed to be numbed to.

Three or four sips, each tasting slightly less strong than the previous, hit the back of his throat with a little jolt, and finally he began to feel a bit of the mellowing it was supposed to provide. He certainly wasn't high, but something was happening. He mustered his courage and took a healthy swallow.

That was a mistake. His friends never

guzzled wine like they did beer, and now he knew why. It was meant to be sipped. But as he wasn't drinking for enjoyment but rather for lubrication, he decided to just finish off the glass. Whew, boy. A little dizzy. Would fatigue follow, the kind that would actually allow him to sleep or at least doze? He could only hope.

As Boone cleared the table and tidied up, he felt light-headed and sick to his stomach. That wasn't all bad. Any feeling other than despair had to be positive. He sat at the kitchen table and breathed heavily for a few minutes. Something was going on inside. Going to bed was worth a try.

Boone staggered heading for the bedroom, and the door seemed to grow smaller as he approached. He had to reach twice for the knob, and he fell onto the bed, rolling over and pulling the covers with him as he went.

There was a part of him, no surprise, unaffected by the wine. He never lost sight of the tragedy, of the crisis he was enduring, of the difficulty facing him in the days to follow. But he for sure had the proverbial buzz now, and he assumed it had come from much less wine than would have affected someone with experience.

His breathing grew even and deep, and while he was still in a dungeon of despair,

Boone felt himself drifting, drifting. Suddenly he was back in the squad with Jack, and Jack was speeding toward Presbyterian St. Luke's while talking and laughing on his cell. He handed the phone to Boone, who was pleased to find it was Nikki wanting to put Josh on the phone.

The boy spoke gibberish, mixing in a few *Da-da*s and *bye-bye*s, and Boone laughed and laughed. And then they were pulling into the hospital and Boone was following Jack to the emergency room admitting desk, where Nikki sat with Pastor Sosa. They greeted him like a long-lost friend and told him the patient he wanted to see was just down the hall. Jack followed him, and they entered a patient room, only to find Boone himself in the bed, his hands thickly bandaged.

"Didn't expect to see you here," the patient Boone said to police officer Boone.

And his eyes popped open. He sat up to see that only thirty-five minutes had passed since he'd tumbled into the bed. The glow of having talked to Nikki and Josh was still with him, but only briefly as reality barged in. Within seconds he was wide-awake and fully aware. The only crazy dream had been the one that had just awakened him. The other nightmare was real. His life, his loves, were gone. He was sleeping in his partner's apartment because he had been left virtually alone in the world. Yes, despite the multitude of people who would offer to do anything for him, Boone felt desperately alone.

When he couldn't fall back to sleep for an hour, he made his way to the refrigerator and drank straight from the bottle. That gave him another forty or so minutes of fitful, crazy-dreamed sleep, and he wasn't sure how restful it would prove to be by morning. At 2:30 a.m., he rose and repeated the cycle. At four he awoke on the couch in the living room, knowing he was drunk and reeking of wine, yet needing another pull or two to allow him to sleep until dawn. Somehow he found enough fortitude to be sure he ended up in the guest-room bed. It was bad enough that there would be no pretending — the bottle was nearly empty. He didn't need to be discovered passed out on the floor somewhere.

Boone awoke at dawn with a raging headache, his mouth sticky and sour. He heard and smelled bacon frying, so he dragged himself to the door and peeked out, asking Jack if he had time to take a shower.

"Sure. You sleep?"

"After a fashion."

Jack displayed the wine bottle and said, "I would have too. Hungover?"

"Yeah, sorry."

"Hey, any port in a storm. Get it? Listen, you don't have to be in uniform today."

Twenty-five minutes later, Boone padded out in jeans and polo shirt and stocking feet, chewing aspirins. His Beretta was on his belt. He felt little hungrier than the day before but knew Jack had gone to a lot of trouble and would badger him to eat anyway. Once he started on the bacon and eggs, he ate a normal helping.

"Don't get used to this," Jack said. "I usually only cook for my girlfriends."

Boone couldn't muster a smile, but he appreciated Jack's trying to be light.

At the District 11 station house, Boone was aware of the sympathetic looks and stares. He just nodded to anyone who caught his eye. It was plain they didn't know what to say but felt awful for him, the way he would have had this happened to one of them.

A heavyset black woman in uniform stood when he entered the conference room, and the district commander, a beefy white-haired man in his sixties named Heathcliff Jones, introduced her as Bonnie Wells from

Human Resources, benefits division. She expressed the obligatory "I'm sorry for your loss," and "Thanks for taking the time to meet with me," then sat before a mountain of papers and forms and notebooks.

Boone assumed there was a lot he would have to know, but when he looked expectantly at Ms. Wells, she looked to the commander, who said, "I'm going to sit in on this, if you don't mind, Officer Drake."

Boone had rarely spoken to the commander outside of a few official recognitions for his service. "Absolutely."

The commander sat next to Ms. Wells and folded his hands before him. "Let me say first, Officer, that you have my sincerest condolences and those of the entire department."

"Thank you."

"And let me also express my apologies for not having been with you yesterday. Very little could keep me away when one of my people is going through something like that. But as you may or may not know, command staff were at a retreat downstate all day, and there was simply no getting back in time to see you at the hospital. I'm sorry."

"Not a problem, sir. I appreciate it."

The commander looked to Ms. Wells, who began. "Officer, I will try to keep this as short and clear and informative as I can. I lost my own husband of nearly forty years last fall, and while it was expected and followed a long illness, I know I was in no condition to be hearing all kinds of policies and such even before the funeral."

Boone nodded.

Ms. Wells reminded Boone that he had twenty paid vacation days and thirteen paid holidays, and that with proper protocol and documents, he could combine these and patch them together with what she called bereavement benefits "to give yourself an appropriate amount of paid time away from the job. You need that, and we assume you are aware of the need as well."

"I sure don't feel like working," Boone said. "And I have no idea when I will."

Commander Jones leaned forward. "We're going to ask you to surrender your weapon, Officer, during the furlough. It's standard procedure."

"You're worried I'm going to hurt myself?"

"No, not at all —"

"Because frankly, I just might."

Boone could tell by Ms. Wells's look that he probably should not have admitted that. She and the commander shared a glance. "To be frank," Jones said, "that is one concern, but primarily, if you are not going to be policing on work time, we don't want you policing off duty during a time like this either. There are emotions and so forth not conducive to typically rational police behavior. I'm sure you can understand that."

"I do."

"I've asked your partner to bring in your M4 from the squad, and I'll be happy to take your department-issue sidearm for safekeeping."

Boone stood and unstrapped it, sliding it across the table. "I feel like I'm being suspended, just like in the movies."

The commander flashed a smile, then seemed to realize he probably shouldn't, and it faded. "I'm not asking for your badge, Officer, but we would appreciate if you would temporarily not carry it. This is to keep you from any temptation to act in an official duty during your time off."

"Now, sir," Ms. Wells said, "there is the matter of psychological evaluation and potential counseling."

"Oh, I'll pass."

"It's not something you should avoid, Officer Drake."

"But really, I'm okay. I'm not happy, and I don't know what my future holds, but nothing will be served by subjecting me —"

"It's mandatory," the commander said. "Just like when you've fired your weapon in the line of duty. It's for your own benefit. Now I can see by your face that you want to argue this, Officer, and believe me, I'd feel the same way you do. But there is only one way out of this, and I think you know what that is."

"Resignation."

The commander nodded. "For all I know, you may lose your passion for the job." There was that word again. "I would certainly understand. But let me urge you to not make any rash decisions. You will have plenty of time to think this all through, and the evaluation and counseling may prove helpful. There will certainly be no harm in it. I realize how fresh this is, Officer. I mean, it hasn't been even twenty-four hours. But your job may prove to be your salvation. We have not interacted a lot, but everything I know of you tells me you're all cop. I know right now you can't imagine going back on patrol. But the day will come when you will need to do just that. Will you make an effort to trust me on this?"

"I'll try."

"And can we schedule you for the evaluation and, if deemed necessary, counseling — let's say within a week after the funeral?"

Boone nodded.

Commander Jones stood and shook his hand. "That's good thinking, son. Now, if you'll excuse me, Ms. Wells will give you some particulars regarding the department's involvement in the funeral."

Boone raised his eyebrows.

"That surprise you?" the commander said as he headed to the door. "Your family is our family. Now you don't have to accept it, but we will work with your funeral director and your church and stand ready to add all the appropriate department pageantry you'll allow. The entire CPD is eager to be represented and express itself to you, Officer Drake, and I hope you'll allow us to do just that."

Ms. Wells outlined a package that called for Boone to be furloughed for up to twenty working days, during which he would be evaluated for counseling, and then it would be determined — between him and the department — when he would be eligible to return to duty. "You may be eager to get back on the job, or you may need more time. Within reason, we will accommodate you."

"And this funeral thing?"

"My advice would be to simply say it's all right to, as Commander Jones said, let us work with your people. You handle the arrangements however you wish, and we will come alongside to add to the program. You may rest assured that it will be dignified, appropriate, and if I may put it this way, impressive. You will be glad you allowed us to be part of it. May I record that you are open to this?"

"I guess; sure."

7

THE WILDERNESS

Boone owed a lot to his parents, Ambrose and Lucy Drake. Whatever he was, whatever he had become, they had helped shape him. Problem was, his father was a know-it-all who pretty much did know it all, and his mother overspiritualized everything and tended toward the dramatic.

Well, that was an understatement. By the time Boone got out of his meeting with Bonnie Wells, he was well aware his parents had arrived. Jack Keller was in the commander's office with them, and Boone could tell from Heathcliff Jones's look that he was doing all he could to tolerate the intrusion. Even before entering, Boone could hear his mother going on about "proud of him," "devastated," "don't know how he's going to cope," "says such wonderful things about his job," and "loves the dickens out of you."

She wasn't beyond embellishing. Boone could not remember having ever mentioned the commander to his parents. He certainly had spoken highly of Jack Keller, so maybe she was confusing the two.

While Boone appreciated his parents to a degree, he believed he had made parenting easy and had said as much to friends and to Nikki. He knew how that sounded, but it was true. When he got to his teen years and his friends were rebelling and doing whatever they could to make life miserable for their parents, he saw no future in that and became essentially a model son.

It wasn't that he idolized them or put them on a pedestal; they were flawed human beings like everyone else. And while there was much to admire about both of them — his father's discipline and consistency and his mother's devotion to God (or at least to the church) — Boone could have easily become a pain to them.

He saw himself as smarter than they, and there were times when he would have loved to poke holes in their assumed logic. He'd had the typical separation issues, wanting early to abandon them and their rules and their antiquated ideas, become a rebel, strike out on his own. But the truth was, he *was* smarter than that. He had the ability to look farther down the road and see that he would only delay his hopes and dreams if he made stupid, regrettable decisions.

And so he had humored them. Besides, they didn't deserve rebellion and opposition. His younger brothers gave them all of that they could handle. To their credit, his brothers seemed to be finally turning out all right too, but for years they'd had to deal with the inevitable comparisons to their straight-arrow older brother. Boone's motives might not have been pure, but he was a hard act to follow.

Nikki had wisely postulated that Boone's form of separation and rebellion had come late and in the form of passive-aggressive behavior. Once he was out of the house, he was really gone. He was the son who rarely called, never wrote, and visited only when he couldn't get out of it. He'd simply had enough of his father's smug wisdom and his mother's assumption that any son of hers would share her enthusiasm over spending every minute of every day "serving and glorifying the Lord." Pastor Sosa would love her.

Ambrose had a dignified, if severely dated, look. Tall, gray, and willowy, he sat in Commander Jones's office looking every bit the almost-retired small-town city manager. It would surprise no one that his daily uniform was suit and tie, never anything less. But now, on a sad day off, he wore tan slacks, a seventies-style turtleneck, and a sport coat with a faint checked pattern and a pocket hankie.

Lucy appeared already dressed for the funeral in a black dress with black purse and accessories — everything, Boone thought, but a mourning veil. She had become matronly with age but retained vestiges of her pretty youth.

When Boone tapped lightly on the commander's open door, his mother leaped to her feet. "Oh! Here he is now, bless his heart! Oh, Boone!"

He surrendered to her exuberant embrace, and both Commander Jones and Jack Keller immediately rose and excused themselves. "Let me give you a few moments here," Jones said. "Feel free to take all the time you need."

Boone wanted to leave the commander's office to him and use the conference room, but he never got a chance to say so over his mother's squalling. With her head pressed on his shoulder, she immediately burst into tears. "We've been praying for you every second. How awful. How horrible. We've lost a precious daughter-in-love — you know that's what I've always called her. And we've lost our only grandbaby. But you —

oh, Boone. God will have to help you get through this somehow. We'll be at your side the whole way."

"Thanks, Mom."

"Standing with you, Son," his dad said, finally getting a chance to embrace Boone — something he hadn't done since Boone was a small child.

The entire morning, from the time he had risen and showered and eaten and ridden to headquarters, Boone had been aware of a strange thing. Something deep in him was working to somehow protect him. He was shutting down emotionally. He no longer felt weepy. The gruesomeness of the deaths was being pushed back, tucked away somewhere he could not access it every moment. Boone would not have been able to survive if those images were ever at the forefront of his consciousness.

But they had been elbowed aside by a resolute coldness that somehow took the rage that had made him want to kill someone — maybe even himself — or to destroy something, and planted in him some seed of deep resentment. That was not a strong enough word for it, he knew. But he was also aware that this was going to manifest itself in a frigid, largely silent persona. No more games. No more cordiality. Unless someone could somehow say something that made sense of any of this, he was not going to even pretend to be comforted.

And it started now. He didn't want to be mean to his parents. Again, there was no question that they, like everyone else, meant well. And they had suffered losses too. Not like his, but losses nonetheless. They would have to be inhuman to not feel deeply for him. But they couldn't help him. No one could. Boone could not imagine anyone saying or doing anything that would change an iota of what had become of his life in one horrible instant.

One moment he had been enjoying the life and marriage and family and career he had always dreamed of and striven for, and the next he had lost everything that mattered to him except his job. And even that, at least for now, held no appeal.

Boone was reminded of a movie that was already old when he had seen it years before — *Catch-22.* He remembered little of the plot, but one scene played out in his mind. A character was standing on some sort of floating dock when a low-flying military aircraft flew into him and tore him in half. He was sure that the way the special effects artists for the picture portrayed it was not likely true to life. The character's body, from the torso down, was left standing on the dock a few seconds before collapsing.

No doubt if someone had been hit by an airplane like that, his entire body would have been obliterated or thrown hundreds of feet. But there was something poignant to Boone now about that ugly scene. It represented how he felt. Standing tall one second, chopped in half the next.

All this rumbling inside Boone's head protected him in some weird way from the awfulness that had plagued him the day before. He could not have gone on living that way, with such sensory overload that he could barely function. It was not lost on him that this new mind-set was poisonous, that he was internalizing the rage, the confusion, the anger at God, and that it would turn him into someone he could not have imagined being.

But, he realized, it was this or suicide. He would work at not hurting anyone. There was nothing to be gained by taking his rage out on someone else, especially Jack or his parents or his pastor. But neither was he going to exhibit any pretense. People would want to hear that he was doing okay under the circumstances, that he was numb, that he knew time was a healer. Well, he wasn't going to say or even pretend that was true.

His plan of action, if he could call it that, was to retreat inside himself. He would tell the truth as dispassionately as he could, and while he would not be intentionally unkind, he would engage in no role-playing.

"I'm sorry for your loss too," he told his parents, and his mother cocked her head and scowled. Clearly she had not expected him to sound so detached and formal. Too bad. He *was* sorry for their loss. "Now let's not take advantage of the commander's kindness and let him have his office back. He's one of the busiest men I've ever known, and we can talk in the conference room."

"Yes, we can pray in there too," Mrs. Drake said.

"Well, you can," Boone said.

She took his arm as they vacated the office and headed down the hall. "Whatever do you mean, honey? You must be praying every minute."

"No, I'm not. I figure if God has something he wants to tell me, like that he's sorry for letting this happen, he can say so. I have nothing to say to him."

"Oh, Boone! You have to know God has some purpose in this! We don't know what it is, and we're in the valley of the shadow of death right now, but —"

"Please, Mom. There is no *shadow* here. It's death plain and simple, and the worst kind you can imagine. I'm not going to tell you not to pray if that gives you some comfort. But it gives me nothing, so spare me."

"This is just a stage," Mr. Drake said as they sat in the conference room. "Perfectly understandable. Be grateful we have a God who can take it when we shake our fists at him and tell him what we really think. He lost a Son too, you know —"

"Dad! Don't start with that. Not now. I don't have the power to raise my son from the dead, okay? And my son didn't die for the sins of the whole world as part of some eternal cosmic plan."

Ambrose held up a hand. "All right, Son. I understand. Let's concentrate on details and logistics. This is all too fresh and painful for all of us."

Lucy sat weeping, and Boone suspected her abject grief had been replaced with horror over her son's blasphemy. As was her wont, she broke into prayer. "Lord, please forgive us and help us and show us your grand design here."

Boone snorted and shook his head.

"Do you have my legal pad, dear?" Ambrose said, and the teary Lucy pulled it from her oversize handbag.

"Boone," his father began, pulling out a pen, "there may be some value in our just getting through some practical things here. Have you settled on a funeral home?"

"No, but I was going to talk to my pastor. There's at least one funeral guy in our church, and I figure Pastor's worked with him before."

"Good. You'll want to get on that today so the bodies can be moved and prepared —"

"There'll be no preparation, Dad. As you can imagine, this will be a closed-casket funeral."

His father nodded, looking grim. And his mother interrupted. "Before we go too far down this road, Ambrose, let's tell Boone what we've arranged at the hotel."

"Oh yes. We understand it will be some time before you could move back home, so —"

"I'm not moving back home. No way I could live there."

"Now, Son, let me caution you not to make any hard decisions while you're, you know, in the earliest throes of —"

"Dad, it's just not going to happen. There may be a few more things I'll want to haul out of there, but moving back in is not an option."

"You know, Boone, widows and widowers often make this mistake. They abandon —"

"End of story, Dad. Now, please, this is my decision, and I've made it."

"They abandon their homes to their eventual regret. It's not financially wise, and in fact, they often too late realize that they have squandered their most valuable asset."

"How many times do I have to say it?"

"If you could just put off any final decision for a month or two. I can certainly understand why you would not want to move back in right away . . . ."

Boone pressed his lips together and stared at his father, shaking his head.

"You're not open to *any* counsel, Boone?"

"You figure that out all by yourself?"

"Boone!" his mother said.

"I can't be clearer. Now let's move on."

"Well, your mother wants you to join us at the hotel. We rented a suite with a separate room and facilities for you, and we plan to be here a full week. You shouldn't be alone, and —"

"I'm not alone; you know that. I'm staying with Jack."

Lucy made a face. "Isn't he the one you told us was thrice divorced and enjoys the ladies?"

"I knew that would come back to haunt

me. Fact is, putting me up will cramp his style, but he's offered and I've accepted. I'm going to get my own place in a month or so, as soon as I'm ready to get back to work."

"Now see," Ambrose said, "there's one reason you should delay your decision about your house. By then it will likely be made livable, and —"

"End of story, Dad."

"Boone," his father said, "this is hard on all of us. There's no need to be testy."

"Well, forgive me if I'm not in a good mood. There's no need to try to talk me out of decisions I've already made."

"Do stay with us for a week, though, Son."

"Dad, I appreciate the thought, but I prefer to be alone. Jack is going to be on duty during the day, so . . . ."

Lucy said, "This is the worst time to be alone. You need someone to talk to, someone who understands, someone who loves you and will pray with you and support you. . . ."

"Let's move on." Ambrose checked his list. "I know this is not something you want to think about right now, but I'm assuming you had insurance policies on your family, I mean besides the little starter thing we bought for Josh."

Boone nodded. "I don't remember all the

details, but yeah, something was in place. The policies are new, so they won't be worth much. Maybe pay for the funeral."

"You might be surprised," his father said. "If you're insistent on leaving your home, perhaps the policies and the homeowners insurance will allow you to, you know . . ."

"Yeah, I know." Boone was grateful his father had finally seemed to surrender to his decision about the house. But the idea of somehow benefiting financially from all this was repugnant.

Lucy had clearly disengaged from the conversation. She had her purse in her lap, had turned away from Boone, and sat staring out the door. He'd known her long enough to know what was on her mind. Plainly he wasn't taking much counsel, making all his own decisions. Their advice and offers of help and companionship were being rejected, so she had nothing else to say or do. Her pouting was fine with Boone. It took the pressure off. He was an adult, and he would decide how to muddle his way through this. He wanted to tell her she ought to be grateful that the only thing keeping him from eating his gun was that he didn't want to inflict even more pain on them.

His father spoke again. "Just know that

we are here, standing by, willing to help in any way you want or need. If you'd like us, or me, to meet with the funeral home people or your pastor, just say the word. Otherwise, we will appreciate knowing when and where the funeral will be."

"Thanks, Dad." Boone told him the Mc-Nickles were in town and wrote down their phone numbers. "Guess we can all get together for dinner this evening."

"And can I at least pray for you one more time?" Lucy said.

"I'd really rather you not," Boone said, rising. "In private, do what you want, but for now, no."

She sighed and shook her head, but she also rose and approached him, arms wide. He let her hug him. "I know this isn't you, Boone, and I understand. It's the devil attacking you."

"He attacked me yesterday," Boone said. "And he wins. I surrender."

Boone felt it only right to see his parents out to their car. His mother was still crying and his father looked stony. "If you change your mind," Ambrose said, "here's where we're staying." He handed Boone a piece of notepaper from the hotel that had the address printed on top.

116

Jack met Boone when he reentered headquarters. "I gotta get on the street," he said, "but you oughta know you've had dozens of calls. Most of 'em, I think, have taken me up on the offer of leaving their messages with me. I'll save them for ya. Mostly just condolences. But your pastor has called several times and really needs to get together with you. He says he'll meet you anywhere. You wanna call him or you want me to get back to him?"

"Yeah, tell him I'll come to the church after lunch." Boone was partly proud of himself that he had stood up to his parents and put into action his new resolve to be brutally honest. On the other hand, what had been the point of hurting people who loved him and cared about him and who had indeed suffered losses themselves? Would he ever again be in his right mind? He couldn't imagine.

His car had been in the district headquarters lot since he had arrived for duty the day before. He drove to an ATM, withdrew several hundred dollars, and found a sunglasses place. If there was one thing he hated, it was people gazing into his eyes, trying to detect something. Did they want to know if he had been crying? Were they trying to determine what was going on in his mind?

Boone asked to see the largest and best wraparound sunglasses, and a girl who appeared to be fresh out of high school showed him the top-of-the-line Maui Jims. He immediately slapped down the cash and rejected all her offers of warranties, cleaning cloths, and other accessories. He had them on before he left the shop.

Boone drove through a fast-food place for lunch, again seeing the food as only fuel, eating less than he was used to, and surprising himself by realizing that he was not out of emotion. As he sat eating, he was reminded that Josh had come to love the kiddie meals and the toys and sharing fries with him, and the tears came afresh. He removed the big sunglasses and wiped his eyes before finally heading for the church.

Boone kept his shades on even in the huge, dark sanctuary, and when he was greeted tentatively and sadly by staff, he responded to their expressions of sympathy with mere nods. He followed the long hallway behind the baptistery to the pastor's office, where Francisco Sosa's secretary told him Pastor was in a meeting but had asked to be interrupted.

"Not a problem. I'll wait."

"No, he insisted."

"It's not like I'm going anywhere."

"Just one second. They're finishing up right now."

Boone stood when the door opened and Pastor Sosa ushered out a young couple. He introduced them to Boone and said they were there for premarital counseling. It was obvious they knew who he was, as they both immediately sobered and told him how sorry they were. It stabbed him to see them so young and in love.

Sosa asked his secretary to get Boone a Coke, and they settled in his office. The pastor asked him how he was doing, whether he had slept, how the meeting went with HR and his parents. Boone admitted he was doing poorly, had not slept well, and asked how Sosa knew about the meeting with the benefits people.

"Your partner has been very good about keeping me informed. Seems like a good guy. You ought to invite him to church. Well, I suppose you already have."

That had never crossed Boone's mind.

Sosa picked up a phone message pad and said, "Actually, I've already heard from a Ms. Wells. She says you authorized her to work with us on some Chicago PD involvement in the service and at the gravesite."

Boone nodded.

"I need to know from you what you want in the program, and then I'll be happy to work with them."

"You know what?" Boone said. "I can't even think about the program. You knew Nikki. You know how special she was. Whatever you want to say is fine with me."

"Did she have a favorite song?"

Boone thought a moment. "You know, she did have two hymns she really liked, but I don't know if we've ever sung them here. In fact, I'm pretty sure we haven't."

"Sorry, our demographic is not big on hymns, but we can sure work them into a funeral service."

"I know 'em because our church sang all the old hymns when I was growing up. 'I Will Sing the Wondrous Story' and 'My Jesus, I Love Thee.' "

Sosa suddenly covered his mouth and shook his head. He pulled his hand away and his eyes filled. "Wow. Didn't expect that to hit me that way. You know, those are two songs we ought to sing around here, quaint language and all."

"Yeah?"

"Whoo. You bet. I'll find someone to sing those. That'll be really special. Anything else you want included, read, said, anything?"

Boone shook his head. "I just want to get through it."

"You want it to be right, though."

Boone didn't want it at all, right or not. This ordeal got worse by the minute, and a funeral service would be the hardest part yet. "You understand I need to leave all the details up to you. I can't deal with it."

"Sure. But I'll keep you posted so there are no surprises, and if anything comes to mind that you want included, let me know."

Boone told the pastor everything about the meeting with his parents.

"I suppose they're just trying to be as helpful as they can, Boone. At some point down the road, you're going to want to make that right with them. Besides their own loss, you can imagine how they feel for you. No one wants to see their child in such pain."

"Tell me about it."

"Sorry."

Boone shrugged.

Sosa gave him the contact information for the parishioner who owned a funeral home. "He also has contacts with cemeteries, unless you already had —"

"No, I need that."

"I'll get with the funeral home and the cemetery," Sosa said, "but only you can pick out the caskets."

"I hadn't even thought about that. Is it too much to ask to have you do that too?"

"Boone, I'm at your disposal, but no, that is something you really must do yourself. I'd be happy to come along, but —"

"Please at least do that. You know I'm off duty for a while, so just tell me where to be and when."

Sosa made some notes. "And I assume you want to take a break from the junior boys."

"Yeah, I don't know about getting back to that at all."

"No?"

"Well, every one of 'em is going to remind me of Josh and what might have been."

Sosa nodded, looking dubious. "Gives you a chance to have positive impact. But that's not something you need to decide now. I understand it'll be a while anyway." They sat in silence for a moment. "I'll want to pray for you before you go."

Boone was afraid of that. "There is something I need to talk to you about," he said.

"Anything."

"I lied to Nikki just before she died."

"You lied to her? You mean you kept from her the truth about Josh?"

"Worse. She asked about him and I told

her he was fine, that she had saved him."

"Hmm."

"It was a flat-out lie; what can I say?"

Sosa looked genuinely puzzled, and Boone appreciated that. He was so tired of snap judgments, especially by Christians. "I'm not a big proponent of situational ethics," the pastor said, "though this is a classic case. Surely nothing would have been gained by telling her the truth. You could have said he was fine without saying it was because he was waiting for her in heaven. The lie was in saying she had saved him."

"Yeah, so what do I do with that?"

"You feel as if you have sinned?"

"I know it's wrong to lie. I lied to the most important person in the world to me."

"She already knows and understands. And there are no tears in heaven, so it's not like she's holding a grudge. But this is what's so great about God. You can take this to him. He understands, and he also forgives. There aren't many people who would hold you accountable for keeping such awful news from a mother on her deathbed. But if you need to deal with it to restore your relationship with God, you know what to do."

Boone hung his head. "It's going to take a lot more than that to restore that relationship."

"Really? You want to talk about it?"

"Maybe someday. Not today."

8

THE ORDEAL

Boone didn't realize until deep into the afternoon that he had made a mistake by going back to Jack Keller's apartment. He wasn't getting together with his parents and his in-laws until dinner, and he didn't want to see anyone until then.

The problem was, there was nothing to do at the apartment but obsess, and Boone was restless. He was getting a picture of what depression was about. For years he had heard of people who suffered from something much worse than the blues or a little melancholy. He knew of people unable to get out of bed in the morning, people to whom absolutely nothing in life appealed. They had no appetite, seemed to forget what gave them pleasure, and lost interest in things that used to entertain them.

Boone had turned his phone to vibrate and checked it infrequently. The calls kept coming, but he would only take the ones from Jack. TV was of zero interest. Boone wasn't hungry. He knew he had to busy himself somehow, but all that was on the horizon was the list of things he and Pastor Sosa had to accomplish before the funeral. Was he expected to be eager about choosing caskets?

He dreaded the dinner, but there was no way out of it. He couldn't begrudge his parents and in-laws their bereavement, but what shape would that macabre meeting take? Would they all just sit there in tears? Maybe there was something to the tradition some cultures had of loudly wailing away their grief.

Boone's mind raced as it had the night before. And while his sleep had been alcohol-induced and hardly effective, he felt exhausted but strangely not drowsy. He desperately needed a nap, but there would be no sleep without wine, and he didn't dare drink before dinner. On the other hand, he was going to need help sleeping that night, so that gave him something to do — an errand.

Finding it hard to believe it had been only twenty-four hours since the horror, Boone tried to refocus. Jack had been good. He wasn't the kind of person Boone would have chosen as a friend, and if it were up to his mother, he would not be allowed to even associate with the man. Jack didn't have the morals Boone had been raised with, but then he didn't claim to be a man of faith, either.

Jack was an expert in his profession, a loyal friend, and generous. Boone wanted to do something for him. He headed for the local grocery, telling himself it was to carry his weight, to stock Jack's shelves, express some gratitude. In truth he was there to load half a dozen bottles of cheap wine into his shopping cart.

Boone knew he should just talk to Dr. Sarangan and tell him he was desperate for sleep. The man had volunteered for a most unsavory task and not only broke the news, but also remained with Boone until he could see Nikki. Surely prescribing a sedative would be nothing for him.

But something else was at work here, and it was not lost on Boone. Much as he tried to tell himself that he was the furthest thing from an alcoholic and that he had no plans of becoming a drinker, let alone a habitual one, he *had* turned to booze to medicate himself. Whether it led to problem drinking or not, he could rationalize it, at least for now. He supposed it was part of his thumbing his nose at God, of rebelling against the cliché-ridden emotionalism of his mother's showy faith.

After rearranging the refrigerator to fit in the steaks and chops he had bought for Jack and storing the wine in the pantry, Boone felt he had accomplished at least one small task. He left a note for Jack, telling him he would be home after dinner and to enjoy the new foodstuffs. None of it appealed to Boone.

Meanwhile, his phone kept buzzing. He recognized names of people he had grown up with, people from his childhood church, his own brothers, people from Community Life, women who had worked with Nikki in the nursery, mothers of other babies, cops, coworkers. They would get Jack's message and call him for memorial service details — which would be settled once Boone and Pastor Francisco Sosa met with the funeral director.

Nikki's parents were about ten years younger than the Drakes, and the two couples had never really socialized with each other much, despite that their kids grew up in the same church. Steve McNickle had worked for the judge advocate at Scott Air Force Base in Belleville until his transfer to Alaska when Nikki went to college. The

Drakes and the McNickles really knew each other only from their kids' engagement party, the wedding, and their paths' crossing when each mother spent time helping Nikki after Josh was born.

By the time Boone showed up at the hotel restaurant, the couples appeared to be longtime friends. All were red-eyed and whispering and touching each other gently, as old dear friends might do. Boone found it all disconcerting. He knew he shouldn't have been surprised at how pale and drawn Mrs. McNickle looked. He had always appreciated his mother-in-law's mature beauty, and it was no secret where Nikki's looks had come from.

He joined them and sat awkwardly, recoiling when his mother tried to remove his sunglasses. "Come on, Boone, those aren't for wearing indoors."

"I'm not wearing them to block the sun, Mother."

The couples ordered soup, but Boone ate just crackers, despite the protests of both women. He hated how all four of his elders probed to find out how he was doing and cooed about what he should do and when he should do it. Worse was when the talk turned to the disposition of the house, and they all wanted to know what shape it was in and whether they could see it.

"Why would you want to do that?"

"Because my daughter and grandson died there," Mrs. McNickle said. "I need some closure."

"Well, I saw it, and it didn't close anything for me."

"I want some mementos, too," she said.

Boone had never had a cross word with her, but that made him flinch. "Mementos?"

"Yes! A piece or two to remember Nikki and Josh by."

It was all Boone could do to keep from snapping that he didn't want anyone in there pawing over the family keepsakes. So it surprised even him when he said, "Feel free. Take everything if you want it. I don't care if I go back there as long as I live."

Steve McNickle started in with the same advice Boone's own father had proffered that morning, causing Mr. Drake to nod and uh-huh. Boone threw up both hands. "I'll decide, okay? I don't want to discuss this."

"Can we talk about the funeral, then?" his mother said.

"What's to talk about? I'm handling the details with Pastor Sosa."

Pam McNickle pushed aside her bowl. "You don't want input? ideas? anything that

130

should be mentioned?"

Boone stood. "Just let me handle it, okay? This is going to be hard enough without too many cooks in the kitchen."

"Where are you going?" his mother said.

"I need to be alone. Do you mind?"

All four looked horrified. "Yes, I mind," his mother said. "You're not the only one suffering here."

"I didn't say I was! Now I will get you all the details, but unless you want to be involved in picking out caskets . . ."

Boone's father shook his head sadly, but Steve whispered, "We need to cut him some slack."

Boone hurried out, feeling both embarrassed and justified. He appreciated Steve's attitude, but he hated being catered to.

When Boone got back to the apartment, he surprised Jack with how early he was. Keller had changed out of his uniform and was already enjoying a big steak.

"There's plenty, thanks to you. Want some?"

Boone shook his head and headed for the guest room. "Got to lie down, Jack. Sorry."

"You don't have to apologize to me, Boones. Ever. You do what you gotta do and let me know if I can help."

That was all Boone wanted to hear from anybody. Why did it have to come from the guy they all thought was a hopeless case? Jack was the only person Boone felt comfortable with just now, and he didn't want to spend much time with him, either.

Boone lay staring at the ceiling, trying to calm himself and think about what was coming. What he really wanted was to grab one of the bottles of wine from the pantry, but he was still too embarrassed to do that in front of Jack. The night before was one thing, but he didn't want to make it obvious that this might become a habit.

It used to be that Boone could lie on his back for ten minutes and drift off. That sounded so inviting — and remote — now.

Jack had the TV on, and soon he turned it off, knocked, and opened Boone's door. "I'm gonna catch a movie. Want to go?"

Boone shook his head.

"I'll try not to wake you when I get home."

Twenty minutes later Boone had rushed through half a bottle of wine and left it on his bedside table. That kind of sleep wasn't much of a relief, but it was sleep nonetheless.

By morning the bottle was empty, Boone was hungover again, and he was getting a picture of what it would take to survive. Good thing the wine was cheap if sleep was going to require a bottle a night. When he emerged from the bedroom, sunlight was already streaming through the curtains and Jack was gone. He had left a note on the kitchen table.

Sorry, but your pastor called and he's coming by this morning. He said he knew you would probably beg off, so he was just gonna show up. If you don't want to see him for some reason, maybe this'll give you enough warning to find somewhere else to be. See you later.

Jack

Great. Boone knew there would be no avoiding Sosa, but he had hoped to put him off until their funeral-planning sessions. As soon as Boone finished with all his obligations, he would disappear from Community Life, at least for a while. Maybe forever. Sosa was the type who would pursue him, and the day would likely come when Boone would have to be honest with him. Meanwhile, couldn't Sosa simply leave Boone alone?

He jumped in the shower, trying to think of somewhere to escape to. He wouldn't hang around headquarters the way some furloughed cops did. Maybe he could just hang out at a public library. Boone needed to figure out how to handle all the legal things that would arise out of this mess. His homeowners policy would rebuild the house, but then he wanted to sell it as soon as possible. The insurance claims on Nikki and Josh would likely be paid after a cursory investigation, but Boone was so repelled by the idea of, in essence, benefiting from their deaths that he could barely stand to think about it. He didn't feel up to studying these things yet, but he needed something to do to keep himself from being so buried by his grief that he would not be able to function. In fact, he was close to that already.

When Boone headed out to his car, he found Sosa's parked right behind it. The pastor sat behind the wheel, reading. There would be no avoiding him. Boone approached and Sosa got out.

"I knocked," he said, "but I didn't want to ring the bell in case you were sleeping."

"I was in the shower. Thanks for coming."

"Let me see your eyes, Boone."

"Nah. They're bloodshot, as you can imagine."

"Not sleeping?"

"Not much and not well."

"You got someplace to be, or can you ride with me for a few minutes?"

Boone shrugged and climbed in. Sosa drove to a park where young mothers watched their kids on playground equipment. The two men sat on a park bench fifty yards away.

"Don't want to spook them," Sosa said. "Nobody trusts anybody anymore."

"Did we have to come here?"

Sosa looked away. "Life hurts," he said. "You're not going to be able to avoid mothers and kids."

"I can try."

"In your job? And in our church? I'm not trying to be mean, Boone. I just wanted to check up on you, make sure you're all right, get you out of the house a little."

"You wanted to make sure I was all right?"

"You know what I mean. I know this has rocked me and so many in our church, and that has to be just a fraction of how awful it is for you. Lots of people are praying for you."

Boone stared at the ground. "It's a little late for that."

"There's never a wrong time to pray."

"Yeah? What are they praying for? That I'll get my wife and boy back? I don't want anything else."

135

"Come on, Boone. You know what they're praying for. That God will come alongside you, make himself known to you, get you through this somehow. I can't tell you how he's going to do that. And I'm not saying how long it will take. But I can tell you that you need to let your brothers and sisters embrace you and gather you in and care for you."

Boone stood and wandered. To his credit, Pastor Sosa let him go without following. Boone turned and called out to him, "I've got to tell you, nothing sounds worse. I don't want to be pitied. I don't want to be cared for. I want to be left alone."

"You know that's not healthy."

"Well, pardon me for not being healthy."

Finally Sosa rose and approached, but Boone was grateful he didn't touch him. "Friend, listen. They didn't teach us in seminary how to deal with stuff like this. I can't make it make sense any more than you can, and you're not going to hear me say that God's got some kind of a master plan and that he'll make it all clear to you someday. He *does* have a plan, but he's not the author of death. All I can make of this is that it's evidence of our fallen world. I'd love to be able to tell you that somehow because of this, a hundred wonderful things will happen that will make it worth it. That's ridiculous and you know it better than I do. You want my prediction: we're not going to know the *why*s this side of heaven. In the meantime, all we can do is put our shaky faith and trust in the God we know is sovereign."

"See? That's it, Pastor! I've believed all my life God is sovereign! I know he's out there. I just don't know what he's doing, and I don't like what he's allowing. Am *I* praying? You want to know that?"

"I know you're praying, Boone."

"You're wrong, because I'm not. Frankly, I'm afraid of what I'd say to him."

"He can take it."

"I've been told that, too. I just have nothing to say to him. I don't want to speak to him, I don't want to sing about him, I don't want to worship him, I don't want to study him, read about him, or even talk about him. I don't want to come to church anymore."

"I know you feel that way now —"

"Do I ever. I'll go to the funeral because Nikki would want me to, and I'd never hear the end of it from my family if I didn't. But it's going to be all I can do to sit through it. I know you're going to worry about me and be praying for me and will keep coming

after me, and I know you'll think you're doing the right thing. But I need the freedom
to back away. Will you give me that right?"

"Of course, Boone. You have a free will.
You're an adult. But again let me plead with
you not to base your decisions on emotion.
Don't do anything you'll regret. If you need
time away, time to be alone, time to not be
the center of attention, I understand that.
I'll support that. But don't tell me I can
never check in on you, see how you're doing, find out what I can do."

Boone nodded miserably. How would it
look to reject even that, much as he wanted
to?

"I can tell you one thing," Sosa said.
"People are going to want to rally around
you, and you'll rob them of a blessing if you
turn them away."

"What do I care about their blessing? They
can get blessed doing something for someone else."

"Fair enough, but just so you know."

As Francisco Sosa drove Boone back to Jack
Keller's apartment, he took a phone call
from the funeral director. "He can see us
this afternoon," he told Boone.

"I just want to get it over with."

"I'm sure he'll make it as easy as possible.

Boone, let me just leave you with one more word. Is that all right?"

Boone shrugged.

"There is such a thing as the nourishment and survival of the spiritual life. If you starve yourself spiritually, you can also die spiritually."

"I feel dead."

"Of course you do. How else could you feel? I'm going to accede to your wishes and leave you alone for a while after the funeral, but you can't keep me from praying for you. And I just hope you'll stay open to God trying to communicate to you, reminding you that he loves you in spite of how things look now. He will do this through friends and Christian brothers and sisters and relatives. I daresay he's trying to speak to you through your partner. Jack's been very good to you, hasn't he?"

Boone nodded. "And he's not even a believer."

"That doesn't mean God can't use him. He can use anyone he wants to."

The visit to the funeral home was every bit the ordeal Boone had feared, though the owner seemed to do what he could to make it easier. They settled on a late Friday morning service at the church, and Boone chose a triple burial site at a nearby memorial garden — leaving space for himself. The man walked Boone through all the logistics and charges, then guided him through a room full of casket choices. Boone couldn't get out of there fast enough. Given a few options, he shrugged and looked to Francisco, who said, "That looks fine," and Boone immediately agreed.

Toughest was seeing the tiny caskets for babies. How was one supposed to select something like that? Boone began to pant, shook his head, and said, "I can't do this. Pastor, just point to one and we'll go with it."

Sosa gestured toward a pure white box that was so small it made Boone hurt just to look at it. He nodded. "Let's get out of here. If something has to be signed, just do it for me, okay?"

The pastor whispered to the funeral director, "You have the church's guarantee. Just see to everything."

Back in front of the apartment, Sosa told Boone when to meet with him Friday morning and what to tell the family about where to be. "I'll handle the coordination with the Chicago PD. I've already heard from your mother."

"No surprise. What did she want?"

"Just wanted to be sure you weren't neglecting anything. I assured her we were working together. She was most interested to know who was singing."

"I don't even know that."

"I assumed you wanted me to handle it. You gave me those two songs, and I've got the lyrics typeset so we can project them. But you know the college girl who worked with Nikki in the nursery?"

"Yeah, Cheryl something?"

"Schmidt. She's a singer and said she'd be honored."

"Perfect."

"You'll spend some time with your family now, won't you?"

"She talk to you about that too?"

"Said you were being independent."

Boone cocked his head. "That's fair. Everybody else, my brothers and other relatives, are all just waiting to hear the date and time, and they'll come in the night before."

"That's nice."

"I hadn't thought of it as nice. Nice would have been having them come for some happy occasion where Nikki and Josh could have been part of it. Now, every time I think of something I need to say or do, the first

141

person I think to call is Nikki."

"I'm sorry."

Boone could see he was wearing on the pastor. He hadn't meant to become so high maintenance. But he was through pretending, too.

"Try to let your family grieve too, Boone. As hard as it's going to be, it's important that they know you at least appreciate their coming, right?"

Boone nodded miserably. "But having to entertain them the night before, you know . . ."

"I don't think anyone expects that. They'll want to see you, sure. But they'll understand that you're in deep waters."

Boone snorted. "That's exactly what it feels like."

"Would it bother you if I prayed for you right now?"

"Would it bother *you* if I said I'd rather you not?"

"No, I understand. I don't need to pray in front of you. But I want you to know that I *will* pray for you. And I'll leave you alone until Friday morning if that's really what you want. You need me for anything, you know where I am."

9
THE MEMORIAL

Until the day of the funeral, Boone made himself miserable, drinking himself to sleep every night, suffering hangovers every morning, and spending his days walking the streets or strolling the North Avenue Beach. He had never been much for idle time. He liked doing things, accomplishing something. All walking the beach accomplished was to bring back painful memories.

A year before, he and Nikki had brought one-year-old Josh to this very beach for the first time. Joshie had sat on a blanket, slathered in sunblock, reluctant to touch the sand. Nikki held handfuls of it in her palm and let it fall gently on his toes. He giggled and kicked, then brushed it off. Finally he reached for handfuls himself.

They walked him at the edge of the water, so cold he avoided the waves like bedtime. Boone now knew that when he could find it within himself to return to their home to mine for keepsakes, tops on his list would be a picture taken by a passerby of him with his hot wife and his fat-cheeked baby under a floppy hat. The question was when he would ever be able to again look at it and smile.

Boone didn't know why he even carried his phone, which seemed to buzz constantly. His parents, his in-laws, and his brothers tried everything to reach him. Even Jack urged him to communicate something to them, anything. "Just tell *me* what to say, Boones. I mean, I understand, but when all I tell them is that I'll pass along the message, you know what they're thinking."

"They're thinking what I want them to think: that I don't want to talk to them. I'll see them at the funeral."

The temperature pushed a hundred Thursday afternoon. Boone trudged the beach, carrying his shoes, and ducked under a concession stand overhang to get out of the sun. His phone emitted the unique chirp that told him he had a text message. It was from Francisco Sosa.

Praying 4 u, as many are. Celebrate the past rather than rue the present. Service will b about Nikki & Josh, not u. Str8 talk, I know.

Empathize with those who suffer w/u.
Singer Cheryl has a question, so take her call.

Boone spent much of the rest of the afternoon sitting and gazing at the water. He wondered how soon he could talk CPD into letting him back on the job. Maybe he was in no condition to be dealing with the public, but this alone time couldn't be healthy either. How he'd love to be forced to solve problems, mediate disputes, interact with people who didn't look upon him with pity.

Boone was walking back to his car when the call came from Cheryl Schmidt. "Hi, Mr. Drake," she said. "First I just want to say how special Nikki and Josh were and how much I'll miss them."

"Thanks." Boone could tell she had started to tear up, and he didn't want that. "Thanks for doing this singing thing, Cheryl. What can I do for you?"

"I'm just wondering if I can change all the *thee*s and *thou*s in the second song to modern words. It sounds really archaic-like with the original lyrics."

"Whatever you think is best."

"Oh, and another thing. I don't, like, perform, you know?"

145

"Sorry?"

"I don't gesture or stroll around. I just try to let the words communicate. Is that all right with you? Because I wouldn't be offended if you wanted someone else."

Boone hardly knew what to say. He couldn't have cared less, but he didn't want to hurt her feelings. "You'll do fine."

His car was so hot from sitting in the sun that he started it and cranked up the air, then closed it and stood outside in the shade waiting for it to cool. Boone used the time to text his family on both sides.

Understand I just can't talk right now. Bear with me & see you tomorrow. Thx.

All that served was to make his phone go crazy on the way back to Keller's apartment. It chirped and chirped and chirped. He dropped into an easy chair, waiting for Jack to get home from work, and peeked at all the messages. They all had the same theme: just-let-us-help-you-love-you-stand-by-you-we're-here-for-you.

I know. I know. I know.

The downside of Boone's nightly sleeping aid, of course, was the daily hangover. He

146

agonized for hours, even after he ate. Friday was, if anything, worse. He had so dreaded this day that, even besotted, Boone had tossed and turned all night. It seemed that more than a half-dozen times he had dreamed of the funeral. In one dream he was late. In another he was the only one there. The worst had him sitting in the front row next to Nikki and holding Josh. He had awakened sobbing.

As dawn finally announced itself through the window and Jack poked his head in to be sure he was up, Boone knew he was no longer dreaming. He sat there with his heart racing, nauseated, shaking, and squinting against the sun. His mouth was dry and his head pounded.

"You look awful, Boones. You need help gettin' ready?"

He shook his head.

"I got coffee on, and you should get some aspirin in ya. You know alcohol and caffeine are diuretics, so I'll put out some juice and water too."

"Ugh."

"Just let me be the doctor this morning, hear? The pastor and the funeral guy called and wanted to set up a pickup time, but I told 'em you were ridin' with me. That still the plan?"

Boone nodded.

"Listen, if you're feeling really bad, believe it or not a light workout will help. It won't feel like it at first, but trust me —"

"Not a chance. I'll suffer through. And I don't feel like eating either."

"You got to. Toast and bananas. Force yourself, or you'll regret it. Today's gonna be hard enough, don't you think?"

Boone couldn't argue with that.

By midmorning he had eaten, hydrated, medicated, showered, and dressed in his only suit. When he emerged from the guest room, he found Jack dressed in his formal blue uniform, his checkered cap on the kitchen table next to his white gloves.

Boone's headache had dulled, but he could tell it was going to be with him all day. He plopped into the comfy chair before the dark TV and said, "I know this is your spot, Jack. Sorry."

Keller pulled out a kitchen chair and sat next to him. "I don't know how many times I have to tell you, what's mine is yours."

"I know, and I appreciate it. But I'm not going to overstay my welcome."

"Don't worry about that."

"I'm already worried about it. What's the old adage? Fish and houseguests start to smell after a while?"

Jack chuckled. "I'm no wordsmith, but I gotta think it's something more eloquent than that."

"Give me another week or so and I'll be out of your hair. I'll get the legal stuff out of the way — the insurance and the house and all — and then find a place."

"Not on my account."

"C'mon, I can't be good for your social life."

"Ah, that's mostly legend, know what I mean? Anyway, I can always go to their places."

Boone sighed. "I need to be by myself, anyway. Nothing personal. I just prefer it."

"It's your call, Boones. Hey, do we need anything? It's been so long since I been to church that I don't even remember. You need a Bible? You know I put Nikki's in the cupboard. Having that with you would be a nice touch."

"Don't need anything. They project verses on a screen. But you know what? Yeah, let me have that."

As soon as Boone had it in his hands, memories flooded him. It *would* be nice to have something of Nikki's with him. And it was a beautiful Bible with a supple leather binding bearing her maiden name. He had no idea how long she'd had it, but it had verses underlined and margin notes on almost every page.

Was he being disingenuous, even phony, to think he should carry it? It would thrill his in-laws and his parents, especially his mother, but that wasn't the point. It was certainly not for show. It was for him.

He'd already promised Francisco Sosa that he would thank people for coming. Boone knew they would tell him how sorry they were, how they would be praying for him, how wonderful Nikki was, how sweet Josh was. And they would mean it; he knew they would.

But Boone would not be able to bring himself to converse about those things. He planned to respond to every comment the same way: "Thanks for coming." He would wear his wraparound shades to hide his eyes, not so much because they were blood-shot from drink or because it might be obvious he had been crying — who could blame him? — but because he wanted to give the impression he was looking people in the eye. And he would not be.

Boone knew and appreciated that regardless of his grief and rage, whoever showed up would have put themselves out on his behalf. People might get tired of his thanking them for coming, but that was all he was prepared to say.

"Tell me what you need from me," Jack said. "I can make myself scarce. I can hang close. Your call."

"Oh, they've got this all-involved seating chart, so I'll be down front and surrounded by both sides of the family. But if you're willing, I'm going to tell them I want you right behind me. If I so much as look in your direction, rescue me from whoever has me buttonholed. Can you do that?"

"You got it. And we'd better get going."

Jack pulled away from the curb with plenty of time to get to the church in advance of Boone's preliminary meeting with the pastor, the funeral director, and the family. The traffic was typically congested, but hardly anything the two cops didn't anticipate at that time of the morning.

About twelve blocks from the church, Boone began noticing more and more Chicago PD squads on the street. "Downtown being represented already?" he said.

"You won't believe it, Boones. The way I hear it, every beat in the city will have someone here in uniform."

"You're not serious. What are there, like almost 280 beats in this town?"

Jack nodded. "Commander Jones wasn't

151

kidding when he said you were family, and that makes your family our family." He grabbed the radio handset and informed the sergeant in charge of crowd control and traffic at the church that he had Boone Drake in the car. The sergeant told him to come in the back way through a side street and that he had someone standing by to park the car so Keller could stay with Boone.

From that point on, the driver of every squad within sight of Keller's vehicle briefly flipped on the blue lights. Bonnie Wells of Human Resources had predicted that Boone would be impressed. That proved an understatement.

When Keller finally pulled in, Boone was stunned to see the parking lot already filling. This was one huge sanctuary, and it was clear it would be full. Thousands of people. Boone toyed with leaving Nikki's Bible in the car, as he was still unsure of his own motives. But at the last minute he decided to hang on to it.

The pastor's secretary was waiting just inside the back door, and Boone introduced her to Jack. "We've talked on the phone," she said, grasping one of Keller's gloved hands. "Sorry to meet you under such circumstances."

She led them through a labyrinth of back halls and staircases, reaching the pastor's office from a direction Boone had never seen. It did not surprise him to discover he was the last one there. The outer office teemed with relatives he hadn't seen since his and Nikki's wedding. The place fell silent when he appeared.

"Thank you all for coming," he said. "This is my partner, Jack Keller."

Everyone began murmuring hellos and shaking hands with Jack. Several embraced Boone, including his brothers, and while he found it difficult to be other than stiff, he began his recitation of the one and only phrase he would use all day. When his mother got her turn, she leaned close to his ear and said, "Surely you'll take off the sunglasses for the service."

He did not respond. She would have to have him tranquilized to get those off.

Francisco held up a sheet informing the family members where they were to sit and asked them to follow his secretary to the first few rows. Boone whispered to the pastor where he wanted Jack to sit, and Sosa told his secretary to make it happen. Then he asked the four parents and Boone to join him in his office.

As they sat across the desk from the

153

pastor, Boone's mother-in-law whispered, "Nikki's Bible. How nice. May I?"

Boone handed it to her, and she immediately broke down. She leafed through it as her husband looked on. "She won that Bible at camp when she was twelve," Steve said.

"Are you going to read from it during the service?" Pam McNickle said.

Boone shook his head. "I would not be able to."

"Me either," she said. "Steve is going to speak for the families, you know."

"Yes," Pastor Sosa said, turning a sheet of paper to face them and sliding it across the desk. "This will be in the printed programs, but just so you can see it. You're sure you're up to this, Mr. McNickle? Everyone will understand if you can't get through it."

"I intend to try."

Boone was impressed. He would not have dreamed of trying. His mother grabbed Steve's forearm. "We wanted to say a few words, but we just couldn't. God will be with you."

"He'll have to be."

Sosa walked them through the order of service. The program would begin with organ and piano music while the caskets were rolled to the front. "The mothers will then place framed photographs atop each coffin. I will read a brief formal obituary for both Nikki and Josh, then introduce Mr. McNickle. After that I'll open the floor for anyone who wishes to be heard. Then we'll have a solo by a friend of Nikki's. I will speak, and then we'll close with one more solo. I will explain the instructions for all who want to join the procession to the gravesites and then announce that all are invited back to the church for food and reflection."

Boone came alive. "For *what?*"

"The church is happy to provide this," Sosa said. "Just light refreshments. Usually about half the people choose to return."

"I knew nothing of this."

"I'm sorry. My error. I didn't even think to mention it. We do it all the time. You don't have a problem with it, do you?"

"I wasn't prepared for it, that's all. The service itself and the gravesite thing are going to be stressful enough. . . ."

Mrs. Drake said, "We can't cancel, Boone. People expect this sort of thing and will want to express themselves. Anyway, the church has gone to a lot of trouble and expense —"

"That is not an issue, ma'am," Sosa said. "This is offered by the church on behalf of the family, so it's entirely up to you all."

"It's up to me," Boone said, feeling slighted.

The four parents began to speak at once. "Not only do we have to do it, Boone," his mother said, "but you must be there. People will expect it."

"I don't care what people expect! It's going to be all I can do to survive, and I don't need a big banquet on top of everything else."

"This is my fault," the pastor said. "I apologize. I can easily just leave out the invitation, and people will understand that the traditional post-service reception is not part of today's agenda. People are flexible."

"No, no," the parents said. "Boone, please."

Part of him wanted to stomp and pound and shout. He was so tired of convention and expectations and worrying about everyone else. Yet clearly there was no way out of this. "Don't expect me to be cordial and cheery."

"No one expects that," his mother said. "Just let people minister to you."

Minister to me? They could better minister to me by leaving me alone.

"Forgive me, Boone," Sosa said. "Totally my error."

Boone nodded. He certainly didn't want this weighing on the pastor.

Pam McNickle handed the Bible back to Boone. "I'm sure you know this, but somewhere in there is Nikki's prayer list. She's kept one there for years."

Pastor Sosa's secretary returned to usher the parents to their seats.

"Boone," Francisco said, "hang back and you and I will walk in together, all right?"

When the others were gone, Francisco put a hand on Boone's shoulder and pulled him close. "Are we all right?"

" 'Course."

"Do I need to apologize again?"

"Please, no."

"Thanks," Sosa said. He pulled open a closet door, revealing a small mirror. He straightened his tie and checked his teeth. "Occupational hazard. Need a last peek?"

Boone was going to decline, but Sosa opened the door farther and he caught a glimpse of himself. Everything was in place, but Boone was sobered to realize how lined his young face was. The last several days had not been good to him. The sunglasses gave him a hard, foreboding look, and that was fine with him.

Following Francisco down the back way to the sanctuary was almost as dreadful as the walk to ICU not so many days before. As they entered from a side door, Boone realized he had never heard such silence in the sanctuary. Usually the place, especially when full, was hopping with music and chatter.

A low murmur began when Boone and the pastor split, Sosa heading to a chair near the steps to the platform and Boone to his seat in the front row next to his mother. Beyond her sat his father and his in-laws, beyond and behind them the rest of the family. Boone was relieved to see Jack directly behind him. Most stunning, however, was that immediately behind the rows reserved for the family was an entire section filled with hundreds of Chicago PD officers, men and women in formal dress uniforms.

A pianist and an organist made their way to electronic keyboards and began playing. When Boone heard a low moan from all over the auditorium, he knew the coffins were being wheeled down the center aisle. People turned as they would for a bride, but Boone sat staring down, gripping Nikki's Bible so tight his fingers felt stiff and his knuckles turned white.

The caskets were transferred to a bier in the front, the tiny white one tucked in next to Nikki's and gleaming under a spotlight. Boone found it hard to breathe. His mother looked to Mrs. McNickle, and they stood together. Pam placed a framed portrait of Nikki atop her casket, and Lucy Drake put a picture of Josh on his. Boone hung his head again, refusing to look.

Francisco Sosa strode to a simple lectern at center stage and solemnly announced the birth and death dates of mother and child, reciting the litany of relatives who both preceded them in death and survived them. "And now Stephen McNickle, father of Nikki and grandfather of Josh, will speak on behalf of the family."

Steve looked shaky to Boone as he took the stage, pulling a single sheet from his breast pocket, fingers fluttering as he spread it flat before him. He cleared his throat to little avail. He had to lean close to the microphone to be heard. And he never lifted his eyes from his notes.

"It is my privilege to speak on behalf of the families. Nikki was a wonderful daughter. . . ."

Steve spoke haltingly, and again Boone had to look away. As his father-in-law told familiar stories and touching incidents, people quietly laughed or oohed and aahed. But when he got to his memories of holding

159

Josh for the first time, of watching the video of his first steps, of his saying his version of *grandpa,* the place was silent except for sniffles and rustling for tissues.

Boone lowered his chin to his chest, pressing his lips tight. He had to hand it to Steve. No way he could have done the same. Boone ran his fingers across the edges of Nikki's Bible, then thumbed through it. There in the back, just as his mother-in-law had said, was a small card titled My Prayer List.

It included several names and situations, but at the very top was, "Boone — that he become a complete man of God and remain a devoted husband and loving father."

On one of the blank pages at the back of the Bible, Nikki had written, "My favorite verse: 'Delight yourself also in the Lord, and He shall give you the desires of your heart,' Psalm 37:4."

Suddenly Boone was aware of his mother leaning toward him. He turned the page so she could see. She reached for the Bible and he reluctantly let her take it. She immediately left her seat and tiptoed over to where Pastor Sosa sat. As Steve McNickle was finishing his poignant remarks, she showed the Bible to the pastor and whispered in his ear.

Sosa took the Bible with him when he replaced Steve at the lectern. "Before I open the floor for comments, I've just been shown something special in Nikki Drake's Bible." He read her favorite verse, then directed people to microphones placed throughout the auditorium. Boone was surprised to see dozens line up to wait their turn. As they began to speak, the pastor returned the Bible to him. Never had anything but his family seemed so precious. Was the first thing listed on Nikki's prayer list the desire of her heart? Had he ever been what she wanted, what she hoped and prayed for? Regardless, it was too late now.

Boone had no idea how far and wide Nikki's influence had spread. She had never been what one would describe as a dynamic personality. Rather she had been a servant, a pleasant people person. And yet friends and coworkers shared story after story of her kindnesses. Boone wondered if he had ever really known her or appreciated her. She had always been wonderful to him, but all this . . . of this he had been largely unaware.

Boone was not sure how she accomplished it, but when the comments from the audience had run their course and the program moved to the first solo, Cheryl Schmidt was already waiting at the lectern. She had apparently slipped up there while the lights were concentrated on the floor mikes. He saw immediately what she had meant by being less than animated. But somehow that made Nikki's favorite songs all the more special.

Cheryl looked to be college-age and was rather plain. But her voice was soft and pure. Apparently without printed music or lyrics, she merely gazed at the audience and sang to simple piano accompaniment:

I will sing the wondrous story
Of the Christ who died for me —
How he left his home in glory
For the cross of Calvary.

Days of darkness still come o'er me,
Sorrow's paths I often tread;
But the Savior still is with me —
By his hand I'm safely led.

He will keep me till the river
Rolls its waters at my feet;
Then he'll bear me safely over,
Where the loved ones I shall meet.

Boone heard weeping from all over the sanctuary. The place fell silent as Francisco

Sosa mounted the stage and quietly traded places with the soloist.

The pastor took a moment to open his Bible and spread his notes. "Dearly beloved, there is a reason that pastors have begun solemn church ceremonies with that phrase throughout the centuries. I call you *dearly beloved* because that is what you are.

"I knew Nikki Drake and her precious baby. I didn't know her as well as many of you apparently did, but I knew her well enough to know that she is dearly beloved by you, and that you would be dearly beloved by her, if for no other reason than that you have made it a priority to be here today.

"As I look out over this crowd and see the grieving family before me, I confess my heart is broken. The remains of the two who are in heaven today lie before us entirely too prematurely. Nikki was a young wife and mother. Josh had virtually just begun what should have been a decades-long journey.

"While we are here to celebrate their too-short lives and to rejoice in their home-goings and the joyous welcome they have enjoyed in the arms of their heavenly Father, you must not wonder whether I am aware of the elephant in the room.

"Believe me, I am aware. There is a villain

in this story. We have an enemy. Some would say this enemy is fate. Destiny. Luck. Happenstance. Others would dare say the enemy is God himself. While no one holds him responsible for these awful deaths, some naturally question how he could have allowed them.

"Do you want the studied, prayer-filled, measured answer from the one who has been charged with trying to interpret God and his Word for you? Here it is: I don't know. Anyone who tells you he knows why God allowed this is a liar. While we rest in what the apostle Paul calls 'that blessed hope' that we will see our loved ones again one day, and while we are instructed not to grieve as those who have no hope, that does not imply that we are not to grieve at all.

"I say grieve. Grieve with all that is in you. Embrace the grief. Ask your questions. I am confident we will not know or understand this whole story until we are in glory ourselves. But I can tell you this: Our enemy, our villain, is Satan, the devil, the prince of darkness."

On the giant screens was projected John 10:10: "The thief does not come except to steal, and to kill, and to destroy. I have come that they may have life, and that they may have it more abundantly."

"The thief is Satan. The one who has come that we might have life and may have it more abundantly is Jesus. You want to blame someone for this, blame the thief. Is your heart broken as mine is? Grieve with all your might.

"If there is any lesson for those of us who remain today, it is that we never know when our end might come. These precious ones were with us one moment and gone the next. Did they want to be used as examples, as visual aids to the brevity of life? Do their loved ones and their dearly beloved friends accept that they have become object lessons? Of course not.

"Our task has become clear. Live life to the fullest, to its most abundant. Grieve with vigor. And come alongside those who remain, loving them, supporting them, praying for them, being there for them. If you have questions, if you're confused, if you hate this and don't understand it and can't comprehend it, imagine their turmoil.

"It falls to us now to be the body of Christ."

Boone sat rigid through it all, fighting to maintain composure, desperate to corral his rage. He gripped Nikki's Bible to keep from shuddering. If he could just bear up through the rest of the message and the one final

165

solo, he could retreat to his rote response for anyone who said anything. And many would. He knew he had to sit there as people filed by the bier and paid their respects and expressed themselves.

Cheryl was waiting in the wings, and she stepped in behind Pastor Sosa as he finished. With a simple piano introduction, again she sweetly sang:

My Jesus, I love you, I know you are
   mine —
For you all the follies of sin I resign;
My gracious Redeemer, my Savior you
   are;
If ever I loved you, my Jesus, 'tis now.

In mansions of glory and endless delight,
I'll ever adore you in heaven so bright;
I'll sing with the glittering crown on my
   brow,
"If ever I loved you, my Jesus, 'tis now."

Boone had been wrung out emotionally. All around him people wept openly. The organ and piano played as first the hundreds of uniformed police officers lined each side of the center aisle, heads bowed, gloved hands clasped behind their backs. More than a thousand people slowly passed by the caskets, some stopping, some touching them, some just brushing their fingers across the tops.

Everyone stopped to shake Boone's hand or hug him or say something. Most just said they were sorry or that they were praying for him; some said something about Nikki or Josh. He couldn't listen. He couldn't smile. He just tried to endure, accepting their touches, their handshakes, their embraces. And he repeated over and over, "Thank you for coming."

The procession to the cemetery, led by more than a hundred squad cars with lights flashing, seemed to take forever. To his credit, Pastor Sosa kept his gravesite remarks brief. To see his loved ones lowered into their graves was almost more than Boone could bear, and he nearly collapsed. At the perfect instant, Jack Keller grabbed one arm and held him up without making a show of it.

On the way back to the cars, the Chicago police officers stood at attention on either side of the cemetery road, and all in attendance strode between them.

The reception lasted two more hours, and by the time Boone had thanked the last person for coming, he wondered if Jack would have to carry him to the car. He couldn't imagine needing wine that night. Maybe for the first time since the tragedy, he would be able to simply fall asleep.

Boone's final task was thanking Francisco Sosa and saying good-bye to the extended families. The pastor pulled him off to the side. "I know you want me to leave you alone for a while, Boone, and I'm going to do that. But listen, you need to be in the Word. Just like with exercise, where anything is better than nothing, the same is true with the Bible. You don't feel like reading or studying just yet, fine. But the Scripture will not return void. Every so often I'm going to just text you a reference. Look it up. Read it. That's all I ask. Will you do that just for me?"

Boone nodded, wondering if he would follow through. Anything to keep Sosa off his back.

Parting from the family was the worst. His mother badgered him to let her stay around a few days, "so you'll have someone to lean on." He promised to keep in touch, but he knew she would do that work for him. He might leave Jack's message on his phone for a while.

Finally back in the car with Jack, Boone had never felt so spent.

10
PROCESSING

"I've got a date tonight," Jack said on the way to his apartment. "You gonna be all right?"

"Yeah. Might turn in early. Just want to get out of this suit. Hey, you bringing someone home? Because I can —"

"Nah, you're fine. Just dinner and a movie. Now if *she* invites *me* home, I might be late."

"I just don't want to be in the way."

"Believe me, I'd tell ya."

Boone was hungry after having ignored the food at the reception. And he continued to feel that he should try sleeping without any help. He changed from his suit to shorts and a T-shirt and was hanging around the apartment snacking while Jack changed into a light sport coat and slacks.

"Call me if you need me," Keller said on his way out. "This gal is an old friend and flexible."

Boone was rummaging in the refrigerator when his phone rang. The readout said it was Steve McNickle. He hesitated, wondering if he should just check the message later. Ah, he'd better take it. What could it hurt?

"Boone, listen, Pam and I were wondering if you could meet us at the house and let us pick through there a bit."

"Oh, I thought you had a flight out tonight."

"No, tomorrow morning."

Pick through Nikki's stuff? Anything but that.

"I'm shot, Steve. How about I choose a few things and send them to you?"

There was a long pause. "Uh, Pam really wanted to see the place. If you're not up to it, maybe we could just drop by and pick up the keys?"

It was Boone's turn to pause. He didn't want them in there without him. "No, I'll go. But I wouldn't mind a ride. Would that be too much trouble?"

"We're on our way."

"One more thing, Steve: would it be all right if I picked your brain a little tonight? Legal stuff."

In the car Pam was still teary from the day's events. "I thought it was a lovely tribute," she said. "Didn't you, Boone?"

It had been one of the worst ordeals of his life. "Uh, it was nice that so many people came."

"You have a lot of friends."

"Well, Nikki did. Me, not so much."

When they got to the house, the front light was on.

"Weren't the utilities down for a while?" Pam said. "If everything else is working, you could move back in."

"Not going to happen," Boone said. "Would you be able to live here?"

"No, I guess I wouldn't."

"You don't want to hear what I think," Steve said. "I agree with Ambrose on this one."

"I know you do," Boone said. "You're thinking primarily financially, right?"

Steve nodded. "Just makes sense."

"That's one of the things I wanted to talk to you about."

Once in the house it was clear this was harder than Pam thought it was going to be. Every picture, every toy, every piece of clothing seemed to remind her of Nikki and Josh, and she just stood caressing things or staring at them and weeping. Steve asked if she was going to be able to do this, and she assured him she would be all right.

Boone said, "If you want a few things, I'd appreciate your showing me first, just so I know where everything is." In truth, the whole idea of her pawing through their things still irritated him, but Boone tried to put himself in Pam's place.

"Thanks, Boone. And what if I choose something, you know, that you wanted?"

I'll let you know — don't worry. "We'll work it out, Pam."

Boone and Steve retreated to the kitchen and sat at the table, Steve pulling a small notepad from his pocket.

"I've got a plan and a few ideas," Boone said, "and I'm not looking for whether you think they make sense. I just want to know if they're doable."

"Shoot."

"I know you and my dad think I should stay here because it makes the most sense from a money standpoint, but here's what I want to do: either sell most everything left here or donate it to charity. I want to use the homeowners insurance to rebuild the garage and fix anything else that was affected by the fire. Then I want a Realtor to sell the place, and within reason I don't want to have anything to do with it. I don't want to be here for showings, sit in on negotiations, any of that. I just want it done."

"Okay," Steve said. "I'm following."

"When the life insurance policies are paid, I don't want to handle those checks either. Can I have them just direct-deposited, along with the proceeds from the sale of the house?"

"Sure, that can be done. You're going to stay with Jack, what, indefinitely?"

"No, I want to find my own place, something very small, maybe two bedrooms at the most and not far from work."

"Uh-huh."

"I'm thinking I can find something that will cost not much more than half the mortgage payment here. I get almost two thousand a year for uniform allowance, and I have plenty of clothes. I'm a rut eater and like cheap food."

Steve was scribbling and nodding.

"My plan is to live as simply and cheaply as possible, putting away every spare dollar."

"That's smart thinking, Boone. It really is. Now what can I do to help?"

"Just tell me who to talk to, to set this all up."

"I'll make a list of potential names. I realize it's way too early to have any idea what the rest of your life will look like, but this makes a whole lot of sense. Just start stockpiling your income, and your options will widen for whatever comes along."

Pam appeared in the doorway, eyes and nose red. Her arms were full. She set a couple of pictures on the table, along with three pieces of jewelry and a tiny pair of Josh's shoes. One of the pictures was the one of Boone, Nikki, and Josh on the beach, Josh squinting under a floppy terry-cloth hat.

Pain stabbed Boone afresh and his voice grew thick. "If I could just get you to send me a copy of that one . . ."

"Of course. It's so precious."

Steve appeared overcome too. He cleared his throat and got back to business. "If you'll just give me your banking information and get me all the other legal stuff, I can make this happen and you won't have to worry about it."

"I didn't want you to go to a lot of trouble."

"I'd really like to do this for you, Boone."

While they were on their way out to the car, Mrs. Gustavson called out from next door. "Mr. Drake! I was wondering when you'd be back."

"Just picking up a few things." He introduced Nikki's parents.

"Oh!" she said, approaching and embracing them both. "I loved her! The baby too! I wanted so much to go to the funeral but just didn't think I would be up to it. I followed it on the news, and it was so big, I think I made the right decision. It certainly looked wonderful, though. It must have been very hard for you all. Well, of course it was. Now, Boone, I wish you'd drop in on me now and then. Don't become a stranger now, and I mean it."

"We'll see," he said. But the truth was he wouldn't likely ever see Mrs. Gustavson again. Coming back tonight made one too many times. Being rid of this place and its horrible memories couldn't happen too soon to suit him.

"We heard about everything you did that day, ma'am," Pam said. "Thanks so much for trying."

"It was horrible," Mrs. Gustavson said, "though I don't need to tell you that. I've been having trouble sleeping. I suppose that's true of all of you, too."

They nodded. Boone wondered if he should recommend wine, but he didn't want to horrify the McNickles. "Ma'am," he said, "would you like a memento or two, something personal of Nikki's or Josh's to remember them by?"

She put a hand to her throat. "Why yes, yes I would. What a thoughtful idea."

"Come on over right now, because if I do come back here, it won't be for a long while. Can you?"

She took his arm and they went back into the house. The woman found a squeeze toy she said "Joshie was rarely without." And she found a picture of the three of them by their car on the way to Josh's baby dedication. "I shot this one," she said. "Remember? You were leaving just as I was getting back from Mass. Look how he's dressed. Can you spare this one?"

"Absolutely."

Boone walked Mrs. Gustavson back home, and at the front door she hugged him tight and long and whispered in his ear. "I know you're not Catholic," she said, "but I'll light a candle for you Sunday. For Nikki's parents, too."

Boone's sleep was not much better than before. His rage had turned to a sorrow so deep it seemed to have no bottom. But he talked himself out of resorting to alcohol. As he had little to wake up for, if he couldn't sleep, he'd just lie there staring at the ceiling or even take a walk. Then he'd doze during the day.

Sunday morning came and went, and Boone had no more interest in church than he'd expected. That afternoon his phone buzzed several times, and Jack Keller, who was on the street, called him during his break.

"That Indian doctor from your church is trying to get hold of you. Sounds important, actually."

Boone called Dr. Sarangan.

"Oh, Mr. Drake! I missed you in church this morning. I spoke with Dr. O'Connor — you remember, the surgeon. She said her people just came across an envelope with some personal items of your wife's that was turned in by the EMTs. Apparently it was overlooked in all the activity."

"Personal items?"

"I have not looked, sir, but she said the envelope is labeled with your wife's name, so if she had any money or jewelry or anything on her person, that's what it would be."

"I, uh, thought nothing survived the fire."

"I am only telling you what I was told. It is at the hospital if you wish to retrieve it."

Curiosity and boredom led Boone to Presbyterian St. Luke's. Sure enough, the woman at the front desk handed him a large manila envelope. It was so light, he wondered if anything at all was inside. He sat among waiting patients and opened it, lifting one end so the contents slid out into his palm.

Three buttons he recognized from Nikki's blouse — still intact because that was where she had pressed Josh to herself in a desperate attempt to save his life.

And her diamond, just the stone and a thin, curled-up section of the mostly melted band. Boone remembered the night he had knelt before her in front of the jewelry store; then they had entered and he had shown her the stone he had in mind. She loved it, feared it was too large and that he couldn't afford it, then selected the band and mounting.

What treasures these were! Boone sat there, streaming tears and ignoring curious stares. He'd never been one for jewelry on men besides rings, but he had an idea for the buttons and the diamond. He would have the buttons affixed to a leather band he would wear as a bracelet. And he would have the diamond somehow mounted on his own wedding band.

Starting Monday and every three days for the next three weeks, Boone met with a fiftyish matronly counselor at CPD headquarters on South Michigan Avenue. She introduced herself as Brigita Velna as she ushered Boone down a long corridor to an office just large enough for her desk, two large file cabinets, and a round table with two chairs. Everything was institutional green.

"What accent am I detecting?" Boone said.

"Latvian," Ms. Velna said, unsmiling. "I do not mean to be unpleasant, but we are not here to talk about me."

She pointed to one of the chairs at the table and sat across from him.

"Fair enough, but as long as you're being direct with me, may I be with you too?"

"Certainly," she said. "One thing you will learn about me is that I appreciate openness above all."

"Good. Frankly, I'm not sure you can help me. You have my file. You know what happened. I just have to get through all of this; that's all."

Brigita Velna looked bored, and her sigh confirmed it. She slid Boone's file folder before her and opened it. "Again," she said, "I do not wish to be adversarial, and I would like that our times together be mutually beneficial. However, it is important for you to understand that I am not here to

179

help you."

Boone realized he was smiling for the first time since the tragedy. "Forgive me," he said, "but that's about the best news I've heard in forever."

"Why is that?"

"Everybody is trying to help me, and of course no one can. But I am curious. If it's not your place to help me, what would you say is your role?"

"The fact is that I am an advocate of the department. I am not unsympathetic to your issues. In fact, I have known my share of personal tragedy and have some small idea what you're going through. I can recommend therapists, counselors, whatever you wish. But I am not here to treat you. I am here to ask questions on behalf of the Chicago PD. I will be asked to determine whether — and when — you are fit to return to duty."

"Interesting."

"I think so, Officer. But you'd be surprised how many misunderstand it. As you can imagine, much of my work concerns officers who have fired their weapons in the line of duty, have been wounded, or have exhibited some unacceptable behavior while on the job. Most can be restored, of course, but the CPD is eager to stay away from behavior that would leave the city vulnerable. The bottom line is, no one wants you back on the street until we're confident you're ready. Determining that is my job. I ask questions."

"Fire away."

Ms. Velna leafed through Boone's folder. "Downstate, mm-hm, church, Scouts, sports." She looked up. "Popular overachiever — would that be a fair assessment?"

"Except in class, I guess. I was above average in grades, but nothing special."

"Pretty nice life growing up?"

"Pretty nice."

"Was this recent incident your first major disappointment?"

"*Disappointment?* Now there's a word choice you could improve upon."

"Granted. I understand this was horrible for you, Officer Drake. It's why you're here, after all. But I mean, never dumped by a girl, had a friend betray you, lost a big game?"

Boone scowled and cocked his head. "Yes, all those, but I'd hardly put them in this category. I bad-mouthed the girl, told off the friend, kicked a watercooler, and got on with my life. But I don't know what to do with this."

Ms. Velna grew quiet and leafed through some more papers, but Boone could tell she wasn't really studying them. She was stalling. Finally she looked up and took a breath. "Officer Drake, are you suicidal?"

He shook his head. "Tell you the truth, I'm a little surprised I'm not, because I don't know what I'm living for now. I won't deny I've had my moments."

She seemed to study him. "You still a churchgoer? Consider yourself a man of faith? I know the funeral was at a church, but how about you?"

Boone hesitated, knowing there was no benefit in being coy. "I'm a Christian," he said. "Fact is, I'm finding out I wasn't much of one, because this has really rocked me."

"Oh, son, it would rock anyone. But, what, you're questioning God now?"

"Of course."

"You blame him?"

"Sort of."

"You do or you don't."

"I don't think he killed my wife and son, if that's what you mean, but I've always been taught that he's all-powerful. I can't get around that he allowed this, and I don't understand why."

Boone had grown emotional with that last answer, and Ms. Velna stood and busied herself tidying her desk and shuffling papers. Clearly she was giving him time to compose himself, and Boone appreciated that.

She sat back down. "I must ask this, Officer. If you had to evaluate your own emotions, as you sit here today, would you say you are more sad than angry or more angry than sad?"

Boone had to think about that one. He sat back and stared at the ceiling. "How important is this?"

"Most important question of the day," she said. "A sad cop is an empathetic cop. An angry cop can be dangerous. You need to be brutally honest with me."

"Can I think about it?"

"No rush. I wouldn't recommend your returning to duty in fewer than fifteen working days anyway. We meet again Thursday. Answer me then."

"And there's no way around that I'm definitely out of service for three weeks?"

She shook her head.

"What am I supposed to do with myself? I can't get this off my mind anyway, but sitting around doing nothing is going to drive me nuts."

"That's beyond my purview. There must be legal things you have to deal with."

"They're pretty much under control. My

father-in-law is a lawyer, and he's handling a lot of that."

"You're living alone right now?"

Boone told her the arrangement with Jack and that he planned to move as soon as he could.

"Have you considered moving back home?"

Boone held up a hand. "Already decided. You can leave that alone. Sorry."

"No problem. I don't recommend your living alone, at least for a while. But that is up to you. I do have an idea for you, though. Is there anything you've ever really wanted to study? It's not a cure-all, but when you find yourself with blocks of free time and you're trying to keep from unduly obsessing over the matter, it's something to think about."

Boone nodded. "I'll try to think of something. But I can't imagine anything taking my mind off . . . you know . . ."

"Of course not. I won't promise this wouldn't be just a temporary diversion. And there will be times you will be wholly unable to concentrate. It's just something to consider."

There was something Boone liked about Brigita Velna. He couldn't put his finger on it, but it had something to do with her straightforwardness, her honesty. And he liked that she didn't fake smiles or pretend that he — rather than the police department or the city of Chicago — was her priority.

By the time he met with her again, Boone had thought through the big question. He'd also heard from Steve McNickle that everything was in place legally and with his bank and the insurance companies. All would happen as he wished, and he could stay entirely out of it. In a month or two, unless the real estate market dictated otherwise, his garage would be repaired, the contents of the house sold or donated, the house closed on, the life insurance policies paid, and all proceeds deposited directly into Boone's bank account.

It was still too early to look for his own place, but as he and Jack discussed things each night, it came to Boone what he wanted to study. Jack told him that things were progressing with his own testing and interviewing, and it appeared that within a month or two he would be transferred and promoted to the role of deputy chief in the Organized Crime Division.

"I'm lookin' forward to serving under the OCD chief, Fletcher Galloway," Jack said.

"A legend."

"Tell me about it. I studied under him at the academy a century ago. You know OCD is under the Bureau of Investigative Services, so I'll officially become a detective."

"Which you've always wanted."

"You know a cop who doesn't? You want to be a detective, don't you, Boones?"

"It's why I'm on the force."

"And I'm going to want you in the Organized Crime Division if I get the job."

"How likely is that, given my age and seniority?"

"Not very, I suppose. But I'll have friends in high places, and you'll bring yourself up to speed. Keep doing what you were doing when you were on the street, and that'll make it easier for me to ask for you. And in the meantime, you better get yourself familiar with the history of organized crime in this city."

Bingo. A subject to study.

Jack recommended a bunch of books, a night school class, and even a training session by a field officer from OCD.

"I don't have to be part of Organized Crime to take advantage of that?"

"All you have to be is a sworn officer."

"Jack, what would you do with me if you could get me into Organized Crime?"

"You kiddin'? You obsess about gangbangers. You'd be a natural in the Gang Enforcement Section."

"I wouldn't work directly for you?"

Jack laughed. "Not till you take Pete Wade's job. He's commander of Gang Enforcement, and he would report to me."

"And how does gang enforcement differ from —"

"Undercover work?"

"Yeah."

"Well, for one thing, *you* can't go undercover."

"Why?"

"Sorry to tell you, but you've been too visible. All your commendations, being in the paper, being on TV, and then, you know, the —"

"Fire, yes, I know. Makes sense. It would be hard for me to blend in."

"Anyway," Jack said, "I like how you interact with bad guys. They know you're a cop, and they know you know all about them. You know how to talk to 'em, get what you need, establish who's in charge, all that. I see you as the Eagle Scout in the communities, engaging with the gangs, enforcing the law. Back when I was doing undercover work —"

"Hold on, Jack! You were undercover?"

" 'Course! You knew that, right? We've

talked about it."

"No! I knew you worked in the gang unit, but not undercover."

"See how good I was? You didn't even know."

"So were you really?"

"You get it so ingrained in your head to not talk about it that it must have stuck with me all these years. You're serious that I never mentioned it?"

"You didn't."

"Well, I've got lots of stories you need to hear, even if I can't use you undercover. Let me know when you're up to it."

Boone told Jack of Brigita Velna's advice.

"Makes sense. But I'll follow your lead. When you're ready, I'll talk."

"Not sure when that's going to be, Jack, but maybe soon. I do have one question, though. Isn't organized crime more about the Mafia or the Mob, or — what do they call themselves here . . . ?"

"The Outfit, but it's nothing like it used to be. If you're going to study it, you'll learn that. In Capone's day, during Prohibition and all that, sure, it was huge. But it's been on the decline ever since, and now it's just a shadow of what it used to be. There are hardly enough 'made men' anymore to even worry about. The street gangs are way bigger and more influential now."

He and Jack agreed to start talking about organized crime in Chicago as soon as Boone was ready and Keller available.

Sheer boredom put Boone in front of the TV for the ten o'clock news. A convenience store proprietor was interviewed in silhouette, his voice technologically camouflaged. For an instant, Boone was distracted from his own turmoil. Even with the effort to hide the man's identity, it was clear he was small and slight. Boone guessed he was Asian or Indian. And the modified voice couldn't hide the man's fear and resignation. "I pay," he said. "Of course I pay. I have family. And I have nowhere to go. What's my choice?"

Gang members would visit the man near closing time late at night, telling him that if he didn't pay for their protection, they could not guarantee his safety. "Windows could be broken, merchandise stolen, maybe even a fire burn my place down. But now protection costs almost all my profits. But I got no choice."

Boone stood and paced. Something deep inside him wanted to find that shopkeeper, have him point out the gang's so-called enforcers, and see how they liked facing terror. He knew they weren't just talking. Small businesses on the edges of gang neighborhoods were torched, looted, vandalized every day. You paid or you suffered — it was as simple as that.

These gangbangers were little more than grown-up versions of the bullies Boone had taken care of as a schoolkid. Oh, for the chance to do that again now, these days, when it really counted.

Late that night when Boone was depressed and unable to sleep — yet still determined to stay away from the wine — his phone chirped. He looked to see that Francisco Sosa had texted him a Bible reference. Psalm 51:10.

He found Nikki's Bible and looked up the verse:

Create in me a clean heart, O God, and renew a steadfast spirit within me.

Boone had to admit, that stopped him. He carried the Bible out to Jack's easy chair and sat reading it over and over. Could that be his prayer? He wasn't sure yet. And what was he going to tell Ms. Velna? Had his rage given way to mostly sadness?

Boone missed Nikki. Missed her touch.

Missed her smile. Missed her laugh. Missed her love. He missed Josh. Missed his giggle. Missed just watching him. Missed his welcome when Boone got home.

He was still mad too, no question. But this missing business — this was sadness. Boone was alone and lonely and pre-occupied. He was still thinking of telling Nikki things, more than once a day. Every time it washed over him that he would never talk to her again, never see her, never touch her, reality bit deep.

At times Boone began to shake and couldn't calm himself. He was not finished crying yet either. He proved that in the middle of the night, every night. And what was that? Just grief? No, it was more. It was longing. It was frustration. It was wanting something like you had never wanted any-thing before and knowing that nothing you could ever say or do would bring it back.

What, Boone wondered, had been wrong with his faith? Had he turned on God when God disappointed him? Or had he never enjoyed a real relationship with God in the first place? His faith had never demanded anything of him, and he couldn't remember ever having been as devout as Nikki or Pastor Sosa. Had he ever just longed to pray, to read the Bible, to go to church, to worship? It was all okay with him, and he was a believer. He didn't doubt that. It's just that his faith had never defined him.

What had he missed? What was the disconnect? Was it simply that he had always been self-possessed, self-reliant? He had heard people begin their prayers by telling God that they loved him.

Do I love him? Have I ever?

Maybe Boone had nothing to fall back on in the time of his most dire need because he had never had anything in the first place. He wondered how he might have felt about God's seeming to abandon him and allowing this, even if he had been devout. It wasn't like a loving God would have allowed this just to get his attention. What kind of a capricious, hateful thing would that be?

His parents and Nikki's parents were good Christians. Why weren't they spared this agony? No way God would have made Nikki and Joshie and the grandparents suffer just because of Boone. Would he?

Boone told Ms. Velna that he had decided what to study, and that he had come to a conclusion about her question. "I think I've gone from being madder than sad to sadder than mad. I'm still mad; I'm still frustrated. I have a lot of questions about faith and

God and all that. But I don't think it's the kind of anger that would affect my work. I'd like to be back on the street as soon as you approve it."

"Well," she said, "do you feel you know yourself well enough to know how you'll respond when you're full of adrenaline, under pressure, and someone ticks you off?"

"I guess I won't know until I'm in the heat of battle."

"As you can imagine, Officer, that's not good enough. My job depends on how accurately I assess these things. I put you back on the street and you wind up hurting yourself or someone else — a partner or a bad guy — because you overreact, and I have to answer for it. And if it's serious, both you and I will be looking for work."

11
Hunkering Down

Over the next few weeks, as Boone tried to busy himself with daily tasks and chores to occupy his mind, he often scared himself. He didn't dare admit it to Brigita Velna, but there were times, in the middle of the night or maybe in the afternoon while Jack was on duty and Boone was tired of reading and studying, when he erupted.

Boone reminisced, grew emotional, and imagined the horror of how Nikki and Josh had died. Then would come the longing. He missed them, wanted them back, didn't understand, couldn't make it all compute. Once he rose from his reading, street gang and organized crime history books tumbling from his lap, and lifted the entire recliner, heaving it into the wall. He kicked it over and over, screaming and crying.

If that was a hint of the kind of hair-trigger emotion he might take onto the street, Ms. Velna could never know. If there was anything Boone yearned for, it was to get back on the job.

He was learning — reading and memorizing, trying to thoroughly familiarize himself with the organized crime world in Chicago. He attended class, and he and Jack talked into the wee hours almost every night. The more he learned, the more he realized that moving quickly into the Organized Crime Division, even if Jack became the deputy chief there, was not likely. The only people his age to land such plum positions were working undercover, and Jack had rightly ruled that out for someone as visible as Boone had been.

One rainy night when Jack got home, Boone asked him straight about the possibilities.

"I told you, Boones. I'm not taking the job if it doesn't mean I can bring you along. Now you can quit asking."

"Sorry."

"Just want you to be sure. Now listen, bein' out there without you has had its moments. Couple of funny ones today and one not so funny. You up to hearing 'em?"

"Am I ever."

"I get called to the Mirage. Remember it?"

"That dumpy little bar down on —"

"That's the one. Barkeep calls in; dispatch says he sounds scared. Bunch of Demon Warrior bikers are in there throwing things around."

"And you go alone?"

"Call me crazy."

"You're crazy."

"I waltz in there and shout for attention. Looks like everybody else has cleared out, so ten, maybe eleven of these guys are winging beer mugs and cans, breaking stuff, laughing. I shout for attention, and when they see me, they burst into laughter. Pretty soon they're chucking stuff at me."

"So you call for backup."

"Nope. I get a better idea. I retreat."

"You did not."

"What was I gonna do, Boones? Start shooting them? I back out of there, and those guys are firing stuff at me from every direction, laughing their heads off. I go to the squad, pull out the double-barrel, grab a coupla shells, and blast one whoop on the siren.

"That brings 'em outside, where I make a big show of loading the shotgun. I point it at the prettiest bike in the long line and say quietly, 'Leave or the hog gets it.' "

Boone closed his eyes and shook his head. "I'm listening . . ."

"End of story. All I saw was taillights."

Boone sighed. "Man, I want to be back out there."

"Soon enough. Wanna hear the other funny one?"

"Sure."

"You see what it's doin' outside?"

"Been pouring since three or so."

"Right at the close of the shift I'm heading back to the precinct and a car blows the light right in front of me. Rain's coming in sheets, so no way the driver even saw me. I pull the car over, throw on a slicker, and venture out, asking this woman for her license and all. Young girl sitting next to her. The girl looks scared but the woman is shaking her head and laughing. I say, 'Somethin' you wanna tell me?' She says, 'Something I shouldn't tell you, but I'm going to. My daughter screamed at me when I ran that light and I told her not to worry, that no cop would pull me over in this weather.' "

Boone proffered a courtesy smile. Stuff like that happened all the time on the street. He wanted to hear the not-so-funny story. "Get to the good one," he said.

"Well, there's good and there's not so good, at least for the vics."

"Talk to me."

"Well, everybody's had an idea that OCD was keeping an eye on an old associate of the head of the Outfit."

"Graziano?"

Keller nodded. "He had a guy that did him wrong, so we figured it was only a matter of time, ya know? So our people are tailing him and tailing him, and nothing for weeks. We finally let up, just a tick, not worrying about covering every shift change, all that, and sure enough, we're not there when he gets it."

"Today?"

"At Midway. Crazy thing is, not one earmark leads this to the Outfit."

Boone squinted and pressed his lips together. "What're you saying? Guy on the outs with Graziano turns up dead and it wasn't one of Grazzy's hit men?"

Keller shook his head. "Dangedest thing. It was the same MO as when that accountant bought it outside the travel agency last year."

"Yeah, but wasn't he connected with the street gangs?"

Keller nodded again and pushed his cap back on his head. "Saw all the dollars and tried skimmin' a few. Chose the wrong clients for that nonsense."

"Duh. But why would Graziano's enemy

die the same way?"

"No idea, but we don't like it. Normally the street gangs stay out of the Mob's way and vice versa."

Boone paused. Then, "It's not like they're in the Mob's way. It's like they're both using the same hit man."

"Never a dull moment, Boones."

"We're losing this war with the gangs, Jack. You know that, right?"

Jack shrugged. "I'm going to get my chance to do something about that. One of these days."

"Me too?"

Jack snorted. " 'Course. If only to shut you up."

As Boone's furlough slowly passed, the legal stuff his father-in-law was handling eventually came together. That was a relief. Boone didn't want to think about it, let alone fret over it. If, by the time he was back on the job, his house was fixed and sold and his bank account healthy, that's all he could ask for.

His leather bracelet had turned out perfectly, and he wore it all day every day. Embedding Nikki's diamond in his wedding band took longer because it had to be tooled so as not to protrude and become a danger.

Boone was thrilled with the result and often found himself studying it as he daydreamed.

Boone was no longer resorting to alcohol to get to sleep, and he hoped he could maintain that resolve when he was back at work. Now it wasn't such a problem if he had a bad night. He could sleep in or nap during the day. When he was back on patrol, with his and his partner's and the public's lives on the line, he would have to be at his best and alert.

"Any idea who my new partner's going to be?" he asked Jack one evening.

Jack snorted. "Your new partner's gonna be your old partner if this bureaucratic logjam doesn't break."

"Any idea when you'll know?"

Keller shook his head. "They were saying a few days, then a week or two, and now they aren't even promising that. Usually when this happens, there are a lot of good candidates or one of the big bosses has a favorite he's trying to shoehorn into it. If Fletcher Galloway has someone else in mind, I'll be stuck where I am. I'll tell you one thing, Boones: if this keeps up, I'll start angling for nights again. This day shift stuff just doesn't do it for me."

Boone was puzzled. He'd been sure Jack would be a shoo-in for the Organized Crime

Division vacancy and that, in due time, Boone would join him there. But if it wasn't to be, it wasn't to be, and second-best would be to get back on the job, working the night shift as Jack's partner. Anything to get out of this torturous desert of boredom, interrupted by grief and rage.

Boone had to admit that Francisco Sosa was keeping his word and maintaining an appropriate distance. There were actually days when Boone regretted having broken from him and wished the pastor would be more insistent about seeing him. But who was he to think he should be a priority for the head of such a huge church? Sosa had a dozen pastors reporting to him and a million other things to think about. And there was the fact that Boone had virtually legislated that the man leave him alone.

Boone came to appreciate that every few days Sosa sent an innocuous text, simply listing a Scripture reference. Boone would haul out Nikki's Bible, peek again at his name at the top of her prayer list, and find the verse. The most recent had been Isaiah 40:31:

But those who wait on the Lord shall
    renew their strength; they shall mount
    up with wings like eagles, they shall run

and not be weary, they shall walk and not faint.

Boone found the language majestic, the promise magnificent. The rub came in the opening phrase. When had he ever waited on the Lord, and why should he now? Yes, his strength needed to be renewed, he needed to be able to fly, to run, to walk and not faint. But what had God done for him lately?

During Boone's visit with Brigita Velna on the fourteenth workday of his furlough, he fully expected to be returned to duty.

"You don't have to like it or accept it, Officer Drake," she said, "but I am recommending that you wait one more week."

Boone sat shaking his head. "Of course I have to accept it. What recourse do I have?"

"I stand corrected. You do have to accept it. I mean, you can appeal it, but that process would take longer than a week, so it's not worth the effort."

"Can you at least tell me why? I've read, I've studied, I've attended classes. I can sometimes think of Nikki and Josh without bursting into tears. And I'm bored out of my mind. I need to be at work."

"How is the apartment hunting going?"

"I'm close to something I like. I should have an answer in a day or two."

"And when you go back to work, you're on day watch, right? You wouldn't likely be able to conduct any personal business in the evenings. This further delay in getting back on the job will give you a week to secure your new place and move."

"I can work that out either way. Now why are you making me wait? Please tell me you're seeing something that can make this make sense to me."

"I wish I could. I'm a scientist, a psychologist, an analyst. There is nothing I would like more than to be able to show you a printout or some research data that proves I am right. In this case, I confess, I am going on intuition."

"So you're convinced I'm not ready."

"I'm not sure, but I fear you are not, and thus I am not willing to risk it. There is something in your demeanor, Officer, something impatient and deeply troubled. Now don't give me that face. I know you have more reasons than most to be psychologically wounded. No one can be expected to just snap back from such trauma. You can protest and try to persuade me, but the fact is that I see before me a man not only understandably devastated, but also angry."

"And why shouldn't I be?"

"I'm not judging you. I am just saying that another six working days before you're back on the job will be to your benefit."

"And to the CPD's and the city's."

"Of course."

"Your real priorities."

"Which I have never denied."

The worst part about all this was that she was right and Boone knew it. He thought he could control himself and that he would not be a threat to the department or the city, but it was coming up on only a month since the deaths. Who could expect him to even be in his right mind by now?

"Tell me about the new living space you have in mind," Ms. Velna said.

"It's nice. Small. About a twenty-minute drive to work. Two bedrooms, one I will use for workout equipment. I have my schedule and routine and regimen all written out. I know what I'll eat and when, when I'll work out and for how long. Everything's going to be just so."

Again she seemed to study him. "You are going to control the things you can control."

He nodded slowly. "I hadn't thought of it that way, but yes. Exactly."

"Does that tell you anything about yourself?"

"Guess I'm a little dense."

"You're anything but dense, but perhaps this is subconscious. You have always been in charge, in control. You work toward what you want, and you accomplish things. Now your world has been shattered by something wholly outside your control, and you are reverting to a place of comfort."

Boone made a face and scratched his head. "That's a little deep for me."

"Is it? Tell me, do you line up your clothes, especially your uniforms, in your closet?"

"Yes."

"Shoes polished the night before?"

"Belt too."

"Work out at the same time each day for the same duration, eat at the same time, leave for work at the same time. You're a man of routine, correct?"

"Anything wrong with that?"

"Of course not. We all have ways of comforting ourselves, making ourselves feel secure. We like things to be predictable. You see how it is a matter of control? You are engineering your own life."

"I can see that."

"Now tell me, what happens when something else invades and interrupts your self-created world, your routine?"

"There's nothing else for me to lose."

"Sure there is. I don't mean to be macabre, Officer Drake, but there are other people in your life you care about, surely. Your parents, your brothers, your in-laws, your partner, maybe other colleagues? people at church? friends? I ask you again, what happens if misfortune or even tragedy attends one of them?"

Attends? Where do people learn to talk like this?

"I guess I wouldn't like it."

"You wouldn't like it because it was beyond your control. You are drawing yourself in, Officer. Retreating to your comfort zone. Your new place, small and smart and efficient as it will be, becomes your personal fortress."

"You think it's unhealthy?"

"Not if you recognize it. You will begin to grow and really mature when you realize that life is capricious. You cannot control everything. You must resign yourself to that."

"Go with the flow?"

"Yes."

"So I should take the loss of my family in stride? It was fate? Nothing I could have done about it?"

"I'm not saying that. Just don't blame yourself — or worse, think you can build new defenses that will protect you from ever suffering again."

"Don't blame myself? I knew Josh could get out of his crib by himself. I should have figured out some way to keep that from happening."

"Yes, and what if it had been your wife who accidentally spilled the gasoline, and then she couldn't get to him in time? I'm not trying to make this more painful for you. I'm trying to point out that you can't think of every eventuality. You can't protect yourself from everything."

This was hard, and part of Boone hated it. She was making him face himself. He'd had the same inward reaction to Francisco Sosa when the pastor pried into the level of his passion for God. What was it about people analyzing him that made him so uncomfortable? *Was* he a self-made man, a control freak? Down deep he wished he *could* control everything. Maybe down deep he also wished he didn't need God. Sosa had once intimated that Boone seemed to give himself credit for a sweet life. Well, it wasn't so sweet now, was it?

Ms. Velna stood and shook Boone's hand. "You're a remarkable young man," she said, "and I wish you all the best. I will send through the paperwork, authorizing you to return to duty a week from Monday. In the meantime, do me a favor. In fact, do yourself a favor. Give yourself a break. I don't say this glibly, and I know it's not easy. But realize that you are not in control of everything and can never be. Cut yourself some slack."

Late the next week, Jack enlisted a couple of off-duty officers to help move Boone into his new apartment. By the end of the day, Boone was exhausted but encouraged. He liked the way the place had turned out, and while he was going to be lonely, there was no way around that. He set up everything the way he wanted it, and when he was done, he had not one inch of wasted space. This was not going to be a place where he could entertain, though Jack could come over and watch a game with him. Maybe Brigita Velna was right. He had built himself his own little fortified castle.

The following Monday Boone was welcomed back to the 11th district with enthusiasm but not the usual horseplay or barbs. He would know the awkward period was over when someone would have the courage to insult him just for fun. He missed that.

Jack Keller quickly dumped his temporary

partner and took Boone back in the passenger seat. While Boone was trying to settle into his old routine, he discovered that it was now Jack Keller who seemed in the worst mood. Every cop in the city knew he was in line for the Organized Crime spot, and it had even been speculated upon by the *Chicago Tribune* police beat reporters.

Yet still it hadn't happened, and there seemed no way to tell when or if it ever would. Boone found himself amused to see Jack short not only with him — which he appreciated under the circumstances — but also with the public. They made a couple of routine traffic stops, and both times Jack wound up berating the drivers, exhibiting sarcasm and condescension. In both cases the offenses were egregious and the drivers worthy of scorn. But clearly Jack had acted outside department protocol and chastised himself all afternoon. "Watch these yahoos complain to downtown, and I won't have a leg to stand on."

"They were in the wrong, Jack. They're not going to complain to anybody."

"If they do, it'll go on my record and will for sure keep me from getting into OCD."

It was all Boone could do to keep from chuckling. He couldn't remember the last time anyone downtown took seriously a complaint from a guilty motorist who felt unduly hollered at. Now if Jack had threatened them or intimidated them or put his hands on them, that would have been a problem. It was clear to Boone, however, that these drivers were relieved to just be ticketed and sent on their way.

Boone and Jack spent much of their downtime in the car talking about the potential of the future. "If it takes this long to see you get promoted, how long will it take to get me over there?"

"Who knows? A year? I hope not more."

Boone was aware that Jack had largely kept him out of sticky situations for his first couple of weeks back on the street. That ended the afternoon Boone was spelling Jack behind the wheel and they were cruising near an elementary school at release time.

Their squad car was second in line facing east, waiting as a crossing guard stopped traffic both ways so kids could cross the street. Suddenly came a westbound motorcyclist, roaring right through the crosswalk. The guard grabbed two kids and held them back, dancing out of the way.

Boone immediately flipped on his blue lights and tried to pop a U-turn, but the cars in front and behind him were too close. Jack turned on the siren briefly, and both cars tried to get out of the way.

"Move!" Jack screamed. "Get that sucker, Boones!"

Boone reminded himself to keep an eye on the crossing guard and the kids as he maneuvered a three-point turnaround and finally headed west. By now the cycle was four blocks ahead and flying. Fortunately the traffic was thick enough that the cyclist had to slow, and the cars ahead of Boone were slowly pulling over.

All Boone could think of was his own son. This guy had missed schoolkids by inches.

"He's gone right!" Jack said. He radioed their position, reported that they were in pursuit of a reckless motorcyclist, and advised where other squads should set up.

Boone had long prided himself in his ability behind the wheel, but while the squad had a high-performance engine, it could not go where a cycle could. Every time he drew within a block or so, the rider shot through an alley or took a turn too late for Boone to follow.

Boone deftly braked, popped U-turns, took sharp corners, and somehow stayed close. Meanwhile Jack was variously shouting, encouraging, swearing at the cyclist, and staying on the radio to direct other squads. Boone knew the best he could do was somehow force the cyclist into a road-block. No way a single squad could catch this guy.

"Right here! Left here! Careful! If we can get him to take a right at the light, we've got him! You're not gonna believe who's in the chase, Boones!"

"Who?"

"Watch Commander Lang. Just got out of a meeting and heard the call."

"How long's it been since he's been in on a collar?"

"Got to be years. Let's get this guy!"

Boone floored the squad from two blocks behind the bad guy, lights flashing and siren blaring. And sure enough, the rider took the right turn. Boone had to slow quickly and pick his way through the intersection. "Brakes are getting mushy!"

"Got to be overheated. Careful."

And as soon as Boone had straightened the car, he found himself within feet of the squads that had stopped the cyclist. He swerved and pushed the brake pedal to the floor, but still he slammed into the back of another squad. Fortunately no one was in it. But he could tell from the markings that it was the watch commander's car.

Lang and his driver were part of a small cadre of officers who had surrounded the cycle, on which the rider still sat. The rider had jerked around at the sound of the crash and was now pointing and laughing so hard he was doubled over.

"Not your fault, Boones!" Jack hollered as he grabbed his hat and nightstick and was sliding out. "Don't worry about it!"

But Boone was already out of the car, leaving his hat and stick. His jaw was set, his eyes afire. He elbowed other officers aside and approached the cyclist, who was grinning so wide he was in tears. Without a thought Boone fired a right cross to the man's chin, and he and the heavy bike went over.

Jack grabbed Boone and pulled him back while the others wrestled the cycle off the man, who lay unconscious.

Boone was still white-hot with rage, now directed at himself. Watch Commander Lang, in his heavily decorated dress uniform, glared at Boone.

"I know you'll have to write me up for that," Boone said, imagining his career being flushed down the toilet.

"For what?" Lang said, a tight-lipped smile growing. "Somebody call the EMTs. This unfortunate cyclist has fallen off his bike and hurt himself."

By the time the ambulance arrived, the rider had roused and asked what had happened. "What happened?" an officer said. "You almost killed a kid in the crosswalk back there. You're lucky we didn't shoot you dead."

The cyclist felt his chin. "One of you guys pop me? I'll have your job."

"That alcohol I smell?" the cop said. "We'd better administer a field sobriety test, hey?"

"I ain't been drinkin', but I'm hurt, so I can't walk no line."

"Then you'd best shut up and let the EMTs check you over."

"Let me drive," Jack said as he and Boone returned to the squad. "I gotta check those brakes anyway." They had cooled and seemed to be operating normally. As he pulled back into traffic, Jack said, "Well, I've seen you act more professionally."

Boone held his head in his hands. "What if somebody taped that? It'll be all over the news, and I'll be dead meat."

"Nobody taped it."

"This day and age? Somebody with an iPhone could have got it from anywhere."

"Worst-case scenario: you take a little heat, few more days off. Grieving widower who recently lost his own toddler goes nuts when a cyclist almost hits some kids. Everybody'll understand."

"Not everybody."

"Don't worry about it until you have to. Nobody on the scene's gonna say anything."

"That doesn't make it right. What if it does come out and some tape shows the watch commander standing right there and then not even reporting it? I don't want to cost him his job."

When they got back to headquarters at the end of the shift, the watch commander asked to see Boone.

"Boss, I'm sorry," Boone said as he sat across from him.

Lang waved him off. "You got to be careful is all. The public doesn't go for that kind of stuff, and if it somehow gets out that this happened, well, you know . . ."

"I get thrown under the bus."

"Well, it would be on you, yes. And I'd have to come up with some reason why I wasn't proactive about it when it happened. Can't say my back was turned. I coulda caught the guy when you drilled him. That was sweet, by the way."

"Can't deny it felt good, but I know it was wrong."

"And you and I both know it may be the

only justice this guy gets. You know what we did back in the day?"

"No, what?"

"You know that elevator down in the garage that goes up to the jail? It didn't always have that electric eye that stops it from closin' on people. The old ones had a rubber bumper that would make the door slide back open when it ran into anything or anybody. Well, we wondered what would happen if that went missing."

"You didn't."

"We did," Lang said, chortling. "The judges and the courts want to slap these guys' wrists? Well, somebody's gotta make 'em pay. We're puttin' a bad guy in the squad, you know how we do it today. We put a hand on top of his head, 'cause with his hands cuffed, he can't steady himself getting in. So we guide that noggin so he doesn't bump himself on the roof, right? Well, we did the same back then, only it wasn't to keep him from hurting himself; it was to make sure he did. Nothing serious. Just a bump he can't rub.

"Then we'd get him into the garage downstairs and head for the jail elevator. Only just as we're crossin' the threshold there, we'd remember something we forgot and hesitate. And here came that door. Only when it hit the guy, it didn't open back up, it just squeezed him between itself and the frame until we could figure out how to get it back open. 'Oops! Sorry, dude! My bad!'

"A few days later we'd see the guy get a slap on the wrist, probation or community service or something or other, and we'd know he at least got some street justice."

"Didn't bother you that he might have been innocent?"

"Innocent? The bad guys we pick up? You know better'n that, Drake. Anyway, I'm not talking about guys we didn't catch in the act, you know. Like the guy you coldcocked today."

"I still feel bad about it."

"Well, if it makes you feel any better, I don't."

Lang mashed a button on his intercom and asked his secretary to check on the health of the cyclist. A couple of minutes later she came in with a note and whispered to him. When she was gone, Lang leveled his gaze at Boone. "Well, would you get a load of this?" he said.

"I'm listening."

"Our guy was bluffing him about smelling alcohol. Turns out it must have been vodka, because none of us smelled it, but he was way above the legal limit. Otherwise he's fine healthwise, except for a sore jaw. Reminds me of when you dropped that domestic abuse guy, the one with the knife. You ought to go into prizefighting.

"Anyway, we got us a real bad guy here. No operator's license. Warrants on him from Tennessee and Wisconsin. Wanna know what for?"

" 'Course."

"DUI, DWI, reckless endangerment, grand theft auto, and armed robbery."

"Seriously?"

"There's more. Wisconsin state police like him for the murder of that teen girl last summer, the one found in the woods off the interstate."

Boone shook his head.

"We're going to inform the press," Lang said. "You're going to get credited with the collar. And you and I are going to go pick him up at the hospital and hold him here until downtown comes for him. He'll be in County by tonight. You got your dress blues in your locker?"

"Sure."

"My driver and I will be out back waiting for you. Be quick. This could make the six o'clock news."

It hadn't crossed Boone's mind to ask which

hospital, but it shouldn't have surprised him when they pulled into Presbyterian St. Luke's. He exhaled loudly and covered his mouth.

Lang turned. "I wasn't thinking, Drake. You gonna be all right?"

"Yeah."

"You want to wait out here? You don't have to go in. They've already got him cuffed and ready to go."

"As long as we're not going in through emergency."

"Nope. In and out through the back. I want to hurry because I hear the press is on their way, and we'd rather they film us going into the station."

Moving the bad guy from the hospital to the car went without incident, and they beat the press. As the only place for the hand-cuffed man was in the backseat with Boone, he removed his Beretta and gave it to Lang's driver. The cyclist sat staring out his window, refusing to even acknowledge Boone until they were within a block of district headquarters.

"Photo op, eh?" he said, turning. "Maybe I ought to tell the press what you did to me on the scene."

"Feel free," Boone said. "Before or after we tell them how close you came to killing schoolkids?"

The man shook his head and looked away again, his knee bouncing. What was he so hyped up about? Looking forward to sitting in a holding cell before his transfer to Cook County Jail?

By the time they got back to the 11th, satellite trucks from channels 2, 5, 7, 9, and 32 jammed the tiny lot. Jack Keller and a couple of other officers held back the crowds and directed Lang's car up to the rear steps.

"I'll lead the way, Drake," Lang said. "You escort the arrestee."

Lang waited briefly while Boone pulled the bad guy from the car and they started slowly up the steps. Boone's antennae perked up as the cyclist tensed. This guy was about to pull something. He was cuffed in front, so he couldn't easily try to get Lang's weapon. And Boone was no longer armed. He held the man lightly, giving him all the rope he needed.

Reporters were calling out questions and cameras were taking it all in as they moved up toward the door. Then, just as Boone had suspected — and hoped — the man spun out of his grip and bounded down the steps two at a time. How he thought he could get past a cadre of officers, the press, and dozens of onlookers was beyond Boone, but criminals have never been known for their brains.

Boone put his right foot on the top step and launched himself into the air, coming down on the man's shoulders just as he reached the pavement. They went down in a heap, the prisoner taking most of the impact on his nose. When he started screaming and swearing, he lifted his head and showed a bloody mess. The press captured it all.

Boone enjoyed watching the news that night, at both six and ten. And yes, the story was made more poignant by who was credited with the collar.

A few weeks later, Boone was feeling better physically, if not mentally. His workouts and his healthy, sparse diet had given him a feeling of fitness and strength and energy he had not enjoyed in a long time. He was still having trouble sleeping, but still also eschewing alcohol. When his longing and grief and depression overtook him, he would pace the little apartment.

Occasionally he would look at the list of verse references he had received from Pastor Sosa. One night he was pleasantly surprised to find that Francisco had sent one since he had last had his phone on. It was Matthew 6:21:

Where your treasure is, there your heart will be also.

Boone sat with Nikki's Bible. He had been wondering why, after all he had been through and suffered and was now struggling with, he never thought to pray. Did he not believe in it? Did he think God would do what God was going to do, regardless of what Boone might ask for?

This verse seemed to have nothing to do with prayer, yet it pricked Boone that if he truly treasured his relationship with God, he would be a man of prayer. Dare he try? What would he say? God knew how he felt about the tragedy, the loss, and the horror of it. Surely he needn't tell the God of the universe what he already knew. But then, God knew everything.

Trying to talk to God certainly couldn't hurt. How long had it been? Too long.

Boone set the Bible aside and bowed his head. "God," he whispered, "I don't even know what to say. Am I hopeless? Do you love me? Do you still care about me? Could you help me survive this? Could you help me understand it?"

As soon as he asked that, he knew the answer was no. What could even the Creator of the world impress upon Boone that would make him understand the unspeakable? Even Pastor Sosa had said there would be no understanding such carnage this side of heaven. He attributed it to a fallen, sinful world.

Boone finished, "Could you show me what it's supposed to be like if I'm a man of faith? Amen."

He felt such a fool that he wasn't sure he would ever pray again. What was God supposed to do with that? He hadn't known what to say or even how to say it. Boone guessed that what he really wanted to know was whether God wanted anything to do with him anymore. Did he dare pray that God would somehow show himself to him?

No, he did not dare.

12
A NEW SEASON

A couple of weeks later, Boone was driving on patrol with Jack in the passenger seat. Boone had been driving more lately, the idea being that when Jack was promoted, Boone would likely get a junior partner who would not be expected to drive.

They were cruising down West Harrison just after noon when the radio crackled and Keller was informed that Watch Commander Lang and District Commander Jones wanted to see him at the end of his shift.

"What do you think, Jack?" Boone said. "Is this it?"

"I'm way past hoping, but I can't imagine what else they'd want. Wish me luck."

Boone was about to when he saw a late-model BMW pull away from the curb a block and a half ahead, pass three cars at once despite traffic coming the other way, and head for the Eisenhower on-ramp at high speed. Too many cars were between him and the Bimmer to accurately gauge the speed, but it was clear the driver was exceeding the limit.

Boone flipped on his blue lights and raced through traffic in pursuit. Fortunately rush hour had not yet begun and Boone was able to use lane openings to close the gap and pull in beside the speeder. The driver quickly pulled over, and Keller called in the tag number.

The driver, a well-dressed, heavyset man in his fifties, opened the door.

Boone flipped on the PA. "Stay in the vehicle, please. With you in a moment."

Dispatch reported no outstanding warrants, no reports of the car being stolen, and that the BMW was registered to a Dwayne White of Burr Ridge. Boone and Jack emerged, pulling on their caps. Jack took a position off the right rear taillight, his hand over the butt of his 9mm Beretta.

Boone slowly approached the driver's window, pausing a foot or so behind the driver. "Operator's license, please?"

The man handed out the card, which had a paper clip affixed to it. "Still live in Burr Ridge, Mr. White?"

"Yes, Officer."

"What's your work there?"

"Import/export. Do a lot of business in the city."

"You in a hurry today, sir?"

"Yeah, late for a meeting. Sorry."

"I appreciate your attitude and co-operation, sir. You were doing more than speeding there on Harrison. That was dangerous."

"My bad."

"I'm going to give you a warning and caution you that in the future . . ."

Boone stopped when he casually turned the license over and noticed that the paper clip was holding a hundred-dollar bill. "What's this?"

"Sorry?"

"What's this on your license?"

Mr. White did not respond.

As Boone continued to speak with an even tone, he began to slide the bill off the clip with his finger. "So, living in a nice suburb, doing business in our fair city . . ."

"Right."

The bill hung from the license by an edge. Boone held it where the offender could see it. "When was the last time you were ticketed, Mr. White?"

"Hmm, oh, couple of years ago. Excessive lane changing, if I recall correctly."

The bill was about to blow away. Boone

said, "This yours, Mr. White?"

"No, sir."

"Hmph. Not mine either." Boone held it up so Jack could see it. "This yours, Officer Keller?"

"Nope, not mine. Is it yours?"

"Nope."

"Is it the driver's?"

"He says it's not his."

"What do you know?"

Boone gave the bill one more nudge and it blew down the Eisenhower behind them in the fall wind. Mr. White wrenched around in his seat to watch it go.

"Sure that wasn't yours, Mr. White?"

"No. Not mine."

"You are aware that bribery is a second-degree felony, punishable by incarceration, aren't you, sir?"

"I wouldn't know anything about that, no, Officer."

"Well, for future reference . . . we don't look kindly on that kind of thing. Do you?"

"No, sir."

"Drive carefully, Mr. White. And have a nice day."

When Boone pulled back into traffic, White's car was still idling. He and Jack burst into laughter when they saw White running down the shoulder of the Eisenhower after the hundred.

"Should we bust him for being out of his car on the expressway?" Jack said.

"Nah. I think it's been an expensive enough stop for Mr. White."

Back at the station, Jack gave Boone a look and accepted District Commander Heath-cliff Jones's invitation to his office, along with Watch Commander Lang and, yes, Fletcher Galloway of Organized Crime. Like Boone, several other officers about to go off duty found reasons to hang around the locker room and the vending machines.

The meeting went on for more than an hour, and when it was over, the others loitered and jockeyed for position near the locker room door, knowing Jack would come there to change back into street clothes.

When Jack didn't appear for another twenty minutes, the others badgered Boone to go find out what was up.

"You're his partner."

"Grab something out of your desk."

"See if Galloway is still here. I didn't hear a car leave."

Boone finally left the locker room and bounded up the steps to the squad room, only to run into the four men in question, standing by the back door. "Excuse me, gentlemen," he said, brushing past. He rummaged around in his desk, folded a bunch of innocuous papers, and headed back down.

"Well?" the others said.

Boone told them what had happened and added, "I honestly couldn't tell from any of their looks — even Jack's — whether the thing got done. I don't know."

"You kiddin'? It has to be a done deal. They wouldn't stand around gassing with the guy if they told him no."

Another officer said, "They might not even have been talking about the promotion. Maybe it was something else."

Others laughed. "Yeah, that makes sense. Your boss and his boss call you into a meeting with the Organized Crime Division chief, and it's about what, crossing guard duty?"

Boone heard footsteps on the stairs, the back door opening, a car pulling away. Everybody in the locker room, now long past the end of their shifts, busied themselves at their lockers. Keller entered with his head down, no discernable expression. Boone saw the others peeking at him.

Keller opened his locker and began to peel off his uniform.

"So?" Boone said.

"So, what? How long's it take for you yahoos to change clothes anyway?"

"C'mon, Jack. We're all pulling for you."

Jack stood with his shirt unbuttoned and was shrugging out of his bulletproof vest. "Let's just say I won't be needing the uniform anymore. First of next month, I'm a detective and deputy chief in OCD."

The others whooped and hollered and surrounded him for handshakes, high fives, and embraces. "Kick some tail over there, would ya?" one said.

"We celebrating?" another said.

"You bet," Jack said. "On me."

They piled into their own cars and caravanned to a local watering hole where off-duty cops from other districts gathered too. The news spread fast, and soon the place was alive with music, singing, dancing, and toasts.

Boone was nursing a Coke and found himself hungry, so he ordered baked chicken wings. He had been so disciplined on his diet that he avoided the loaded potato skins, onion rings, deep-fried fish-and-chips, and other bar fare. He was teased unmercifully by the others, but all that only meant things were getting back to normal. He had grown so tired of being treated with kid gloves.

At the end of the evening, Jack was clearly too tipsy to be driving, so Boone prevailed on a couple of other guys to take his car back to the station. "I'll run you home and pick you up in the morning."

"Oh, I'm okay, Boones."

"You know better than that. No arguing."

Fortunately, Jack wasn't so far gone that he had to be led to his apartment or put to bed. He was just buzzed, and by the time they got to his place, he was also hungry. Boone liked having something to do and not having to face the prospect of another lonely evening at home. He had been, as Francisco Sosa always liked to put it, "redeeming the time." He was reading about gangs and the Chicago Outfit, studying organized crime, brushing up on stuff he'd learned studying criminology. And none too soon. Jack kept talking about how street gang violence was at record levels and that it seemed something was about to blow. "I can't get to OCD soon enough," he said.

"Me either," Boone said. "I know most guys would love to be in the 11th with all the action we get, but I'm not going to be happy until I'm on full-time gang duty."

"Well, don't worry. The work will be waiting for us when we get there. And I hope you know we're never going to solve the problem. Gangland stuff is never over."

"You sound defeatist, Jack. If we can't win, what's the point?"

"You serious? Just frustrating the bad guys and neutralizing them is a worthy enough goal."

Boone was also looking up the verses Sosa occasionally sent. Strangely — to him anyway — Boone continued in his own awkward way to try to pray.

Every time he did, he was reminded what an empty Christian he had been all his life. He believed the Bible, believed in God, trusted Christ for his salvation — all of it. But he had never been passionate about any of it. He had never memorized Scripture or even read much of it outside church. And besides saying grace, he virtually never prayed. Well, now he was trying. He wasn't sure of the benefits or what he was trying to accomplish, and he didn't tell a soul. But if there was something there, something more, something he'd been missing, he was willing to pursue it.

Boone was still angry. He still had deep, unanswerable questions. But he wanted to do his part. In some weird way, Boone wanted to be available and open if God really wanted to communicate with him.

And that wasn't all. He wanted relief, rest, some sense of peace and happiness. He would never be giddy, as he had been when he had it all — the job he'd always wanted, a beautiful wife, a precious child. But down deep he hoped there was some modicum of something out there — anything — that would spark something in him.

He was doing as Brigita Velna had deduced. He had created a routine, a structure, a life for himself that protected him from outside forces. And there were benefits. He was as healthy as he had ever been — fit, toned, chiseled even. And he was back in the groove on the job, able to corral his emotions and perform his job the way it was supposed to be done.

He was being recognized again, and while that didn't bring the same joy it brought when he had been able to share it with Nikki, there was some sense of satisfaction in it, of having accomplished something.

"I know this is your day, Jack," Boone said while tending a steak in Jack's oven. "And you know I'm thrilled for you, but what happens to me now? Who do I get stuck with as a partner, and how long do I stay assigned to the Siberia of day watch?"

"You're gonna love me," Jack said, having changed into a robe and planted himself behind a TV tray, turning on a Cubs game from San Diego. "I mean, I haven't got you transferred yet; that's going to take a while. But I think I convinced Jones to switch you back to nights. And I laid it on thick for Lang, too. I told him the only thing you were going to miss was working for him."

"Beautiful. Not true, but beautiful. No sense burning that bridge, that's for sure."

"You like Lang, don't you? I mean, he did you right on that motorcyclist murder suspect."

"Oh, no question. But I can't say I want to stay on days just to work for him."

"Looks like your new partner's gonna be Fox."

"Garrett Fox from OCD?"

"Yeah, he's been through the wringer, undercover for too many years. Wants back in uniform, if you can believe that."

"Wants?" Boone said. "Or is being forced? He's got a reputation."

"Don't we all? He can be a hothead, thinks he knows it all and is God's gift to police work, but you can work around that. If you could put up with me —"

"Don't start, Jack. Everybody envied me getting to ride with you, and you know it."

"Hey! You know I get to wear a suit and tie and share a secretary with Galloway?"

"For real?"

"Yeah, I've met her a few times down there. Got a funny first name and some kinda ethnic last name. 'Bout your age. Young mother."

"I think you're going to want to get a handle on her name before you become her boss, Jack."

For the next six months, everything Garrett Fox did made Boone more eager to transfer into the Organized Crime Division. For one thing, Boone missed Jack. Despite his rough edges, Jack was a cop's cop and — for all his ability — humble. No one had ever described Garrett Fox as humble. Maybe he had been so good undercover because he knew how to keep his mouth shut. But now he was making up for it.

Fox was squat and muscular, about five years older than Boone, with short black hair and a pointy face. Boone decided his name fit. The man seemed unable to talk about anything or anyone but himself. Fox told Boone of his every case, every caper, every exploit in the years he had been undercover. According to him, no one came close to being as good, as insightful, as aware.

Fox was also impressed with his own

libido. He was already separated from his wife, fast heading for divorce number two. Thankfully, no kids. He wanted to talk about his nearly nightly sexual conquests, and he also asked if Boone had met the secretary from Organized Crime.

Boone shook his head.

"Now there's one I can't crack," Fox said. "Not a model, but you know, attractive, young. Gets hit on all the time. I mean, we have to be careful with all the harassment rules and everything, but there's not a guy in OC who wouldn't want to . . ."

"Not available, eh?" Boone said. "Isn't she married?"

"That never stopped me. Sometimes they're the most grateful, know what I mean? But no, Haeley's never been married, far as I know anyway."

"I heard she had a kid."

"Well, yeah, a little boy. Under three, I think. Cutest little guy. But that was from some boyfriend who ran out on her, if I heard it right. She ought to be ripe for picking, but I think she's a religious wacko or something."

"Yeah?"

"She's got some Bible verse on her desk. Well, not the verse, because they don't allow that, but the numbers — whatever they call it. Besides that, she pretends not to know when someone's coming on to her — I mean, she's smart and everything, so I'm not buying that she can be that dense."

"Interesting."

"Maddening."

Fox started in on all his other prospects until Boone finally asked him to quit. "I'm missing my wife, if you don't mind."

"Lighten up, dude. It's been almost a year, hasn't it?"

Lighten up? Just like this idiot to think time heals this wound.

Boone grew weary of hearing the same stories over and over, but he had not learned how to imply that he was not as impressed as Fox thought he was. Anytime Boone responded at all, with a nod or a *really?* or an *uh-huh,* Fox took it as rapt interest and kept going, plainly embellishing every story before moving on to another.

Fox also seemed convinced that he knew more about street patrol than anyone else, and while Boone did most of the driving and was in essence the senior partner, Fox treated him as a rookie. He reminded Boone of all his years on the street before going undercover, and after each call he would debrief, explaining how he would have done things differently. Boone prided himself on being open to input and able to discern when Fox, though obnoxious, was right.

And he had to admit that Garrett was a by-the-book cop. Boone never felt vulnerable or insecure with Fox in the passenger seat.

In December, closing in on midnight, Boone and Garrett received a call to a bar where a man was drunk and disorderly. As Boone sped toward the address, he said, "I don't know what these tavern owners expect with the kind of clientele they serve."

"Tell me about it," Fox said. "I remember one time when I had to take on four Seabees from Great Lakes, on leave in the city for one night. They were all over six feet and about two-forty. Lucky for me, they were too drunk to counter all my moves. Single-handedly cuffed all four of 'em before backup arrived."

"That so?"

"Dang straight."

"You're telling me the truth?"

"I don't have to lie. I can show you the commendation I got from downtown."

"You carry four sets of cuffs?"

"Well, no, I mean . . . You know what I mean."

"You subdued 'em until backup helped

238

you cuff 'em all."

"Right, but believe me, it was me against four."

When Boone double-parked in front of the bar, Fox leaped out and waited for him at the door. They would enter together. But as soon as Boone reached him, two other bar regulars spilled out. "Watch it, Officers. The guy's armed!"

"What's he carrying?" Boone said.

"Big blade."

Fox laughed. "You don't know Drake's reputation. Got your move ready, partner?"

"Shut up, Fox."

"Just sayin' . . ."

Both cops unholstered their Berettas and pushed into the bar. The place reeked, of course, and most of the patrons had backed into a corner. One slept at the bar, and two others dozed at a back table. The drunk-and-disorderly — a thick and shabby alkie about sixty years old — leaned across the bar, wielding a bowie knife and slurring threats at the bartender, who was keeping his distance and still had a 911 dispatcher on the phone.

"They're here!" the barkeep said. "Thanks." He hung up the phone as the bad guy slowly turned to face Boone and Garrett.

"I can throw this thing faster'n either of you two can shoot," he said.

"I'd love to see you try that, Freddy," Fox said.

"Let's go, Freddy," Boone said. "We've got your cot ready and a chocolate on your pillow. Now drop the knife so we can check you in to the District 11 Hotel."

"Very ffffunny," Freddy said. He shifted the knife so he was holding it by the blade and reached up as if to throw it. He was so unsteady that it was slipping in his fingers.

"You're going to cut yourself, Freddy," Boone said, approaching and holstering his weapon. "Now give me that, and don't you dare even try to throw it or you'll be charged with assaulting a police officer. Believe me, you don't want that."

"Or the one I'd put between your eyes," Fox said.

Freddy's eyes grew wide as he tried to hang on to the knife and defend himself, but Boone was on him in a flash. The knife clattered to the floor, and Boone grabbed a wrist and wrenched it around behind him, nearly making the drunk topple. Freddy swore and began crying as Boone kicked the knife to Fox and finished cuffing him. Soon they had Freddy in the back of the squad.

"What was the trouble in there, Freddy?" Fox said.

"He cut me off! 'Leven o'clock, and he says I had more'n enough. You b'lieve that?"

"You sound like you've had plenty," Boone said.

Freddy leaned forward and awkwardly flashed him an obscene gesture, cursing.

"Behave yourself," Fox said. "You know you're not going to remember any of this tomorrow."

"I'll get my other knife and cut you both before then."

"You want me to write you up for threatening a police officer?" Garrett said. "You keep your nose clean and you can keep wasting your life drinking all night instead of rotting in County or Stateville, you hear me?"

Freddy waved him off and seemed to fall asleep.

At the station Boone opened Freddy's door to help him out. But when Freddy got onto one foot, he drove the door into Boone as hard as he could. Boone kept hold of the handle and pressed his hand against the window, but as he tried to position himself to subdue the drunk, he slipped on the ice, and all his weight transferred to the squad car door. It slammed on Freddy, who was half out of the car, and Boone heard bone and tissue give way. When he righted himself, he discovered what he had feared and swore aloud.

Freddy lay against the floorboard, shin torn open to the bone, a wrist artery splashing, and his face appearing to have been ripped open from his eye to his chin. Fear filled his eyes.

"Help me get him onto the seat!" Boone said as Garrett raced to them.

Fox was on his radio calling for an ambulance and reporting a drunk in danger of bleeding to death. He turned to Boone. "That was a little overkill, don't you think?"

"I slipped, man! You think I wanted to hurt this guy?"

Onlookers approached from a nearby bus stop, and a middle-aged woman began bellowing, "Look what you did to that poor man! That's police brutality! I saw it! I'll testify! I'll press charges! You better hope he doesn't die on you, slamming the door on him like that!"

Freddy the drunk was rushed to the hospital, where he was patched up and held for several days. Meanwhile, Boone was suspended pending an investigation by Internal Affairs.

■ ■ ■ ■

Boone hated the downtime. It reminded him of the weeks of furlough that had followed losing his family. Garrett Fox assured him he would say whatever Boone wanted him to say when questioned by Internal Affairs.

"Tell the truth, Garrett. You know me. You think I tried to kill that guy?"

"You don't want me to tell the truth, Drake. I saw him try to ram you with the door. But he was way drunk and half-asleep, and it was more funny than menacing. You weren't in any danger from that old coot."

"I know that."

"Then you slammed the door on him so hard, you almost did kill him. Now I'm your partner. You tell me what went down and that's what I'll run with."

"I told you. I slipped on the ice and all my weight hit that door. He was in the wrong place at the wrong time."

"So 100 percent an accident."

"Exactly."

"You got it."

"But you don't believe me."

"I know what I saw, but don't worry. We're all brothers under the blue, right?"

"Let me tell you something. If I thought you did what you think I did, I wouldn't want to be your partner anymore. And if I thought you expected me to lie for you, I'd be sure of it."

"That's how you thank me for standing up for you? What's the matter with you, Drake? You've got citizens who are gonna say they saw what I saw. If I say the same, you're done."

For several days the story was all over the news, dominating even the increased gang violence accounts. Somehow the origin of the case, a drunk threatening a bartender with a bowie knife, was lost in the shuffle. What it became was a story of a routine arrest gone bad, when a short-tempered cop meted out street justice on a harmless drunk. The eyewitnesses' accounts were on the news every night, while Garrett Fox said he was not allowed to say anything before the case was investigated by IAD.

Things looked bad for Boone. And in his hour of need, Francisco Sosa called, texted, e-mailed, and insisted on coming to see him. Boone finally gave in.

"I like the place, Boone," the pastor said, sitting next to him in the small living room. "You're looking good, by the way."

"So are you."

"Yeah, but you're working out and eating right. It shows. We've missed you, man."

Boone wished he could say the same, but he didn't want to lie. "Maybe one of these days I'll get back to church."

"You're not going anywhere? I hoped that maybe, you know, you'd found a place without the hard memories, something like that."

Boone shook his head. "I read Nikki's Bible once in a while. Try praying. I'm not too good at this stuff."

"You know, don't you, Boone, that you're not the first to suffer like this? Is it still too soon for me to get tough with you?"

"What do you mean?"

"Something's got to shake you out of this, man. I'm never going to tell you to quit thinking about your loss. But the Bible is full of people who suffered for no apparent reason. You remember what happened between Adam and Eve's first two sons? One murdered the other. We feel bad for Abel, but he was in the right. What had Adam and Eve done to deserve that?"

"They sinned, right?"

"Well, sure, but they were already paying for that. Was it really necessary for them to lose their beloved son at the hands of their other son?"

Boone shrugged, but apparently Sosa had just begun.

"Abraham was instructed to sacrifice his own son. Can you imagine?"

"He didn't have to in the end."

"So you think he didn't suffer? Isaac's twin sons, Jacob and Esau, hated each other. Joseph's brothers threw him into a pit and left him for dead. Moses was not allowed to see the Promised Land. The list in Scripture goes on and on.

"People suffer. Sometimes there's an explanation, but lots of times there isn't. We all deserve death and hell. Why should you or I be spared? What did we ever do to deserve what we have?"

"I don't feel sorry for myself anymore," Boone said, knowing as soon as it had passed his lips that he was not being entirely honest. "But Nikki and Josh didn't deserve to suffer that way, especially if the whole reason for it was God getting my attention."

"Do you think that was the reason?"

"I don't want to think it."

"Neither do I, Boone, because that wouldn't sound like God."

"Can you put any spin on this that makes it sound like something God would allow?"

Sosa hung his head. "I told you, Boone. I'm not pretending to have the answers

246

here. I just want to see you back in church, back in the Word, back in prayer. You don't have to come to our church, but go somewhere. You need brothers and sisters. You need to nourish the inner life. Here, let me leave you with a reference." He scribbled it and handed it to Boone.

When Sosa was gone, Boone had to admit to himself that he appreciated the man. He was trying. And he was sincere. There were certainly plenty of reasons to give up on Boone. There was nothing in this effort for the pastor or his church. With its size and resources, it didn't need Boone Drake.

He sighed and looked at the slip of paper. Psalm 23. He knew that one and could probably quote it or get pretty close. He reached for Nikki's Bible.

The Lord is my shepherd; I shall not want. He makes me to lie down in green pastures; He leads me beside the still waters. He restores my soul; He leads me in the paths of righteousness for His name's sake.

Yea, though I walk through the valley of the shadow of death, I will fear no evil; for You are with me; Your rod and Your staff, they comfort me.

You prepare a table before me in the

presence of my enemies; You anoint my head with oil; my cup runs over.

Surely goodness and mercy shall follow me all the days of my life; and I will dwell in the house of the Lord forever.

"I will fear no evil." Well, there was some truth to that. Boone was no longer afraid of dying, because what lay on the other side had to be better than this.

"He restores my soul." If only that were true. How Boone longed to have his soul restored.

"God," he said quietly, "can you really restore my soul? And can you let the truth come out in this investigation?"

Again he felt foolish after praying.

The next morning, still suspended, Boone called his parents to tell them why he wouldn't be home for Christmas.

"If you're innocent," his mother said, "God will protect you. I'm confident."

"I'm glad *you* are."

"Oh, Boone . . ."

"And listen, I need to apologize for how nasty I was to you before the funeral. You didn't deserve that."

"Honey, that was a year and a half ago. I understood then and I'm over it now. Are you sure you can't get away? You need your family, and we miss you."

"Next year for sure. Promise."

Boone visited Jack Keller in his new office downtown. He saw the nameplate for the secretary Jack shared with Fletcher Galloway, but Haeley Lamonica was not at her desk. There was a photo of a blond-headed boy, and sure enough, there was a tiny frame with a Scripture reference someone had handwritten in calligraphy. Jeremiah 29:13. He'd have to remember that one and look it up.

Keller was packing up to head to a meeting but took a minute to let Boone run through the IAD case.

". . . So Fox thinks I'm guilty but will stand up for me anyway."

"As he should. But that's not going to carry any weight against other eyewitnesses, especially more than one. And you know Freddy's got it in for you."

" 'Course. Could I lose my job over this, Jack?"

"You sure could. I won't lie to you. And even if you somehow survive it, there won't be any plum transfers for a while."

"It's been more than a year already since you left."

"And it'll be another half, regardless. But this could kill it altogether."

"Any advice?"

"All you can do is tell them the truth, Boones."

To his surprise, Boone found himself praying more frequently, and not always late at night before going to bed. He chastised himself, telling himself he was falling into old ruts, praying only when he had a crisis. But this *was* a crisis. And while he hadn't done his part in the relationship with God thing, he really did need help. Would God help him? It seemed he needed a miracle now, and he couldn't imagine one on deck.

He looked up the verse Haeley Lamonica had referenced on her desk:

You will seek Me and find Me, when you search for Me with all your heart.

13
INTERVENTION

Wearing a civilian tie for the first time since the funeral nearly eighteen months before, Boone bounced a foot and tugged at his collar. The Internal Affairs Division investigation into his abuse charge had dragged on and on, mostly due to the fact that a key witness had gone on vacation at the wrong time. It happened to be a female police officer who had pulled her squad in behind Boone's at the same time Boone was attempting to extract Freddy the drunk from the backseat.

When Boone first heard that her dashboard video cam had been running, he was certain he would be exonerated. Unfortunately, especially for Garrett Fox, the angle of the camera did not clearly show what had happened with Boone and Freddy. The door was at the edge of the shot, and while the ugly impact was plainly recorded, only Boone's hands could be seen on the door, not what propelled all his weight against it. The recording did, however, show that Garrett Fox had his back to the action for several seconds before the impact and had turned only at the sound of Freddy's screams and Boone's hollering for an ambulance.

Garrett had, as promised, sworn on the record to IAD that he had seen Boone slip on the ice and that the incident was unequivocally an accident. He had gone on to testify that Boone was the finest young officer he had ever worked with, that he knew him to be a man of character and integrity, and that he was anything but the type of public servant who would intentionally harm an arrestee.

That was all well and good until the dash cam revealed the lie. To their credit, according to Boone's department-assigned defender, IAD investigators stipulated that the recording had impugned only Fox and not Drake. While the female officer said she had seen the incident and corroborated Fox's account, eyewitnesses, especially the noisy middle-aged woman, told an entirely different story.

The female cop was in no trouble because nothing could prove that she did not have the vantage point she claimed. But Boone realized, short of a miracle, he didn't know how in the world he could prove his story.

The Internal Affairs Division was to conclude its investigation with this final hearing at police headquarters downtown, at which Freddy himself would testify. He was suing the department and the city for more than a million dollars.

Boone, too, had been given his day in court. "Is it not true," one of the panelists had said, "that at the time of the arrest you were heard to threaten, and I quote, 'to put one between your eyes,' speaking to the arrestee?"

Boone had hesitated. "I believe we threatened that as a last resort, yes."

"We," the moderator said, "meaning you and your partner, or *you,* Officer Drake?"

"Regardless which of us said it, we communicate as one. And we are trained to use verbal commands to help subdue anyone resisting arrest."

"Did you or did you not threaten to shoot the offender between the eyes?"

"We did."

"Again I ask, *we* or *you?*"

"That's all I care to say, sir."

Now, as Boone sat waiting with his counsel, he was running through his mind the Scripture reference that had been displayed on Haeley Lamonica's desk outside Jack Keller's office. *Am I seeking you with all my heart?* he prayed silently. *I want to, I really do, and I don't want it to be because my job is on the line.*

And his job *was* on the line. It was likely that Garrett Fox would be fired for lying under oath. While there was huge sentiment within the Chicago PD supporting an officer for standing up for his partner, the video had been shown ad nauseam on the local news, and the public had plainly made up its mind. In every poll, the citizenry wanted Fox gone. Most assumed Boone guilty as well.

"What should I have done?" Garrett said to the press and TV news teams. "Supported the eyewitnesses' accounts? Fine, I didn't see what happened. But I know Boone Drake, and there's no way he abused the arrestee."

Now, waiting for the final hearing to be called to order, Boone was certain from the look on his counsel's face that all was lost. The man didn't even try to encourage him. Freddy would soon drive the last nail in his coffin. Boone turned at the sound of the door opening and was moved to see that Garrett Fox was there — looking peeved — as were the female cop, Jack Keller, and

Francisco Sosa. Boone feared they had all come to see his end.

Being there was way above and beyond the call of duty for Pastor Sosa, given that Boone was no longer an active member of his church. Sosa had explained that he saw something in Boone, something worth fighting for, but Boone couldn't understand it. In truth he felt pressured that a man as busy as Sosa spent so much time trying to woo him back to God.

Freddy was on his way in, limping painfully even with the aid of a walker, his face puffy and red and bearing a jagged scar from which stitches apparently had only recently been removed. Was it possible that besides losing his job, Boone could also be prosecuted for assault — even attempted murder?

Freddy and his counsel — a local ambulance chaser known to most as Fast Eddie — sat at a table across the aisle, and as Boone peeked at him, the injured man glared. He looked ready.

The IAD panel whispered among themselves, and during the lull before opening, Boone felt a tap on his shoulder. Francisco Sosa handed him a sheet of paper and retreated. Boone laid it in his lap and quietly unfolded it.

At the top Sosa had written, *Praying for you. This is for today.* Beneath that were lyrics from an old hymn. *And at the bottom is a passage to look up later, no matter what happens. It's the Scripture the hymn was based on.*

Fear not, I am with you, O be not
　　dismayed,
For I am your God, and will still give you
　　aid;
I'll strengthen you, help you, and cause
　　you to stand,
Upheld by my gracious, omnipotent hand.

When through the deep waters I call you
　　to go,
The rivers of sorrow shall not overflow;
For I will be with you, your troubles to
　　bless,
And sanctify to you your deepest distress.

When through fiery trials your pathways
　　shall lie,
My grace, all-sufficient, shall be your
　　supply;
The flame shall not hurt you; I only
　　design
Your dross to consume, and your gold to
　　refine.

The soul that on Jesus still leans for
  repose,
I will not, I will not desert to his foes;
That soul, though all hell should endeavor
  to shake,
I'll never, no, never, no, never forsake!

What was it with Pastor Sosa and the Bible and hymns and their constant references to trials as fire? Was that supposed to be comforting to Boone? All it did was remind him of the pain and horror of his loss, though he tried to glean something meaningful from it too. He wanted to believe that God would be with him throughout this and would never forsake him, but he still hated that Nikki and Josh had been through fire, and that it had done way more than hurt them or refine their gold or consume their dross, whatever that meant.

Boone held his breath as Freddy made his way to the witness chair. The panel asked for his full name and his account of the incident, from arrest to injury.

"Name's Fredrick A. Macintosh, and I was drunk. I'm not disputin' that. The bartender cut me off, and I was mad. I pulled my knife and threatened him. He got on the phone, and I knew he was callin' the police. I was trying to reach him over the bar, and I could tell I had him scared. When the cops showed up, I raised that knife on 'em, but I wasn't gonna throw it. I know better'n that. They woulda shot me, and the one even said so."

"Which one?" a panelist said.

Freddy pointed at Garrett Fox, sitting in the back. "You can make all kinds of jokes about how loaded I was and how I shouldn't be able to remember any of this, but b'lieve me, I do. When somebody threatens to put one between your eyes, you remember. Like I remember the other one, this guy Drake here, 'bout cuttin' me in two with the car door."

"If I may?" Boone's lawyer said, standing. "Mr. Macintosh, is it your testimony that you remember every detail of exactly how you suffered your injuries?"

"Absolutely."

"You understand that Officer Boone Drake remembers it otherwise?"

"He saying he didn't do it?"

"No, he's stipulated what happened. But his contention is that he slipped on the ice and that it was entirely an accident, that there was no malicious intent."

"Yeah, well, I know Drake. We've had our run-ins before. Same with Fox."

"Has there ever been another incident where either of these officers has treated you with anything but respect?"

One of the panelists said, "Let me interrupt here. Mr. Macintosh, you should answer this question as it relates solely to Officer Boone Drake. Officer Garrett Fox's conduct is not under examination at this particular hearing."

"Ever had any problems with Drake? Is that what you're asking me?"

"Correct."

"Matter of fact, I haven't. He always treated me just right, the way he should. I know who I am and what I am, and there are a lot of cops who like to knock me around. I'm not really a threat to anybody, even with my knife. Nobody needs to be mean to me."

"But it's your testimony that this time, for some reason, Officer Drake changed the way he treated you?"

"Look at me."

"There's no question you were severely injured, Mr. Macintosh. The question is whether it was intentional on Officer Drake's part, and if so, why?"

Freddy was silent for so long that those on the panel looked at one another and his lawyer beckoned to him silently with his hands. Freddy shook his head. "I can't do this, Ed," he said. "Drake wouldn't have hurt me on purpose. Truth is, I tried to hurt him, and I could tell from the look on his face that he was just disappointed in me, not mad. And I saw him slip. I think I knew before he did that he was gonna fall into that door and I was gonna be in trouble. Don't punish him for this. It was an accident."

Freddy's lawyer shot to his feet and asked for a recess so he could consult with his client.

"Is that necessary?" the moderator said, turning to Freddy. "Sir, is that your own testimony and not the result of coaching or threat or fear?"

"Yeah, it is."

"Then I see no reason to attempt to amend it."

Freddy said, "If that means change it, I don't either. Drake's a good guy. Let him be." He turned to his lawyer. "It's okay, Ed. What would I do with a million bucks anyway?"

"That's the sole reason for this charade?" a panelist said. "We have spent a good deal of expensive time —"

"I ask that that last statement be stricken from the record," Freddy's lawyer said.

"I'll just bet you do."

Despite the panel's efforts to keep order, members of the press were having a field day with the turn of events, shouting into their cell phones as they headed for the door.

Francisco Sosa and Jack Keller rushed to Boone, clapping him on the back, but he shushed them and insisted they not overreact. "C'mon, Boones," Jack whispered, "It's over. There's nothing they can do to you now. You'll be moving over to OCD before you know it. Come back to my office as soon as you're done here."

It had happened so fast that Boone had trouble taking it in, and he certainly didn't want to jinx it. The last thing he wanted was to celebrate in front of the panel. Most cops under IAD scrutiny grew to hate the investigators and ended up feeling used and abused. He thought they had done what they had to do under the circumstances. And to Boone's mind, Freddy Macintosh's sudden attack of conscience was no less than an answer to his own fervent, if awkward, prayers.

The IAD panel spent nearly twenty more minutes posturing, in Boone's opinion. They thanked Freddy Macintosh for his help, reiterated that the case against Garrett Fox was still pending, and quickly voted to drop all charges against Boone and restore him to full privileges as an officer.

Finally it was time to celebrate, and Keller and Sosa approached again. "Show me a smile, Boones," Jack said.

"In a minute. I've got to talk to Freddy. He just saved my entire career."

"He told the truth," Francisco said.

"And if he hadn't . . ."

Boone thanked his counsel and left Keller and Sosa for a moment, heading toward Freddy. Macintosh shook his hand and said, "Sorry about all this. I know you've had enough problems in your life."

"You do?"

" 'Course. Who doesn't?"

"Hey, you didn't give me a break just because of that, did you, Freddy?"

"I told the truth, man. I'm still broke and dyin', but I know who I am."

"So do I, Freddy. Thanks. Try to stay out of trouble now, you hear?"

The man nodded and turned away.

"Wait. What do you mean, you're dying? Your wounds aren't life-threatening, are they?"

Macintosh motioned Boone closer and whispered, "Truth is, I'm pretty sick and I

don't have much time. Cancer. Ed here
thought a settlement would help me pay the
doctor bills — and pay him off too, of
course."

"Freddy, you were hurt while in our
custody. Surely there'll be a settlement of
some sort, at least to cover your bills. Maybe
more than that."

"Nobody told me that."

"I'll make sure of it."

"No, *I* will." Freddy turned to his lawyer.
"Ed, is it true the cops have to pay for
everything anyway, 'cause this happened
while I was under arrest?"

"Uh, yeah, the city made an offer. I told
you that."

"You did not."

"Oh, I'm sure I did."

"What was it?"

Ed rummaged in his briefcase, looking
stricken. He showed it to Freddy.

"You kiddin' me? I woulda settled for this
in a blink. It's way more than my bills."

Ed whispered, "Yes, but it's nothing like
what a real settlement could have been. And
you know you signed an agreement, so I
still get my third of this."

Freddy glared. "I wonder."

"We have a contract."

"But you never showed me this offer."

"Stand firm, Freddy," Boone said. "If he didn't show you everything, your agreement may be null and void."

"You stay out of this!" the lawyer said.

"Just do the right thing, Eddie," Boone said. He pulled Freddy aside. "Offer him 10 percent and don't budge. Then get yourself into rehab."

Freddy appeared overcome. Lip quivering, he said, "I'm glad I didn't get you in trouble."

"Me too."

"On to my office to celebrate," Keller said, finally dragging Boone out of the hearing room, past a glaring Garrett Fox.

"Can Pastor Sosa come?" Boone said.

"Sure! I won't even break out the booze."

A few minutes later Boone got his first look at Haeley Lamonica as they came to her desk. She was tall and dark-haired with high cheekbones, and her business suit showed a flair for fashion. She looked at Jack Keller expectantly.

He gave her a thumbs-up and said, "We win."

She offered a closed-mouth smile and said, "How nice," and Boone didn't know what to make of it. Maybe she had assumed him guilty all along.

"This's him, my former partner and maybe new colleague soon, Boone Drake."

Haeley nodded but was slow to shake his hand after he had extended his. "Congratulations," she said flatly.

He introduced Francisco, and Haeley seemed to come to life. "*Pastor* Sosa? What church?"

When he told her, she said she was well aware of it and that she attended a small storefront church in a depressed area. "We call ourselves North Beach Fellowship, and there's only about fifty of us, mostly street people."

"I've heard of that work," Sosa said. "I'd love to visit sometime, but you can imagine how weekends are for me. Oh! Who's this?" Sosa turned a framed photo to face him. "He sure looks like you."

"He should. My son, Max. He's three."

"He's beautiful."

Boone was glad she wasn't looking when he grimaced at the photo. The boy was about the age Josh would have been. Pastor Sosa handed him the photo, and when Boone put it back on the desk, he turned it a little farther than it had been originally so it wasn't facing him dead-on.

"I'll look forward to working with you if things turn out," he said. Haeley turned back to her work.

Boone knew he should have said something nice about her son's picture, but he just couldn't. *Beautiful* was right. But so was Josh. He was glad when Keller pulled him and Sosa into his office. "You ought to see that kid," Jack said. "He's in day care nearby, and sometimes she goes and gets him and brings him back in here before going home. A real charmer."

Boone sat heavily.

"What happened to the smile, Boones?" Jack said. "You won, man! You won!"

"I feel lucky, but it was only right, you know."

"Lucky?" Pastor Sosa said. "How about you give the Lord a little credit, Boone? You know as well as I do that that was a direct answer to prayer."

"I do."

"And when you get home, be sure and check out that Scripture I gave you."

Boone nodded.

"Hey," Sosa added, "I've got to go, and you guys have a lot to talk about." Boone stood and the pastor embraced him. As Sosa left, Boone noticed he stopped at Haeley Lamonica's station and chatted.

"Can you concentrate, Boones," Jack said, "or are you totally wiped out?"

"Concentrate on what?"

"The future. Your coming here."

"You think it's going to happen?"

"What's standing in the way? You've been exonerated, and now I push through the paperwork. I want to get it done before they team you with a new partner."

"You think Fox is history?"

" 'Course. I'd vote that way. Backing up a partner is one thing. Perjury is another."

"Imagine how it makes me feel. Freddy as much as said Garrett was right, but Fox can't deny he was only guessing. He stood up for me, but he lied. Got to admit, I never liked him much, but I don't wish this on him."

"It's his own fault." Jack switched gears. "Sorry to change the subject so fast, but the timing couldn't have been better. We need you bad over here. If we don't get a handle on what's happening with the gangs — including the old-timers in organized crime — I could be back on the street as quick as I got here."

"You're talking my language, boss. I haven't been able to concentrate much the last few weeks, but I couldn't ignore the papers and the TV news. This is the reason I became a cop. Get me over here and turn me loose."

Keller beckoned him with a nod and Boone followed him to a thrice-locked room full of file cabinets. "Everything in here is ultraconfidential," Jack said. "I shouldn't even bring you in here until you're officially transferred, but you need to get started."

He pulled from the files several folders containing the rap sheets on the most notorious gangbangers and members of the Outfit. While Boone had looked forward to just getting home and celebrating alone what had happened at the hearing, now he couldn't wait to dig into these records. Nothing in his life had satisfied him more than standing up to playground bullies. The chance to do that to the nth degree was more than he could ask for.

Jack led him back to Haeley Lamonica's desk and had him sign for the files. It was not lost on Boone that the woman seemed very hesitant about that and kept staring at her boss. Finally she whispered, "Sir, there are only two divisions who are supposed to be privy to these, and he's not employed by either one."

"That's my girl," Jack said. "Always lookin' out for me. Let me sign right alongside Boone's name so I take the heat, okay? You're off the hook."

"I wasn't worried about being on the

hook, just protocol."

"I 'preciate it, Haeley. We okay now?"

"Of course."

Boone couldn't help but feel responsible for the woman's discomfort and tried to smile an apology. But she wouldn't catch his eye.

As he followed Keller back into his office, Jack said, "I've been talking with Galloway and Pete Wade, and if you can get up to speed and we get this done as quick as I hope, we have an office I think you'll like."

"Seriously?"

Jack nodded. "Want to see it?"

Jack took him just a few feet down the hall past Haeley, still not smiling, to a small office with one window.

"Hang on a second, Jack. You didn't know before I did that I was going to survive this investigation, and yet you've got this office for me already?"

Jack pressed his lips together and shrugged. "All right, you caught me. We had a backup candidate, and I swear, I wasn't giving you a nickel's chance before Freddy gave it up. But as soon as he did, I called Haeley and had her arrange an appointment with the losing candidate. I'll be breaking that news later this afternoon. I'm not looking forward to that, but I'm glad it turned out this way."

Keller walked Boone out, files under his arm. They were waiting by the elevator when Haeley told Jack there was a call he would want to take. "Be right there," Jack said as the elevator arrived. "You got to celebrate, Boones, even if it means whooping and hollering in the car by yourself, kicking up your heels, eatin' some dessert without working out, something."

"I'll try."

"And I don't need to tell you, those records are for your eyes only."

"I should leave them on the table at Starbucks, is that what you're telling me?"

"Hilarious."

As he descended to the lobby, Boone realized that his victory was hollow without Nikki to share it. He was glad, sure, and as an old justice freak, he simply felt this was right. It was what should have happened. But he couldn't deny that God had intervened.

Boone hesitated by the exit, knowing he had left things awkward between himself and Haeley Lamonica. Garrett Fox had told him everybody was always hitting on her. Maybe her defenses were up. Or maybe she was disappointed he had done the opposite — he had not acted impressed by her at all.

And there was no hiding that he had neglected even a polite comment about her son.

He headed back up, only to find her on the phone. When she noticed him, Haeley seemed to idly turn Max's photo toward her and away from Boone. When she hung up, she said, "Forget something, Officer?"

"Uh, no, I just wanted to say again that I would look forward to working with you, if this whole thing works out and I get transferred here."

She cocked her head, looking dubious. "That so? You don't even know me."

"Yeah, but I've heard good things about you. If Jack Keller likes you, I know I will. And your son is cute. You didn't need to turn the picture away."

She blushed. "Sorry. Your pastor reminded me who you were, so I understand. A lot of us on the job were praying for you back then when . . . you know."

"Thanks. I still need it."

"Well, there must be a lot of people praying for you at Community Life."

"I don't go there anymore."

"Oh? Well, I thought . . . Pastor Sosa —"

"Still a friend."

"Where *do* you go? I'd think it would be hard to find a better church than —"

"Let's just say I'm between churches."

"You're looking? Because —"

"Not really. Not yet."

"Oh, that's not good. Sorry. Listen to me. I'm just saying, when you're ready, you know where we are."

"No, I don't."

Haeley fished in her purse and pulled out a business card with her church's information. Boone put it in his pocket and thanked her. "No promises, but you never know."

"Hey, some weeks if you showed up, you would double the attendance."

Boone snorted and she grinned, and he had to admit it was a nice smile. "I hope my transfer comes through."

"I wouldn't worry about that. You wouldn't have gotten out of here with those files otherwise."

When he got home, Boone looked up the passage Sosa had jotted down for him. It was from Isaiah 43.

Fear not, for I have redeemed you; I have called you by your name; you are Mine. When you pass through the waters, I will be with you; and through the rivers, they shall not overflow you. When you walk through the fire, you shall not be burned, nor shall the flame scorch you. For I am the Lord your God, the Holy One of Israel, your Savior.

"God," Boone said quietly, "thanks for what you did today. I know it could have easily gone the other way, and then I don't know what I would have done with myself. I'm so tired of all this. Pastor Sosa says that one prayer you will never ignore is a request to reveal yourself to someone. Well, I need that. I want that. Please."

Boone sat there feeling foolish, realizing that God had shown himself that very day in the hearing. *Guess I just need a little more of that.*

14
DEEP NIGHT SHADES

Over the next several months and into the late fall, Boone found himself mired in a cycle of encouragement and depression, and he couldn't get a handle on it. He studied for the detective exam while also immersing himself in all the stuff Jack Keller had given him about Chicago street gangs and the Chicago Outfit, the local version of the Mob, the Mafia, or what was known elsewhere variously as "the families" or *La Cosa Nostra* ("this thing of ours").

Much of the street gang stuff he already knew from his time on patrol in the infamous 11th district. Only the latest Outfit material was new to him, as he had already brought himself up to speed on its history. Most intriguing was what appeared to be a relatively new connection between the street gangs and the old Mob. Where it might lead, no one knew, but Boone found himself restless, eager to play a role in finding out and maybe even putting a stop to it.

Call me an idealist, he thought, *but I want the bad guys to be as afraid of the Chicago PD as the bullies were of me in junior high.*

Meanwhile, Boone was lonely. He breezed through the detective exam and enjoyed a nice going-away fete and the congratulations of his colleagues at the 11th. But after switching to plainclothes and being awarded his simple but dramatic five-point star with *Detective* across the top, *Chicago Police* in a semicircle, and his service number across the bottom, Boone found himself living for the workday.

In his new office he was getting to know his colleagues, spending a lot of time with his new boss, Pete Wade, and learning more than he thought there was to know about Chicago's underbelly. Wade, like Keller, was no-nonsense and old-school, a born teacher. In his midfifties, black, and already white-haired, he was articulate and rapid-fire in his delivery, and Boone found himself drinking in everything.

But when the day was over, it was as if his lights went out. He and Wade did not socialize outside the office, as Pete was a family man. And Jack had a new live-in girlfriend who seemed to monopolize his off-duty time. So Boone spent his late afternoons and evenings working out, studying, and watching TV.

Mostly he was in a funk, feeling sorry for himself. Sleep was so elusive that he was tempted to resort to wine again. But Boone had spent so much time and energy working out and eating right, he found himself in the best shape of his life and didn't want to do anything to jeopardize that.

He was still trying to pray, but his pleas disgusted him. It seemed all he did was ask for relief or something else for himself. He wanted rest, peace, something to look forward to besides the job. Boone was not looking outward, as Pastor Sosa kept encouraging. "You're not going to be happy until you're doing something for somebody else," Francisco had texted him.

The pastor was still inviting him to church and encouraging him to go somewhere, if not Community Life. He also sent him Scripture references occasionally, and strangely, Boone found himself actually looking forward to them. One night as he sat watching another inane late show, he muted the TV and looked up Sosa's latest verse, Matthew 11:28:

Come to Me, all you who labor and are heavy laden, and I will give you rest.

Boone was glad he was sitting when he read that familiar verse. It washed over him with such power and left him with such longing that he felt he might collapse under it. It was all he could do to keep from weeping, and then he wondered, why not? Who was there to see if he cried? "I'm coming to you, God. I'm laboring and heavy laden, and I need rest. Tell me where to find it."

He finally turned off the TV and stumbled to bed, only to lie there staring at the ceiling and realizing that the answer to yet another prayer was no. Either that, or he was looking in the wrong place for rest. By now he thought the pain of his loss should have dulled, and at times perhaps it did. But deep in the night it was often as sharp as ever, and all he could do was bury his face in his pillow and scream and sob. He wanted Nikki and Josh back with such fierceness that he wondered if life was worth living. And people said time was supposed to heal all wounds.

Some evenings Boone wondered if he should take Francisco Sosa up on the free counseling offered at Community Life. But every morning was a new start for him, and

277

he eagerly dressed and headed for the office. Boone was intrigued by the fact that Haeley Lamonica was cordial and sometimes friendly, but never overtly so. She kept the photo of her son closer to her and not showing as she had in the past, and while Boone was tempted to ask if that was for his benefit, he didn't pursue it.

He was also struck by the number of times other police personnel — in fact just about anyone in the building for any reason — seemed to flirt with Haeley. Every time, she just sighed and hesitated, ignoring them as Garrett Fox had reported. She responded only to those who were clearly inappropriate, and her tone indicated a warning that she would not put up with harassment.

To one senior executive who mentioned what he'd like to do with her after hours, Haeley said, "If you'll forgive me for declining, I'll forgive you for suggesting it."

"Come on! I know you're single and would appreciate a man of experience."

"And I see you're married."

"But not dead."

"No, but unemployed if you say one more thing I can report to Human Resources."

When the man huffed off, Boone emerged. "Impressive."

Haeley snorted and shook her head. "I

only play tough. That stuff makes me quake."

"You really shut him down."

"I have a lot of experience."

"Sorry."

"Comes with the territory."

"Would you even know how to respond if someone asked you out and you *wanted* to see him?"

She squinted. "Don't start. Please. After all these months of barely speaking to me . . ."

He smiled. "Don't jump to conclusions."

"Don't flatter myself, you mean?"

"I didn't say that; you did."

"How about those Chicago Bears, eh?" Haeley said, and they both laughed.

Keller and Wade spent much of the day working with Boone either in a conference room or on the street, keeping an eye on the gangs. Of course there was no hiding a so-called unmarked squad car with three suit-clad men in it.

It didn't matter which of the big three street gangs' territories they ventured into — the Gangster Disciples, the Vice Lords, or the Latin Kings — the members immediately busied themselves looking the other way when the police officers rolled into view.

The Disciples had become the largest of the three factions, and they consisted of more than thirty thousand blacks in the Englewood area on the South Side. The Jewish Star of David and the upturned pitchfork were their symbols. All over their neighborhoods, graffiti read, "All Is One," and "What Up G?"

"I'll tell you what's up, G," Pete Wade told Boone. "These guys pull in more than nine figures a year."

"You're not serious."

"As a heart attack. They're bigger than the Vice Lords, though the Lords have been around longer. The Lords have about twenty thousand members in the Lawndale area. You believe that? They started as a little club more than fifty years ago at the Illinois State Training Center in St. Charles."

Boone saw all kinds of graffiti symbols on the West Side for the Lords, including the initials VL, a pyramid, dice, a bunny head, a crescent moon, and a top hat with gloves and a cane. The Vice Lords had gained control of their neighborhood when they appeared to turn over a new leaf in the 1970s and became community leaders. They were given federal grants to run a center for youth and job-training classes.

"When the grants were rescinded," Wade said, "the Vice Lords reverted to their old ways."

Even the so-called smallest of the three leading gangs, the Latin Kings — made up primarily of Puerto Ricans and Mexicans — numbered nearly twenty thousand members. Their symbols — expressed in graffiti all over the Southeast Side and Humboldt Park — included crowns, stars, a cross, a lion's head, five dots, and their initials.

"These neighborhoods and their gangs freak you out, Drake?" Pete Wade said, swinging around in his seat as they headed back to headquarters late one Friday afternoon. Keller was driving with Boone in the backseat.

"Sure. Give me the creeps. You couldn't pay me enough to venture in there alone. But give me the right tools and backup, and you couldn't pay me enough to stay away."

"That's as it should be. Now it's quiz time. See if you've been studying. Where are we on Chicago Outfit and how do they interact with the gangbangers?"

"Well, let's see. It's been one disaster after another for the last two decades for the Outfit. Worst came earlier this decade when a bunch of Mob bosses and their associates, including three made guys, were indicted.

They're down from six street crews to four and some say as few as three. They're still big in loan sharking, debt collecting, extortion, and street taxes, but the old days of making a lot of money from vice and gambling are gone. Too much of that has been legalized, and it's cut into their action. They still lend to casino gamblers the bank won't touch, and the vigorish on those loans is exorbitant."

"Good," Wade said. "How big is the Outfit now, compared to what it was?"

"Around a hundred made guys and associates, down from about four-fifty twenty years ago."

"Uh-huh, and in your opinion, from what you've read and we've taught you, what's the biggest organized crime threat to the city of Chicago?"

These were softballs, Boone thought. Clearly something else was coming, once he had established that he had all this down. "Well, seeing as how the Chicago Crime Commission figures there have been around eleven hundred Mob hits in the last century, and the last one was more than twenty years ago, while the street gangs — who monopolize the drug trafficking — have murdered about two thousand in the last decade, I think it's obvious. We still have to stay atop the Outfit, with all its ties to the unions and embezzling and all that. But the street gangs are clearly worse."

Pete Wade settled back, facing the road. "Jack," he said, "I think the boy is ready for the next step."

"Yeah?"

"Don't you think he's ready for the assignment?"

Keller shrugged. "In due time."

Pete held up both hands. "Sorry. Didn't mean to be premature. And it wasn't my place."

Jack laughed. "I just want to wait till we're back in the office. I want to see the look on his face."

Whatever this assignment was, Boone was eager to get it. But when they got back to the office, the workday was nearly over. Haeley had her son in a chair next to her desk. Apparently she had persuaded him to be both quiet and still, as having him sit there was a privilege she couldn't afford to lose.

Keller retired to his office with Wade, while Boone stalled in his own office, waiting to be summoned. As he tidied up and stacked files, he heard Keller emerge and instruct Haeley to set a meeting for the three of them Monday morning. Why did it always have to be this way? If there was one thing Boone no longer looked forward to, it was a weekend with nothing to do.

Boone was pulling on his trench coat when Haeley poked her head in to tell him of the meeting. He thanked her and made a show of jotting it down when Max scooted away from his mother and ran to him. He reached up with both hands, and Boone froze.

"Max, no! Come here!"

But the boy stood there, looking puzzled, still reaching. Boone finally welcomed him into his arms, not prepared for the wave of emotion the little body evoked. He bit his lip and looked away as Max laid his cheek on Boone's shoulder.

Haeley quickly pulled the boy away. "I'm so sorry, Boone. Forgive me."

"It's all right," he managed, feeling his face flush. "Hey, listen, you got plans for dinner?"

Haeley gave him a look. "Don't do this. You don't have to, and I'd rather you not be like everybody else. Trying to get a sitter on a Friday night —"

"No, I meant you guys, you two, both of you."

She hesitated. "Are you sure?"

"Nothing fancy. Maybe pizza."

"Well, okay. I guess. Max, you want pizza?"

"Pizza!"

"That's a yes."

They walked to a place nearby, and as they sat waiting for their food, Max climbed into Boone's lap. "Max!" Haeley said, looking mortified.

"Nah, it's all right," Boone said, putting his hand on the boy's back to steady him. So many memories. Such pain. He was impressed that this seemed natural for Max. He played with stuff on the table, ignoring Boone.

"He doesn't do that with most people," Haeley said. "Despite being a day care kid, he's kind of clingy."

"Maybe because of that, huh?"

"Maybe. I hate leaving him every day, I can tell you that."

"No family nearby?"

She shook her head. "Deep South."

"I don't hear any accent."

"We're from Michigan, but when my parents retired, they moved to South Carolina."

"Does his dad get to see him?"

Haeley exhaled loudly through pursed lips. "There's no dad in the picture."

"And you don't want to talk about it. No

problem."

"Ah, I don't mind. I was stupid, a bad judge of character. Away from God, you know?"

Boone nodded. He knew, all right.

"I let him move in," she said, "supported him for a while. The day he found out I was pregnant, he was out of there. Haven't seen him since."

"You ever hear from him?"

"Oh, sure. I know where he is. Works at a casino in Indiana. Last time I heard from him it was just him telling me not to expect a dime, that the baby was my *fault,* and that he didn't feel any responsibility."

"Quality guy."

"My poor choice. Pushed me back to my faith, though, I'll tell you that."

"That's good then, I guess."

She fell silent when their food came. She made Max sit next to her, and Boone enjoyed watching her with him, making sure the pizza was placed far enough from him so he wouldn't burn himself. She looked expectantly at Boone.

He smiled. "Dig in."

"Max is used to praying before a meal," she said. "Want to do the honors?"

"Uh, no, go ahead."

She held Max's hand and he reached for

Boone's.

"Dear God, thank you for this food and for a new friend. In Jesus' name, amen."

"Amen!" Max said, smiling.

How nice that she had been quiet and not showy so Boone didn't have to feel embarrassed, except that he had declined to pray. Haeley didn't eat much, then seemed to study Boone, making him feel self-conscious.

"What?" he said.

"You ever feel unforgiven, even though you know better?"

"Humph. When I feel unforgiven, I know I deserve to."

"Come on. You a new Christian or what?"

He briefly told her his history.

"So," she said, "like me, you were raised in church, and like I say, you know better. I knew better than to live with a guy too, but while I really came clean about it and asked forgiveness, there are times when I don't feel forgiven."

Boone wanted to tell her that he was having trouble forgiving God, but it seemed way too personal this early in their friendship. "I'm no saint," he said. "I use language I never used and never thought I would use before I became a cop."

"I don't know how Christian officers can

avoid that, with what they hear from criminals and their fellow officers every day."

"Yeah, but it's no excuse."

"So then you do know we're forgiven even if we don't feel it," she said.

"I should."

"You would if you were hearing it every week in church. I bet that's what your pastor what's-his-name preaches."

"Francisco Sosa? Yeah. It is. Far as I can remember."

"Shame on you, Boone. You've got to get back to church."

He was surprised he could take this, but she was so easy to talk to. "I know."

"But?"

"Lots of reasons."

"Painful memories."

"Yeah, but more than that."

"None of my business, but if it's too hard for you to go back to Community Life, there are other places —"

"I know."

"Listen to me, advising you. Sorry."

"No, you're right," he said.

"And as I told you a while ago, you know where I am on Sunday mornings."

"That an invitation?"

"Well, what else would it be? Should I watch for you?"

"Nah. Not this week. Maybe sometime."

"Otherwise engaged?" She looked at him as if she'd caught him.

"Pretty busy," he said.

"Uh-huh," she said, a tease in her voice. "So busy you can make dinner plans at the drop of a hat."

He laughed. "What does that mean, anyway, 'at the drop of a hat'?"

"Don't ask me. I don't even own a hat."

When they finished and were on their way out into the darkness, Max suddenly wrapped his arms around Boone's thigh, and he had to slow himself to keep from tripping over the boy.

"He likes you," Haeley said. "He's got the instincts of a puppy that way."

"Guess I should be glad he isn't barking at me."

Boone walked them to her car, and she thanked him for "doing the pizza thing on short notice."

"At the drop of a hat?"

"Exactly," she said.

"Can we do it again sometime?"

"Maybe."

At home Boone found himself obsessing about Max and how he reminded him of the tactile joys of just cuddling Josh. He hauled out some pictures and made himself miserable.

When his phone chirped, he had a fleeting hope that it might be Haeley. But why would it be? He hadn't even given her his number. Rather, it was another reference from Pastor Sosa. Psalm 62:7:

In God is my salvation and my glory; the rock of my strength, and my refuge, is in God.

How Boone wished that were true for him.

15
THE ASSIGNMENT

Boone had to admit that Saturday proved one of the strangest days he'd had since he'd been alone. His mind was its usual jumble, but for the first time his thoughts were not dominated by his losses. Memories of Nikki and Josh were still ever present, as they would always be, but for once his mind was occupied by the future.

He knew it held a new assignment, and he was so eager for Monday morning's meeting that he could barely think of anything else. And yet he found himself intrigued by Haeley. Not everyone was so easy to be with and talk to, and while Boone wanted to move slowly and not get ahead of himself, he simply wanted to see her again, away from the office. And he couldn't deny, painful as it was, he was enamored of Max too.

Boone's daylong restlessness got him out of the house, spending much of his time just driving around and talking himself out of asking Jack Keller for Haeley's phone number. All he needed was to come on too quickly and too strong and scare her off. It wasn't as if he saw some long-term future with her, but he needed a friend — and so did she. And he didn't want to be one of "those" guys. She'd had enough trouble with them.

Boone's curiosity took him past her church — just in case he needed it for future reference — and Haeley's description of it as a storefront proved an overstatement. A tiny window between a fast-food chicken place and a laundry bore a simple sign announcing North Beach Fellowship. A peek inside revealed rows of folding chairs facing a small riser and a screen.

Boone told himself it was high time he got back to church, but he wasn't fooling himself. He would be there the next morning to see Haeley . . . and Max. On his way home, his phone buzzed; it was a text message. He pulled off to read it and was glad to see that it was from Haeley.

Sorry, got your number from the boss. Didn't want to bother you, but you said your pastor sometimes texted you verses? After what you said about language, I have one for you. Proverbs 13:3. Hope

292

I'm not overstepping. Thanks again for the pizza at the drop of a hat. See you Monday.

Boone looked up the verse when he got home:

He who guards his mouth preserves his life, but he who opens wide his lips shall have destruction.

Boone texted back a simple thanks, grateful to have Haeley's number. Sleep again proved elusive that night, but for a different reason than before. Boone was more eager than troubled. Haeley thought she would see him Monday. He hoped she would be pleasantly surprised to see him sooner.

There was little Boone hated more than the awkward moments in a new place when he would not know what to do. So the next morning he parked far across the parking lot from North Beach Fellowship and waited till starting time before even approaching the door. Apparently the little church was informal about time, because a couple of minutes after they were to begin, people were still milling about and talking. Boone hung back, away from the door and out of sight, until the music started and people

293

began taking their seats.

Boone slipped into the back row behind an enormous black lady in a flowery dress and festive hat who held a little white boy in her lap. Boone was glancing around looking for Haeley when the boy jumped to his feet on the woman's thighs and reached toward him, squealing, "Pizza!"

The woman fought to hang on to him, and Boone put a finger to his lips. As Max continued to try to wrench free and get to him, the woman turned and scowled at Boone. "You ain't going to no stranger, Maxie. No, sir."

"I work with his mom," Boone whispered.

"Maybe you do; maybe you don't," the woman said. "I'll know soon enough."

Max was causing such a ruckus trying to get to him that Boone moved across the aisle to another back-row seat and quit looking at the boy. Up front a guitarist who introduced himself as Sean, a keyboard player, and a drummer kicked up the volume as lyrics appeared on the screen. The band and a couple of singers — one was Haeley; despite the cramped quarters she had apparently not noticed him yet — led out in a rousing, folksy rendition of an old hymn Boone remembered from his childhood.

The noise and the beat distracted Max, and the woman got him turned around and bouncing as the little congregation stood and began singing.

Boone found he was able to sing along, but he had to admit he'd never heard singing quite like this. There seemed no self-consciousness on anyone's part. Some in the congregation played along with tambourines and maracas, and people seemed to sing full-throated and emotionally. He had memories of having his nose in a hymnbook as a child, singing this same song as a dirge.

When about twenty-five minutes of singing had ended, a young man who introduced himself as the pastor made announcements and asked for prayer requests. The band members and singers found their seats, and when the woman watching Max whispered to Haeley and pointed, Haeley turned quickly and gestured for Boone to join them.

He slipped across the aisle next to her and Max immediately climbed into his lap. The woman leaned over and said, "Sorry, son, but I don't just hand him over to people I don't know."

"You did the right thing," Boone whispered.

Meanwhile, people stood one at a time to

either express thanks for prayer or tell of current needs. A couple mentioned money problems, and another woman said her son was back in jail. Finally an elderly woman stood, and Boone could tell from the sympathetic sounds from the others that she was known and that they knew what was coming.

"Dorothy," the pastor said.

"You all know," she said just above a whisper, "that my beloved Henry passed last Monday. I appreciate so many of you coming to the funeral. We would have been married fifty-three years come next month. I just want to praise God for the time we had together, but most of all for being with me these last few days. I won't lie to you. This has been the worst week of my life. There were times I wondered if Jesus cared, if he knew how empty I felt. Many of you have been there and know there's no hole in your heart like when you lose somebody you love. If I didn't have the Lord, I'd be lost."

As she sat, many reached to pat her on the back. The pastor whispered to the song leader, who immediately rose and plugged in his guitar. The pastor said, "Normally we would have prayer now and one more song before we dismiss the kids to their class, but I've asked Sean to sing a special song just for Dorothy. While he sings, the children can go. Their teacher this week is Miss Haeley."

A wave of disappointment rolled over Boone as Haeley reached for Max and they began to leave. She flashed him an apologetic look, and just like that he was alone.

With the first haunting chords Sean strummed, Boone was mesmerized and all but forgot where he was. His peripheral vision left him, and all he could see was the lone guitarist under a cheap spotlight as he closed his eyes and sang earnestly:

Does Jesus care when my heart is
    pained
Too deeply for mirth or song;
As the burdens press, and the cares
    distress,
And the way grows weary and long?

Does Jesus care when I've said good-bye
To the dearest on earth to me,
And my sad heart aches till it nearly
    breaks —
Is it aught to him? Does he see?

Dorothy stood and raised her arms, tears streaming, and all over the room, others did the same as Sean sang the refrain. Boone

297

stood and edged to the door, knowing he
would be unable to stay another minute
after the song was finished.

Oh, yes, he cares; I know he cares,
His heart is touched with my grief.
When the days are weary, the long nights
    dreary,
I know my Savior cares.

Boone hurried to his car and shut himself
in behind the wheel. He sat unable to move,
knowing he had to pray. But what could he
say? He did not understand God, and he
was finally learning that no one did or ever
would. He didn't like what God allowed,
but Boone had also learned that it wasn't
his place to try to do God's job for him.
"I asked you to reveal yourself to me," he
said hoarsely. "And you remind me that you
care. I confess I've been doubting that. But
I believe it. I know it. I know you care. For
whatever reason, you allowed the dearest on
earth to be taken from me. I'll never understand or know why, but I will rest in the
fact that you know what it's done to me.
And that you care."
Boone was left so frazzled that he didn't
feel he had the strength to even drive home.
He recognized Haeley's car and decided to

wait for her and Max and see if he could have lunch with them. Meanwhile he sat resolving to do something about his new realization. Boone was suddenly aware that he was finally willing to return to his faith. He also recognized that his faith had never been vibrant or fervent, and that had to change.

North Beach Fellowship, though he hadn't even stayed for the message, hit him as so much more personal and inviting than Community Life that he wanted to try it as his church home, at least for a while. Francisco Sosa would understand. In fact, he would encourage it. Boone wasn't sure he would ever be comfortable in the church where he and Nikki had served and Josh had been dedicated.

More than an hour later, Haeley and Max were among the last to emerge from the little storefront. Boone waited near her car.

"Pizza!" Max said.

Boone laughed but feared his red eyes would give away that he had been crying.

"No, honey," Haeley said. "Lunch at home today."

"Aw, will it keep?" Boone said.

" 'Fraid not," she said. "I need to get Max down, and I have a lot to —"

"But there's so much I want to talk to you about."

"Today's not going to work, Boone. I'm sorry."

"You sure? Maybe later, after he's up?"

"No, not today."

Boone was stunned and couldn't hide it. Had he misunderstood something, offended her?

"I'll see you at the office tomorrow," she said. "Maybe we can talk on break."

"I don't take breaks," he said. "And I need more than a few minutes."

Haeley put Max in his car seat and stood by the open door. "Boone, it's obvious you're working through some pretty deep stuff."

"I am. That's why —"

"Well, I am too, and I'm not sure it's a good idea for two vulnerable people to lean on each other."

"Don't make it more than it is, Haeley. I just want to talk, be friends. . . ."

"We can be friends at work for now, okay?"

Well, no, it wasn't okay. What was this? Part of how God was revealing himself to Boone? Was it too much to hope that a new good friend might be part of the deal?

"So, no more meals — the three of us, I mean?"

"I didn't say that. Just, let's not get ahead of ourselves. Neither you nor I have much going outside the office, so . . ."

"Play it by ear?"

She nodded, looking eager to escape.

"I don't want to become a pest," he said, "but I can't promise I'll quit asking."

"I didn't ask you to quit asking, but you'll do yourself a favor if you slow down."

"Got it."

"How did you like our church?"

"I liked it. Will it bother you if I come back?"

"It's no place to see me. You can see how busy I am there. But no, it wouldn't bother me at all. In fact, it would encourage me to see you here."

Bitterly disappointed, Boone texted Francisco Sosa and asked if they could get together for coffee late that evening.

I would almost any time, Sosa wrote back, *but after multiple services this weekend, Sunday night is family crash time. Pick another time and I'll make it work. Meanwhile, here's another passage to look up. Romans 8:38-39.*

All Boone had wanted was to tell Sosa of his new resolve and his interest in what the pastor had once referred to as the nourishment of his spiritual life. He knew he had been remiss, even in all the years before the tragedy, in his devotional life — reading the Bible every day and praying. He wanted to do something about that and wanted some kind of an aid. Was there a book or a list of passages or a guide for, say, reading through the Bible in a year? He knew there was. He had heard of those, even a through-the-year Bible that had it all scoped out for you. That seemed perfect.

Boone knew he could find all this stuff on his own, but after the brush-off by Haeley, he needed the kind of feedback he knew he'd get from Francisco. Ah, who was he kidding? He had brushed off Sosa ten times. He was surprised the guy hadn't given up on him already. Boone certainly couldn't expect special treatment by someone in charge of so many people.

Boone looked online for a book on prayer and for a one-year Bible, ordering them both. Meanwhile he thanked God for a most unusual day, for revealing himself to Boone and even for the response he'd gotten from Haeley. "I don't understand that either," he said, "but I'm trusting you and accepting it for now." He also prayed about the assignment that was coming in the morning and for the ability to sleep so he would be alert and ready to respond to his bosses.

Then he looked up the Bible passage Francisco Sosa had recommended:

> I am persuaded that neither death nor life, nor angels nor principalities nor powers, nor things present nor things to come, nor height nor depth, nor any other created thing, shall be able to separate us from the love of God which is in Christ Jesus our Lord.

So often Sosa's references resonated with something Boone had experienced that very day. This one he could not put into that category, but something about it gave him such a sense of deep peace that he knew God must have nudged Francisco to suggest it. Boone's biggest fear, as he haltingly and cautiously made his way back to his faith, was that he himself had somehow caused a separation between him and God. But if none of those things listed could separate him from God, how could he himself?

These were verses he wanted to memorize, and he decided he would try to memorize at least one verse a week. He read them over and over before he went to bed, and with the promise rattling in his brain, slept deeply and soundly for the first time in ages.

Boone awoke at dawn thanking God for peace and rest, which surprised Boone after his disappointment. What struck him was that he was still wounded, still alone, still confused about many things, and yet he looked forward to the future.

He had planned to work out before leaving for headquarters but decided instead to go for a run. Boone felt better than he had in a long time as the cold morning air filled his lungs. By the time he arrived at the office, he was ready for whatever the brass had to offer. He greeted Haeley, who seemed warm enough, and grabbed the picture of Max. Boone just smiled at it and put it back, angling it to where he could see it from his office.

He was sitting at his desk when Haeley called out, "Detective Drake, it's time for your meeting. Deputy Chief Keller and Commander Wade would like you to bring just a legal pad."

Maybe it was his imagination, but Boone thought Keller and Wade looked even more excited than he did. He sat across from them in the small conference room off Jack's office, his pen ready. Keller had his suit coat off, revealing his 9mm strapped in a shoulder holster. Wade, his pure white hair shining, wore a dark suit, buttoned up despite that he was sitting, and was fingering a stack of file folders.

"Ready, Boones?" Keller said.

"If I was any more ready, I'd burst."

Wade opened the top folder, revealing a large mug shot of a dapper, elderly man. "You recognize him?"

Boone nodded. "Jacopo."

"Graziano Jacopo," Wade said. "To the best of our knowledge, still boss of the Chicago Outfit."

"Don't let his age or his look fool you," Keller said. "He's still the most feared man in the Mob. And as you know, we suspect he has kept his nose clean the last few years by outsourcing his hits."

"To the gangbangers," Boone said.

"That's why the Crime Commission doesn't lay some of the Outfit deaths personally at his feet or hold his most established hit men responsible," Wade said. "The deaths have not had the quick and clean characteristics of Mob hits. You remember some of these?"

"Sure," Boone said. "Ripped to shreds. Overkill. Some by AK-47s. The way the street gangs do it."

Jack stood and placed both palms on the table. "The public tells us to quit looking for the killers. To just thank them. I understand that sentiment, but it's not what we're about. The problem is, these kinds of murders don't reveal the modus operandi of the Mob or any specific hit men. They could have been committed by any one of tens of thousands of gangbangers."

"The proverbial needle in a haystack, huh?" Boone said.

Keller smiled grimly. "Welcome to Organized Crime, Boones."

"What, that's my assignment? Find these killers out of the whole Chicago universe of street gangs? We can't even differentiate between the black gangs and the Hispanic gangs in their methodology. Or at least I can't."

Wade pulled out another folder and opened it to reveal another photo. Boone turned it upright and slid it in front of himself. "That's Pascual Candelario, right? Didn't he do time at Stateville?"

Wade nodded. "Armed robbery and assault with a deadly weapon, but as you can imagine, that was just what we could get him on. You remember what he did almost as soon as he got in there?"

Boone racked his brain. It was coming

back to him. "Just about cleaned up all the gang stuff at Stateville, didn't he?"

"*Between* the gangs, at least," Wade said. "God help you if you were white, a skinhead, an Aryan, or unaffiliated. But anybody in there from the Disciples, the Lords, or the Kings was invited to join Candelario's new coalition, the DiLoKi Brotherhood. There wasn't so much as an injury to one of them after that."

"But they wreaked havoc on everybody else."

"They did. And now he's out and heading up the same kind of coalition in the city."

It was Boone's turn to stand and stretch. "You know what the new coalition reminds me of? The Jamaican Shower Posse in New York and Toronto in the eighties."

Boone felt Pete Wade looking at him with admiration. "That's a good thought," Wade said. "The posse was one of the first coalitions of smaller gangs."

Boone shrugged. "So what are we doing about that? Do we think the DiLoKi is easier to manage than three rival gangs?"

"They could even wipe out the Outfit," Wade said. "Candelario's genius is that he welcomes everybody. No turf. No colors. All for one and one for all."

"Is it working?"

"Seems to be. Intergang violence is almost nil."

"What are they doing to everyone else? Seems they'd be just as hard to control — maybe harder."

"They would," Jack said. "Except Pascual Candelario — he goes by PC — wants to work with us."

Boone sat back down. "I'll bite. What happened?"

"Two things," Wade said. "The DiLoKi, specifically Candelario, made a pact with the Outfit to protect any of their guys in Stateville. Imagine that coalition now, on the outside. The Chicago Outfit and the three biggest street gangs in the country working together against everybody else."

"Wow. But you said two things."

"For that you'll have to come with us. Get your coat."

A few minutes later, in the backseat of an unmarked squad with Keller driving and Wade in the passenger seat, Boone said, "Does this all have to be cloak-and-dagger, or can I ask where we're going?"

"You've been there," Keller said.

Okay, so this was how it was going to be. Boone sat quiet until he recognized the route and Keller finally pulled into a parking garage near the U.S. Customs building on Canal Street. Among other things, the structure housed the Chicago Division of the Federal Bureau of Investigation's Gang Crime Unit and crime lab.

There the three were greeted by forensics expert Dr. Ragnar Waldemarr, a tall, graying man of about sixty. He took them to an anteroom off the crime lab, where he pulled from the shelf a large, white storage box and carefully set it on a table, at which they all sat. Despite how little Dr. Waldemarr jostled the box, still it rattled and tinkled.

A crime scene location and date were felt-tip marked on the side, identifying the evidence from the last big gang shoot-out on the Northwest Side, six months before. Boone remembered seeing the story on the news, but the DiLoKi Brotherhood was not named. Reporters merely mentioned that a coalition of gangs had engaged in a brief but bloody war with one of the lesser Hispanic gangs, a lagging holdout against the merger. Word was, the new alliance had vowed to persuade whatever few survivors there might be to join peacefully. There hadn't been many, but they had meekly joined.

Dr. Waldemarr began removing handfuls of large-caliber shells, and soon more than two hundred were scattered on the table, some rolling, and all three cops gathered them to keep them from dropping onto the floor.

"You want them all?" the doctor said. "There are more than a thousand."

"That's plenty, Rag," Keller said. "Just show the new guy."

The doctor turned to Boone. "Drake, is it? Do you know the assault weapon of choice of the head of the DiLoKi?"

"Some kind of Nazi rifle, but I couldn't tell you much more about it."

"Well, let me tell you, it's something distinctive. It's called the StG 44, the Sturmgewehr model 1944. It's widely referred to as the first modern assault rifle. The Nazis used it for only about a year at the end of World War II, and less than a half million were produced. Where Candelario got one, we have no idea, but someone who knew what they were doing has it in tip-top shape."

As he spoke, the doctor was separating out and setting on their broad flat ends the shells for cartridges that looked like — with bullets inserted — they would have been close to eight inches tall. The hollow end made Boone guess, "32mm?"

Dr. Waldemarr nodded. "Close — 33.

Gas-operated, the thing will shoot more than five hundred rounds a minute, emptying a thirty-round magazine in less than four seconds. Velocity of more than two thousand feet a second with an effective range of three American football fields."

Boone snorted. "Candelario would never shoot that far."

"More like twenty feet," Wade said. "That thing rips people in two."

The doctor and the two older cops glanced at each other. "Show him," Keller said.

Waldemarr stood and pulled a small envelope from another box on the shelf. He emptied into his hand a half-dozen similar shells. "Compare one of these to one of those," he said, sitting and sliding one to Boone.

Drake examined one from each group. "These," he said, referring to the ones the doctor had taken from the envelope, "make the others look as if they haven't even been fired. I don't get it."

Dr. Waldemarr smiled at Keller. "Can you spare him for lab work?"

"Not on your life."

"Very good, Detective Drake," the doctor said. "We have determined that of all the shells collected from that battle scene, only the few dozen from Candelario's StG 44

311

were blanks."

Boone let his eyes close and shook his head. When he found his voice, he said, "I'm lost."

The doctor stood and began putting all the evidence away. "Now he is in your territory, gentlemen. Not mine. I show you the forensics; you make of it what you will."

On the way back to headquarters, Boone sorted and shifted the news in his head and simply couldn't make it compute. "I give up," he said finally. "I don't get it."

"PC got religion," Keller said.

"No way."

"He did. Nobody knows quite how or why, but we have inside information that this guy is a born-againer and the real deal. Won't kill anybody, but he can't let on to his compatriots either. He'd be a dead man."

"Inside information?" Boone said. "How solid?"

"The Protestant chaplain at Stateville. Claims it's legit and that he's the only one who knows about it. That's where you come in."

"I'm listening."

"We'll set up a meeting between you and this chaplain. He says the new PC isn't really that new, that he's been a secret Holy

Roller for more than two years. If that's true, it could be that PC came up with the DiLoKi idea as a way to help make amends for all the stuff he's done."

"That's a lot, isn't it? Wasn't he high up in the Latin Kings?"

"Among the top three for a decade. We figure he personally killed at least a dozen rivals. Maybe more."

"What's his angle now?"

"That's for you to find out from the chaplain. But in broad strokes, it involves PC getting the big coalition solidly established and out of each other's hair. Then they plan something big, and at the right time, he gives 'em all up, the leadership of all three big gangs and the Outfit."

Boone drew a hand through his hair. "Talk about writing your own death sentence."

"Of course he wants to do it in such a way that it'll save his own skin."

"Which won't be easy."

"Tell me about it," Keller said. "You're born-again yourself, aren't you, Boones?"

"Yeah, why?"

"You'll understand this guy. And you can keep him alive so he can testify before a grand jury."

16
AND SO IT BEGINS

"Something's not adding up," Boone said.

"Oh no," Pete Wade said, looking at Jack Keller. "Don't tell me I've lost the bet."

Keller smiled. "Fifty. Hand it over."

"Now just hang on a second. Let's see if he really knows what's not adding up."

"Do me proud, Boones," Jack said. "Tell 'im what's not in place here."

"Hey!" Wade said. "Quit coaching him. A deal's a deal. You're the one who said he was so sharp; let him prove it."

"I must be missing something important," Boone said, "because this doesn't take a genius. I'm just wondering where the U.S. Attorney, the Chicago Crime Commission, and the FBI fit in here. Surely we're not running solo with this."

Wade swore and pulled two twenties and a ten from his wallet. Jack plucked them from his hand with a flourish and said, "Thank you for shopping at Keller."

Boone squinted at Pete Wade. "All due respect, Commander, but you really thought so little of me that you bet I'd miss that?"

Wade laughed. "It wasn't that at all, Drake. I just thought you'd be so overwhelmed by what was going down that you'd forget to ask about it."

Boone shook his head. "I ought to charge you fifty myself just for the insult."

Keller pulled his chair closer. "Here's the deal. Candelario has this thing about the CCC and the FBI. Can't stand 'em, doesn't want to work with 'em. Fact is, he's the biggest fish we've ever had, so that gives him a lot of bargaining power."

"Enough to keep those guys out of it?"

"So far the only people who have any knowledge of this whatsoever are the chaplain — and all he knows is that PC wants to go legit and work with us — Chief Galloway and the three of us."

"What about the crime lab guy, Dr. Scandinavia?"

"Waldemarr? All he knows is that Candelario was shooting blanks. He doesn't know why, and we haven't hinted."

"You're really going to keep everyone else out of it?"

"They have to be informed, of course; even PC knows that. But he won't meet

315

with us without assurances that the Crime Commission and the feds keep their distance."

"And the U.S. Attorney?"

"He'll be up to speed, but he won't be officially brought in till we're on the other end, for the indictments, if we get that far. You have any idea how big this is, Boones?"

"Well, 'course I do. What, is there another bet on the table? Somebody thinks I can't get my little mind around the biggest informant deal in history?"

Pete Wade made a show of pulling out his wallet again before collapsing into laughter. "Sorry, Drake. Just pulling your chain. We have to have a little gallows humor, don't we? This is going to consume all of us for a long time. You especially. It's going to be the most difficult thing you've ever accomplished — professionally, I mean. Any mobster or gangbanger anywhere in the world gets a whiff that Pascual Candelario has flipped, and he's a dead man, simple as that. We can't let that happen."

"Needless to say," Boone said.

"Okay," Keller said, "we've got a meeting scheduled with the boss in a little while. But he wants you up to speed before he signs off on this. Here's what's going to happen: You know that three-story parking garage six blocks south of your apartment? The one people use when they're heading for —"

"Wrigley, yeah. Next to the brownstones. I know it."

"We're going to give you a half-dozen sets of keys for six used cars we're going to plant in there, so you can be constantly mixing up your rides. Don't use the same car two days in a row. No more suits for a while, unless you're coming down here in your own car."

"I'm infiltrating? I thought I was too recognizable to be used that way."

"No. You're not dressing like a gang-banger. More like a casual grad student, something like that. You're not trying to fool anybody. You're trying to be invisible. We're not sure where and when or for how long you'll meet with PC, but you should look nondescript and no one should even wonder who you are."

"Got it."

"You'll start with a meeting in Joliet with the chaplain." Keller found a slip of paper in one of Wade's file folders. "Name's George Harrell. You'll meet him at a Billy's, the chain restaurant on the main drag there, heading into town."

"Been there," Boone said.

"This'll be like a scavenger hunt. Get what you can from Harrell, and tell him enough to get him to sell Candelario on trusting you. He'll tell you where to meet PC, if and when they're both satisfied that you can be trusted."

Boone nodded, scribbling notes. "Then . . . ?"

Pete Wade sat back and crossed his arms. "Then you work out with PC how we're going to take down the leadership of the DiLoKi Brotherhood, the big three street gangs, and the Outfit."

"That's it?" Boone said.

"That's not enough?"

"We're not trying to find bin Laden and win in Afghanistan too?"

"I hope you still have a sense of humor by the time this is over," Wade said. "You know this is classified top secret confidential. No one else can know a thing about this. No family or coworkers or colleagues, past or present."

"Really? I shouldn't put it in my Christmas letter?"

"Only your life depends on it."

"Give me a little credit. I got that. And I need to say, I appreciate your confidence in me, wagers aside."

"This could be a career maker," Jack said.

"Or a career breaker," Pete said. "Any more questions before we get the chief's blessing?"

"Yeah. How does Candelario survive this?"

"That's your job, Boone," Pete said. "I thought you understood that."

"No, I mean in the end, when it's all said and done. We get everything we need on all these guys, everything goes like clockwork, and we cripple them by putting away their leadership. Normally a rat goes into the Witness Protection Program, but where are you going to hide a guy like PC?"

"Good point, Boones," Jack said. "You don't. He'll have to be overtly protected, not try to hide or blend in somewhere."

"That's no kind of life."

"But it's *a* life, anyway. He has only one other option, and he doesn't want that."

"What else is in this for him? There has to be some sort of a deal. I mean, obviously he'll get immunity from whatever's hanging over his head. But what else? Anything?"

"I'm going to leave you with all these files," Wade said, "but here are some of his bargaining chips."

Pete pulled out several pictures of young Hispanics. "These are relatives of his, mostly nieces and nephews. Within reason we're going to exonerate them and somehow get them out of the Latin Kings and Queens."

"That's it?"

"That's all he asks. Well, and protection for the rest of his immediate family. He's got a mother and some aunts and uncles he wants kept safe."

"Not a bad deal for us," Boone said.

"You kiddin'?" Jack said. "If this goes down the way we hope it will, it will be the best deal the Chicago PD has ever had."

The three passed Haeley Lamonica's desk on their way to Organized Crime Division Chief Fletcher Galloway's office. She glanced up only long enough to acknowledge them with a nod, and Boone had to wonder how much she knew about all this. He couldn't imagine she would want to be burdened with even one detail of it, and yet it seemed inconceivable that in her role she would have no knowledge. Problem was, he couldn't ask. If she *was* aware, at some point the brass might ask if Boone had ever broached the subject with her. And if she was not aware, he would violate the code of silence to mention it.

Despite having an office just down the hall from the chief, Boone had seen Fletcher

Galloway only in passing during the whole time he had been with Organized Crime. It did strike him, however, that he had never seen the man in anything but his formal and heavily decorated uniform. Boone didn't know whether a chief was required to dress that way on duty or if Galloway simply preferred it. He thought he had seen other brass in business suits occasionally.

Galloway was tall and thin, in his late sixties. He reminded Boone of an older version of his own father. The man stood to greet the three, then pointed to chairs around a conference table in his office. He spoke softly as if he expected them to pay attention.

"Your reputation precedes you, Detective Drake," he said. "Stellar service in the face of deep personal tragedy."

"Thank you, sir."

"Thank *you* for taking on this assignment. I'm assuming from your presence that you have agreed."

"That's affirmative, sir."

Galloway turned to Keller. "You going with the cell phone setup, Jack?"

"That's our hope, though we have not discussed that with Drake yet."

Galloway stood suddenly, causing the others to do the same. "I'd better let you get

321

back to it, then. Thanks again, Drake, and I'll look forward to being kept up to date."

Not knowing how late his meeting would go with Chaplain Harrell, Boone headed home early in the afternoon and ran through what was to become his daily routine. He worked out, prayed, and read from both his devotional book and his one-year Bible. Wearing thick-soled shoes, jeans, an untucked flannel shirt, and a heavy winter parka, Boone strapped on an ankle holster and set out, briskly walking the six blocks to the parking garage.

There he found a nine-year-old Chevy with a lot of wear and junk in the backseat and on the back shelf. Knowing how the CPD worked, this would be an impounded vehicle whose owner was doing time somewhere. And the car would have had all its invisible needs met to a T by the department mechanics. It would have healthy tires, shocks, struts, transmission, electrical system, and be freshly lubricated and tuned. It only looked like a junker.

Settling into rush-hour traffic, Boone had a sudden urge to call Haeley and just talk. He resisted the temptation; he didn't want to blow whatever chance he might have had to establish a relationship, even if it was destined to be merely a friendship.

Instead he called George Harrell and settled on where they would meet inside the restaurant. "Nobody ever wants the booth back by the kitchen," Harrell said with a Southern lilt. "So look for me there."

The traffic was heavier and the drive farther than Boone had anticipated, to the point where as he was pulling in, Harrell was calling to see if he'd gotten lost. "That would give you a real sense of confidence, wouldn't it, sir?"

Harrell chuckled. "Well, I was gonna say . . ."

The chaplain didn't rise from the booth when Boone finally approached, but he reached with a long bony arm to shake hands. He reminded Boone of a carpenter from the church he grew up in. With a lined, chiseled face, Harrell looked to be pushing seventy, but his crew cut was still dark.

"Hungry?" he said. "This place is all right if you like big, unhealthy portions."

"Sounds perfect," Boone said, despite that he had been on a healthy eating regimen for months.

"I recommend the meat loaf. Comes with mashed potatoes scooped with an ice cream scooper, dark gravy, and old-fashioned white bread and butter. The beans are canned, almost gray, and probably lethal, so it's your call on those."

Boone liked the man already. He was sitting there with a cup of coffee, and when the waitress came to refill it, she asked if Boone wanted any.

"Coke," he said.

"Man after my own heart," Harrell said. "Caffeine or sugar, I say go for the poison straight up. And you goin' with my recommendation?"

Boone nodded, and Harrell ordered two meat loaf dinners.

While they waited, Harrell got straight to the point, leaning forward and nodding for Boone to do the same. "Now, listen," he said, "they tell me you're a Christian man. Can I take their word for that?"

"Yes, sir."

"When the food comes, I'll say grace, 'cause folks round here know who I am and it won't look out of the ordinary. For all anybody knows you're some friend or relative. I reckon you need to hear my side of this story, but then you're on your own, and leave me out of it.

"That's important to me, 'cause I'm coming up on retirement and the wife and me want to get out of Illinois and enjoy ourselves somewhere that costs less to live. I been in this game a long time, so I know danger when I see it. You don't need to be telling me how bad this thing could get.

"Now, I want you to know I've been played and conned by so many inmates over the years that I've got a 360-degree bull detector. Past decade, I don't think a one of them has pulled a thing over on me, though they keep tryin', you follow?"

"I do."

"I've had gangbangers show up for chapel a lot, and I can usually tell within five minutes what their deal is. Best-case scenario is that they're scared out of their minds, know their days are short, and want to get back to their faith or try it for the first time. Then you've got the ones who think something religious is going to look good on their record. Worse-case scenario is somebody showing up because someone he's after comes to chapel thinking he's going to be safe there. I try to assure safety, but we've had violence. If somebody's out to kill somebody, there's enough opportunities.

"I don't get too many Hispanics because most of 'em, if they've got any church background at all, it's Catholic. And they got their own chaplain. Good guy. I like him. But like I say, I don't get too many of 'em. Well, one morning, who shows up but Pascual Candelario himself? Even I was scared. You ever see this guy?"

"Only in pictures."

"Biggest Mexican I ever saw. Goes about six-six and three hundred pounds, tattoos telling his whole history. Bald with ink around the eyes, tiny crosses encircling his neck — I guess one for each murder — and every gang symbol and image you can think of on his forearms and hands. Besides all the Latin King stuff with the crowns and lions and such, he's got the DiLoKi Brotherhood symbol near his eyebrows and a permanent teardrop.

"And a scowl? This guy looked like he'd rather tear you in two than look at you. Well, we had maybe fifty or sixty guys for chapel that morning, and PC plants himself dead center of the second row, arms crossed, staring straight at me. I have a simple little routine each week where we'll stand and sing a couple of choruses, have testimonies and prayer requests, and then I do a short message. Well, PC doesn't stand when everyone else stands, and he has no interest in sharing a chorus book or looking on at one of the Bibles we issue. In fact, he won't even pass stuff down the row.

"The place was quieter than I've ever seen

it, and if there was a guy in there who didn't know PC was among us, I'd be surprised. Some left before we hardly got started. The singing was quieter, the testimonies and prayer requests shorter, and I admit I got right on with my part of it too. I don't know if I looked as scared as I was. I've learned to hide it pretty good. But I saw a lot of terrified faces that morning, every one of 'em wondering if he was the reason the king of the DiLoKi himself was there."

George Harrell quieted when their meals arrived. Then he bowed his head and said, "Lord, thanks for this and please protect us. In Jesus' name, amen."

The chaplain began eating quickly. Boone said, "Take your time, Reverend. I'm in no hurry unless you are."

"Nah, force of habit, and I don't want to keep you. Already told the wife I'd be late."

"Then slow down and enjoy."

Boone found the meal delicious but so heavy that he ate only half of it — eschewing the beans at Harrell's suggestion — and passed on dessert while urging the chaplain to have some. And he did. A huge piece of cherry pie à la mode. Boone almost wished he still had that kind of an appetite.

"That's really kinda awful," Harrell said.

"What, the pie?"

The man nodded but finished it anyway. "Not sure what's wrong with it. Not spoiled, but old, you know? Like me, I guess."

When the waitress came by again, Harrell said, "You got any more of that pie?"

"Why, yes I do!"

"Well, you'd better throw it out."

Harrell roared at that one, and when the waitress looked horrified, he assured her it was probably all right but just didn't sit well with him. She offered to take it off the bill, but he said, "No, no. I was able to force it down, wasn't I?"

Boone found the whole exchange puzzling, and Harrell must have noticed. He shook his head. "Sorry, but I gotta keep things light outside the joint. Pretty depressing in there, day after day, year after year. In a lot of ways we correctional employees are in prison too, you know?"

"I can only imagine."

"Well, take it from me." Harrell maneuvered his rangy frame till he was sitting sideways in the booth, his feet jutting into the aisle. "Anyway, I got Pascual Candelario himself in chapel, and we're all on edge. So it's finally over and everybody's startin' to leave, except for the two or three guys who help me pick up the chorus books and Bibles and fold the chairs. Only PC says to them, 'I got this,' and they immediately take off. Now there I am, alone with him. Just terrific."

"What're you thinking at this point?"

"Well, I don't know what to think. I say, 'Thanks for your help, man.' He says, 'No problem,' and I have to admit, I was kind of stunned by his tone. I mean, I had never heard him speak before, but you see a guy that huge and you know his reputation and all, and you assume he's gonna sound scary, right? But he sounded gentle."

"For real?"

"Gave me courage. I said, 'To what do we owe the pleasure of your presence this morning?' That made him smile. He said, 'My presence gave you pleasure, man?' Well, he'd caught me, and I had to laugh. That really seemed to amuse him, because a guy like that is certainly aware of how people respond to him. It broke the ice.

"I said, 'Are you interested in the things of God?' He nodded, shy-like. I said, 'Well, you came to the right place, unless you'd be more comfortable at Mass.' He said, 'You tryin' to get rid of me already?' I assured him I was not and that if he wanted to join us, he was certainly welcome. He said, 'Wonder what that'll do to attendance.' "

"So PC is that engaging, huh? Doesn't

sound scary at all."

"Oh, I was still scared, and I was hoping he wasn't really planning on becoming a regular. Which he wasn't. He looked around and asked if we could talk in private. I said sure, but I wasn't excited about it. I took him into my office, which fortunately has a security camera and a panic button. 'Course a guy like that coulda broke my neck and had me dead before anybody came to help, but I've always known the risks of a job like mine."

"I'm dying to hear what he told you."

"And I'll tell ya, at least the basics. But you should hear most of it from him. It's quite a story, and you'll be as intrigued as I was. Bottom line is he was raised dirt-poor in Guadalajara, his dad died when he was young, and the rest of the family somehow found their way to the States and migrated to Chicago. He got involved in the Almighty Latin King Nation when he was pretty young, committed his first murder as a teenager."

"Wow."

"Well, it was blood in and blood out, you know? If you want in, you've got to shed blood, and if you want out, you're gonna shed some of your own. Came up through the ranks. As he got bigger and stronger and had no qualms about murdering his rivals, he became the most feared gangbanger in the city."

"That's pretty much common knowledge."

"I know, Detective, and like I say, I want you to get the details from him. But the bottom line is that he was raised in a Christian home. Maybe not Christian in the way you and I think of it, but they were sort of outcasts in their own community because they weren't Catholics. They weren't traditional evangelicals either, more charismatic or Pentecostal. His mother, he says, was into speaking in tongues and healing and all that, and while Pascual turned his back on church, he remembered what he was taught about being saved."

"It obviously didn't affect his life."

"No, it didn't. Broke his mother's heart. Anyway, you know several years ago they finally got him on a laundry list of lesser charges, and he gets sent up. He's still running things from Stateville and gangbanging even inside, then comes up with the idea of the DiLoKi Brotherhood. It just makes him bigger and more powerful and more feared than ever. The DiLoKi are open to just about everybody, and you're either in or you're in trouble.

"But if you can believe him — and frankly at first I didn't — he says his conscience started working on him because of the constant letters and visits from his mother, telling him she and her little church were praying for him. In every letter this little lady spells out the gospel, how he can repent of his sins and be saved from hell. Funny thing was, he says his motto used to be — you know, to his fellow gangbangers — 'Let's all go to hell together.' He really believed that was what was going to become of them. They didn't care about anything or anybody, and they weren't afraid to die. They just figured it was inevitable."

"So he finally decided he was afraid of hell?"

"You know, I never gathered that from him. I don't see this as a deathbed conversion or something to make things easier for him in the future. He tells me that he finally waited till he knew his cellmate was asleep and nobody was watching, and he knelt by his bunk and prayed the prayer. Asked forgiveness for all the murders — would you believe more than twenty?"

"We had him down for twelve or thirteen."

"He tells me close to two dozen. And he asked Jesus to come into his life and save him."

"And you believe him."

"I told you, at first I didn't. I know finding Jesus is a common ploy for the worst of these guys, and I was looking for all the holes in the story. I know God can save even the worst of sinners if they are sincere, no matter what anybody else thinks about how easy and convenient it is for a multimurderer to get assured of heaven. The reason I came to believe PC is because of how conflicted he still was, still is."

"And this has been how long?"

"More than two years. I gave him the Scripture about how you accept, believe, and confess, and he said he had confessed to God. I told him, no, you've got to confess with your mouth to someone else that Jesus Christ is Lord. He told me, 'Reverend, that's going to be you and my ma. Nobody else would believe it, and I'll be dead in a week if they think I mean it.' "

"But you said he wasn't afraid to die even when he thought he would go to hell. Why would he fear death now?"

"He told me he was scared to death he would never get to make amends to all the people he had hurt and killed and stole from."

Boone sat back. "He sincerely wants to do that?"

"I believe he does. I gather that dealing with his remorse was way more important to him than escaping hell. From that day to this, he has kept the whole thing secret, but he has poured himself into the DiLoKi. So far it seems none of the other leaders have suspected a thing or figured out that the whole idea has cut way back on violence, especially on the inside. Sure, there are still horrible things that happen between various factions. But the three major gangs used to kill each other inside and outside Stateville. You hardly even hear of that anymore. But to PC, it's not enough. He wants to start making amends."

"By ratting out the leadership."

"Exactly."

"And he has no second thoughts about that?"

"Good question, and I asked him that. Because there's a code even among killers, you know. There was a day when a gang-banger wouldn't even rat out an enemy, let alone a friend. But PC says these gangs, the DiLoKi included, are so out of control, the fear and the dread and the horror they inflict on the community will never be checked until the hierarchy is disabled. This is the only way he knows to do it."

"And he's got a plan?"

George Harrell nodded. "He's no dummy, Detective. He didn't get where he is through intimidation alone. PC knows what it will take to make this work the most thoroughly, and once he's assured a deal is in place, he's ready to put his plan into action."

"And once you hook us up, you want out of this?"

"Completely. Maybe there's a way I can communicate some kind of encouragement to him through you. And wherever he winds up, I might try to get word to him that I'm still praying for him. But after I tell him he can trust you, I've got to be left out of this. He asked only that I make the contact with the Chicago PD and said he would take it from there."

"I think we can honor that."

"You have to."

"You have my word, Reverend. What else do you need to know about me so you can endorse me to him?"

"I know who you are, Drake. And so will he. That you're still on the job after what you went through tells me all I need to know."

"How do I meet him?"

"I thought you'd never ask." Harrell pulled from his pocket a sheet from a tiny spiral notebook. On it he had jotted an address. "He holes up above a garage not far from the old headquarters of the Kings at Beach and Spaulding."

"Northwest Side. I'm going to look kind of conspicuous in that neighborhood."

"Yeah, but PC assures me it's a place you can slip into after dark, if you follow the route he's outlined here on the back. He'll be waiting for you at two in the morning Friday. I don't mean to treat you like an imbecile, but that's after midnight Thursday."

"Got it."

"He wants you to just stop at the stop sign at this corner and wait fifteen seconds. He'll climb in, and then you can take him wherever you feel you'll both be safe."

Boone folded the sheet and put it in his pocket. "And so it begins," he said. "Reverend Harrell, on behalf of the Organized Crime Division of the Chicago Police Department, I want to extend sincere gratitude. This was a thankless but courageous task."

Harrell scooted out of the booth and stood to shake Boone's hand. "I appreciate it, Detective, but you'll understand if I say I hope we never see each other again, at least this side of heaven. What say I meet you at the eastern gate sometime in the hereafter?"

"Works for me," Boone said.

17
LION'S LAIR

Tuesday morning Jack Keller and Pete Wade came to Boone's office for a debriefing about his conversation with the chaplain. They didn't shut the door and lowered their voices only when they heard footsteps in the hall. Boone could not imagine that Haeley was out of earshot. Did that mean they weren't keeping this from her because she had already seen a lot of the paperwork anyway?

Boone asked them what Fletcher Galloway had meant about using a cell phone setup. Finally, Keller pushed the door shut. "You know, as tiny and sophisticated as clandestine recording has become, we can't risk someone as high-profile as Candelario wearing a wire. Somebody from another gang or the Outfit frisks him and finds that, he'll be dead before we can get to him. But you know what cell phones are capable of these days, don't you?"

"I hear they can be programmed to record even when they're turned off."

"Bizarre, isn't it?"

"It gets better," Wade said. "By the time you meet with PC, we'll have a high-tech phone for each of you that has so much built into it, it'll do everything but cook your breakfast. In fact, say Candelario is in a meeting with someone and we're recording. They get suspicious and ask to see his phone. Two things can happen. We can remotely hit a button that completely wipes that phone, while we would have already remotely recorded everything up to that point. Or if there's been interference and he isn't sure we're hearing the demand to see his phone, as he hands it over, he can casually hit a button on the keypad that does the same thing."

"Impressive," Boone said.

"Besides that," Wade said, "these phones are untraceable, are encrypted to the point where no one would be able to hack into them for a million years, and so they are secure for you and him to communicate with us or each other — or anyone else for that matter — at any time from anywhere."

"I like that."

"Boones," Jack said, "I've seen this done from halfway around the world, and I'm not kidding. One of our techies proved it to me. He's chatting with me, right, and during the conversation I get a text message from a mutual friend of ours in London. Curious, I excuse myself and check it, and it has an attachment. I click on it and what do I hear? A recording of the conversation I'm having with the techie right then. I take it to him and say, 'Explain this!' He laughs and tells me that he did it without even the knowledge of our London friend."

"The future is here," Boone said.

"If he can do that via satellite internationally, just imagine what we can do with these phones right here in the city."

That night at home Boone pored over the files on Pascual Candelario, thinking that two in the morning Friday couldn't come soon enough. The monumental importance of the case was one thing, but even getting to hear the story of the man's spiritual journey made the danger worth it to Boone.

He was about to turn in at 11 p.m. when Haeley called. "I'm so sorry to bother you," she said, "but I need help. A neighbor lady just getting home from work saw my light on and came to my door to tell me I had a flat tire. I don't know if it was slashed or what, but I can see it from here."

Boone was tempted to ask if she had a AAA account, but if she did, she wouldn't have needed him. Plus, he was glad. Of all the people she could have called . . . well, he was encouraged.

"I'll be right over."

"Oh no, it'll wait till morning. I thought maybe you could come by before work."

"I'd rather do it now, if you don't mind."

"Whatever works for you. Thanks so much."

"You'll just need to get me into your trunk so I can get the spare and jack and all."

"Oh, I wouldn't want to leave Max even for a minute. I know that's crazy —"

"Just watch for me and use your remote from the window to open the trunk."

She hesitated. "You think of everything. All right, but when you're finished, you have to come up for a cup of coffee."

"Don't feel obligated, Haeley. Really."

She laughed. "I call you probably out of bed in the middle of the night and I'm not supposed to feel obligated? Anyway, I'm not just being polite. Now promise me."

Like he was going to turn down that invitation.

An hour later he had changed the tire and sat in her living room trying to warm his hands with the cup. "You didn't bring gloves?" she said.

"Hard to screw on lug nuts wearing those."

Their conversation was awkward and halting. Boone started giving signals that he was about to leave. Haeley kept thanking him for coming and helping.

"You're welcome," he said, laughing. "Don't make me say it again. Glad I could do it. Now we'd both better get some sleep, don't you think?"

She walked him to the door. "Boone, I know what's going on at the office."

"Sorry?"

"You heard me."

"You know I can't talk about it."

"And I wouldn't want you to. I just wanted you to know that I'm aware, and I understand the weight of it. And of course, the danger."

"So you'll pray for me."

"I pray for you anyway."

"You do?"

She nodded. "Don't embarrass me. I know *I* need prayer. Don't you?"

He shrugged, feeling his face flush. Boone was glad she hadn't asked whether he prayed for her. He prayed *about* her but hadn't thought to pray *for* her. Which was pretty shortsighted, as he thought about it. Here was a young, vulnerable, single mother with a lot tougher life than he led. How self-ish was he that he didn't think to include her in his prayers?

"What do you say we agree to pray for each other from now on?" he said.

She smiled. "That would be great, since I'm already doing my part." She paused again, appearing to search for words. "Boone, I was a little hard on you Sunday. I wasn't trying to be mean. It's just that I heard you didn't stay for the service and it made me think you were there only to see me."

"Yeah, well, you were wrong about that." He told her how the song had overwhelmed him.

"I should have realized that," she said. "I'm sorry. Anyway, it wasn't my place to chastise you."

"Just tell me I can see you and Max now and then away from the office, and all will be forgiven."

"Of course you can."

"And that if the brass asks what I've said about my current assignment —"

"You haven't said a word."

Haeley took his hand in both of hers as he was leaving, and he stopped and turned.

"Now tell me the truth, Haeley: don't you have AAA?"

She nodded, looking resigned. "I *would* try to pull something over on a cop, wouldn't I?"

He laughed. "At least tell me you didn't flatten your own tire. I saw a nail in it."

"Of course not! But I have to say it didn't break my heart to have a reason to get you over here. My biggest fear was that you would take me up on the suggestion that it wait till morning. I was saying one thing and hoping another."

"Well, that's about the nicest thing I've heard for as long as I can remember. Makes me want to ask you out."

"You catch on fast, Detective."

"How soon?"

"Weeknights are bad for me, obviously."

"This weekend? Saturday?"

She nodded. "That gives me time to get a sitter."

Much as Boone wanted to see Max too, he couldn't have been more thrilled to get time alone with Haeley. They agreed on an early dinner Saturday night.

On the way home, Boone got a text from Francisco Sosa.

Up working late and thinking about you.
I'm going to stop pestering you, but feel
free to call or drop in anytime. One more
verse for you. Isaiah 26:3.

Boone couldn't wait to get home and look
it up in Nikki's Bible.

> You will keep him in perfect peace, whose
> mind is stayed on You, because he trusts
> in You.

Boone lay on his back in the stillness of
the night, too excited to sleep. He had
prayed that God would reveal himself and
help him find peace and rest. Those prayers
were being answered. Well, except the rest
part. But how could he sleep now?

As risky and terrifying as his assignment
was, he looked forward to meeting the
infamous Pascual Candelario. And while
Francisco Sosa was backing off, Boone had
a feeling PC was going to need a pastor
someday too. Was it realistic to think he
might be able to get the two of them together? Maybe Candelario couldn't be seen
in public at a megachurch like Community
Life, but Boone was certain Sosa would be
happy to have an influence on someone like
Pascual, especially considering their common ethnicity and mother tongue.

The prospect of getting to know Haeley better was risky and terrifying too, in its own way. And Boone knew it was the real reason he found it hard to sleep.

"Is there such a thing as being overprepared, Jack?" Boone said at work the next day. "I don't know what else to do during a week that drags like this."

Keller smiled. "You implying you have experience with this sort of a case?"

"Hardly."

"Well, me either, so how would anyone know if you're overprepared? I can't imagine a downside of knowing everything there is to know about our man."

"I feel like I've memorized all the files."

"Take a break."

"You serious?"

"Sure. Go somewhere. Do something else. You're gonna drive yourself nuts otherwise."

"What'm I going to do, go to the aquarium?"

"You could do worse. Run, work out, read a book, see a movie. By the time this is over, we're likely to owe *you* hours, not the other way around."

Boone knew Jack was right, but he still couldn't pull himself away from the files and surveillance videos supplied by the Chicago Crime Commission. And of course there were the photos from CSI and his own copious notes about the strange crime scene and the shells that had fired only blanks.

He slid from a folder the picture of the man Pascual Candelario had usurped to become the most powerful gangbanger in Chicago history. Jazzy Villalobos was a bald, thin-faced razor of a man with a soul patch and two neat rows of crosses tattooed around his neck. He also sported a tattooed teardrop under each black, soulless eye.

According to the Crime Commission, Jazzy had somehow become PC's most loyal soldier, unusual for a man who had been enthroned before Pascual rose. The man seemed, so said informants, to enjoy his first lieutenant's role even more than he had enjoyed being king.

Was it possible PC had somehow kept his most dire secret from Jazzy? Did he have a choice? If Villalobos caught wind of the boss's flip, wouldn't Candelario be vaporized, not a drop of DNA to be found?

Boone sat watching the CCC recordings over and over until it was time for the techies to deliver the phones for him and Candelario. That gave Boone something else to play with.

For the rest of the day, he found himself

wandering in and out of his office and inventing things to chat with Haeley about. He could tell by her look that she knew he was suffering from anticipation. Boone looked forward to their date, but of course meeting the DiLoKi Brotherhood king monopolized his mind.

Keller ordered Boone to stay away from the office Thursday. "Everything is in place. We'll have personnel in the area, and we'll be monitoring your conversation via the phones. Just trust your support system."

"Let me ask you something, Boss. Am I right that there's a manual override on these phones?"

"You mean to keep us from hearing you?"

Boone nodded.

"You know there is. You planning on using that?"

"For some personal stuff, maybe."

"Nothing can be personal here, Boones."

"Hear me out, Jack. One of the advantages of me doing this is that spiritually, Pascual and I are brothers. You don't want or need to hear us talk about that."

Jack sat back and rubbed his mouth. "Everything's instructive to us. But if you think there's some value in you guys connecting on some personal level, I don't have a problem with it. But don't be off the air

348

for too long at one time. What are we supposed to do then, with no idea whether
you're in trouble?"

"I'll keep that in mind."

After midnight Thursday, Boone was ready.
More than ready. He was dressed similarly
to when he had visited the chaplain. With a
.22 strapped to his ankle, his and Pascual
Candelario's new phones in one pocket and
his own cell in the other, he set out for the
parking garage, having settled on an old
Buick LeSabre to get him there.

A couple of blocks from the garage, he
received a text from Jack.

Green light. All systems go?

Boone texted back:

Roger.

Just as he reached the garage, he got
another text and was stunned to see it was
from Haeley.

Mark 10:27.

Boone was ahead of schedule, so he lin-
gered outside the garage to be sure his

signal wouldn't be interrupted.

No access to a Bible. Anyway, what r u doing up?

Like I could sleep.

U need 2.

Worried about u.

Thanks. Got 2 go. What's the verse?

A minute later she responded:

With men it is impossible, but not with God; for with God all things are possible.

Just what I needed. Thanks. Pray 4 me.

You're master of understatement, Boone. Looking 4ward 2 Sat nite.

C u tomorrow.

Well, that 2.

As Boone drove toward the Northwest Side, he felt a tingling from the back of his legs to the top of his head. He found that encouraging, needing the edge. He had been an officer long enough to have faced nearly every danger one could imagine. But this was beyond anything almost any Chicago cop had encountered. Gangbangers in the city had progressed far beyond the days of rumbles and vandalism and petty crimes.

Local gangs had gone national and become bigger and more widespread than even the Chicago Outfit, controlling heroin, cocaine, PCP, marijuana, and weapons trafficking. Murder, extortion, protection rackets, and every form of underworld activity could be laid at their feet. While the Outfit still intimidated businesses and was heavily involved in racketeering, embezzlement, and hijacking truck and ship cargo while also infiltrating the trade unions, not even they were feared like the violent street gangs. The gangs were as heavily armed as any military, never ratted on each other, threatened any adversary, and seemed to have zero respect for human life, their own included.

In this instance, Boone and his superiors were counting on the veracity of one prison chaplain. There was the very real possibility that this whole thing was a setup. Boone didn't think Pascual Candelario would personally expose himself to the danger of the Chicago Police Department swooping down on him if his aim was some sort of attack. But who knew if the whole idea of this meeting with one of the top gang kings in the country was just a way to get a decorated officer in the wrong place at the wrong time?

It was not beyond the DiLoKi Brotherhood to make such a statement. Boone imagined the headlines in the *Tribune* the next day. "Officer Slain in Street Gang Ambush."

Even in the darkness of the wee hours of a December morning, Boone — his senses fear-heightened — could make out the change in the tapestry of graffiti that blanketed the community. For years the Northwest Side had been the bailiwick of the ALKQN (the Almighty Latin King and Queen Nation). Its initials and symbols had long dominated the region.

But with Pascual Candelario's release and the advent of the brilliant idea he had formed while at Stateville, turf wars had virtually ended. Blacks, whites, Crips, Bloods, People, Folks, P. Stoners, Vice Lords, Gangster Disciples, you name it — all were welcome under the banner of the DiLoKi Brotherhood. Boone had not seen anyone but Hispanics in this neighborhood for years, but now, even during the witching hours, he saw a rainbow of races.

Their colors, tats, hats, do-rags, and gang signs had one thing in common: DiLoKi. Even the streetwalkers, trying desperately to look sexy while bundled against the cold, were apparently sponsored by and protected by DiLoKi pimps and muscle. Street corner pushers brazenly flashed packets of dope and signaled prices, while at the same time clearly on the lookout for marked or unmarked squad cars.

A pure white bread like Boone in a Buick would have created a firestorm of attention in this neighborhood not so many years before. But while Boone drew curious stares, he heard no shouts, no threats, saw no automatic weapons brandished. In the past, someone having made the wrong turn or taken the wrong exit off the expressway would have had about sixty seconds to find their way out of the neighborhood. Otherwise, he and everything he owned was fair game to the Latin Kings.

Boone rolled to the stop sign in question. He'd hoped the streets would be deserted, but with no cross traffic, stopping for more than an instant drew immediate attention. A streetwalker approached from one side, a pusher from the other.

Boone tried to wave them off, but while the girl turned on her five-inch heel to look for other fare, the pusher reached into his waistband. Boone slid his hand down to his ankle holster, knowing he would be better off just speeding out of there.

But suddenly the pusher held up both hands, palms out, looking terrified. "PC!" he said. "My brotha!"

"I ain't your brotha," Pascual Candelario said as he opened the passenger door. He called the pusher a vile name and told him to disappear as he slid into the car. The man ran off, but the hookers began squealing and waving and even the pimps got out of their cars to salute the king.

"Let's get out of here, *amigo*," PC said. "Up three blocks and right four."

Boone stole a glance at the mountain that had invaded the car. Pascual was so huge that the LeSabre seemed to drift to the right. The man was wearing sneakers, socks to just below his knees, basketball shorts, and an oversize jersey under an unzipped coat. Boone was tempted to ask how he kept his legs warm, but for now he was just doing what he was told.

The area Candelario had directed him to was deserted, the buildings boarded up. He pulled to the curb and sat idling outside a chain-link fence that enclosed a vacant lot.

"You carrying?" PC said.

" 'Course, what do you think? I'm on duty."

"What you got, man?"

"An ankle toy."

Candelario laughed. "A .22, right? Tell me I'm right. Am I right?"

"You're right."

The big man hooted and leaned over, almost smothering Boone. He reached down and found the weapon, pulling it up and examining it in the light of a streetlamp. "I don't think this would even pierce a man my size, do you?"

Boone smiled weakly. "Maybe not."

"You wanna see what I'm carrying?"

"I'm afraid to ask. I felt it when you leaned over me."

The DiLoKi king reached into his coat and produced a sawed-off shotgun. Only a man that big could conceal such a weapon. It was nearly three feet long.

"Is that what I think it is?" Boone said, accepting his own weapon back and breathing a sigh of relief. He holstered the .22, which looked even more like a toy now.

Pascual was still chuckling. "I don't know, man. What do you think it is? How well do you know your straps?"

"Looks like an Ithaca. Is it? A 37 Stakeout?"

"*Bueno, hombre.* With a pistol grip."

"Nice."

Before Boone could even think about reaching for his .22 again, Candelario pressed the barrel of the Ithaca to his temple. "Look straight ahead, man."

So was this it? Over before it began? Boone fought to regulate his breathing. Pascual Candelario had to know Boone wasn't alone. Did he have his own people nearby and a way to escape after executing a police officer?

No, this had to be a test, and Boone was determined to pass it.

"Scared, man?"

"You hold all the cards, Pascual."

"You just meet me and you call me by my first name?"

"We haven't even been introduced," Boone said. "But we're going to be working together, so . . ."

"So you thought you'd be familiar."

"I'll call you whatever you want. But you can feel free to call me Boone."

"You're a brave man, Boone. Come in here, knowin' who you're talking to."

Boone shrugged. "I believed what I was told about you. If it's true, it's true; if it's not, it's not."

PC pulled the weapon away and laid it

across his lap. "It's true. Sorry I had to do that, but you know. . . ."

"I know," Boone said. Then he snatched the .22 and pressed it against Pascual's bald head. "Don't move. This feel like a toy to you now? You realize that Ithaca in your lap is all the justification I need, right? Felon in possession of a deadly weapon? I wouldn't be off the job longer than two days. And I'd be celebrated."

The big man wasn't moving, but Boone didn't detect fear either. Finally PC started to chuckle. "Okay, *amigo,* okay. Now we both know neither of us is afraid to die. I know your story, and you know some of mine. We work together, we're gonna have to trust each other. Put the cap gun away and shake my hand."

"How 'bout we also put the Ithaca in the backseat?"

Boone holstered the .22 and Pascual tossed the shotgun in the back.

"So we stared each other down," Candelario said. "We good to go now?"

"I am."

"Take me somewhere safe where we can talk."

"Where would *you* be safe, PC? You're not exactly a man I can hide."

Candelario glared at Boone. "That was

part of the deal. You were supposed to have a place picked out."

"Calm down. I do."

Boone drove six miles north to an industrial park where security had been temporarily replaced by the Chicago PD and the local district squads had been instructed to keep their distance. He pulled in behind a metal fabrication plant that produced wire, staples, and nails. It had recently moved from three shifts to two and was closed until eight in the morning.

"Now I got to trust you," Candelario said as they emerged from the Buick and headed to the back door.

"We've got to get to know one another, PC," Boone said, producing the key. "You hungry?"

"Do I look hungry? Man, I stay ahead of hunger."

Under the light over the back door, Boone got his first good look at the man. With his huge frame and tattooed neck, Pascual was a walking nightmare. "You are one scary dude."

"I hope so," Candelario said. "The whole package has to work, and it always has."

They entered a combination break room/locker room, and Boone dug a Coke out of the refrigerator. "They've got whatever you want, PC. What'll it be?"

"Mountain Dew? Got to have my caffeine, man."

Boone tossed him one.

PC shed his coat and slowly sat, his massive body spilling over both sides of a plastic chair. Boone sat across from him and rested his elbows on the table. "I've actually been looking forward to this, Pascual," he said. "I can call you Pascual, right?"

"Yeah, man, that back there was just posturing, you know. I had to see if I could make you wet your pants. I should have known better. They weren't gonna put a child on this assignment. Now, listen, my people know better than to question me, but they're gonna be suspicious if I'm gone too long. I got a plan and I know you got questions, so let's get to this."

Boone said, "I think we both have an idea where we want to go, but I want to hear your story, know how you got to this point, hear what you're about."

Candelario sighed and stared at the ceiling. "Some of it I like talking about. Some of it I don't."

"I want to hear it all."

"Okay. But then let's get down to business."

359

18
THE RENDEZVOUS

For the next Few hours, Pascual Candelario told Boone a sad but typical story of a young immigrant who found love and acceptance and respect and a sense of belonging in a street gang. The difference was that as Pascual began to mature, he admitted he became intoxicated with the fear he saw in others' eyes.

"My *madre* was beside herself, man. She knew I was up to no good, and she was goin' to church all the time and praying for me. But I wouldn't listen. I was mad at God because my father had died. And I didn't like church anyway. It was too crazy for me."

Pascual said that as a teenager he told the leadership of the Latin Kings that he wanted to be a full-fledged member. "One of the dudes just told me flat out, no. He told me I was primitive. I didn't even know what he was talking about. He said I had to grow up and be more mature before I could understand Kingism. It was like a religion to those guys.

"But you know what I loved to do? I loved to show off. So I asked him, what do I got to do to get some respect, and he told me the LKs had a blood-in, blood-out policy, just like all the other gangs. I knew what that meant. You had to fight somebody, maybe even within the Kings, to show that you weren't afraid to make somebody bleed or bleed yourself, prove you were tough. I didn't want to stop there. I told the guy, 'Tell me who needs to be killed, and I'll do it.'

"He laughed at me, man! He told me the LKs had a hit list, but it wasn't for primitives. That was disrespect, man. I was so mad I could have killed *him!* I begged him to show me the list, but instead he just gave me a few names. Well, I knew who these guys were. They were big shots with the Disciples and the Lords. I said, 'Let me get this straight: I kill one of these guys and I'm in?'

"He said, 'Sure, primitive, if you don't end up in a box yourself.'

"I got one of my friends, and we stole a video camera. Then I got him to record me sticking up a gun shop. You believe that? I was lookin' at Glocks, but I knew they would be asking me for ID and all that before they'd even let me test it or anything. So my friend went to another register and bought ammo. Then, while he's taping again, he tosses me the box, I load the gun before the guy can even say anything, and I point it right at him. I'm on tape, man, stealing a Glock. It gave me such a rush, I can't tell you."

"You weren't afraid of anything?"

"Nothing!"

"But didn't the gun shop have cameras too? Wouldn't the guy recognize both of you?"

"I wasn't a King yet, but my friend was, and the owner knew it. He didn't want to bring anything like us down on his head. All it cost him was one gun and one box of ammo. You wouldn't believe what I did next. I was too young to even have a driver's license, but the older guys let us drive all the time. My friend and me, we hot-wired a car, and with him recording still, I drove right into Vice Lords territory and asked for one of the guys whose name I saw on the hit list."

"You're not serious."

"I am!"

"You're lucky to be alive. We've heard of rival gang members being murdered without

362

a word, just because they drifted into the wrong neighborhood."

"You don't know how bad I wanted in, man. I sat behind the wheel of that car and a bunch of Lords surrounded us, guns out. I held up my hands and said I just wanted to talk to this guy. They laughed and threatened me and called me a crazy fool, but then they went and got him.

"He was impressed, you know? I could tell. Young LK wannabe comin' onto his turf and just asking to talk to him. He told me to get my fat rear end out of the car so his boys could search me, and I said, 'Sure.' I got out and lifted my hands, but as a guy came to frisk me, I just grabbed my strap and started shooting. Hit List Man was the first to fall, then the guy who wanted to search me, and I don't know how many others. They were all screaming and running, and I just jumped in the car and headed back to King territory. Would you believe we still show that recording to recruits?"

"And you were how old?"

"Not even sixteen yet."

"And you're what now?"

"Thirty-six. A lot more killing since then, *amigo*." He pointed to the tattooed crosses encircling his neck. He had started on a second row. "Twenty-three."

"How did you feel — right after that, I mean? Any trouble sleeping? Any conscience over it?"

"I only had trouble sleeping because of the excitement. I was still livin' at home then. I was proud of myself, lying there a murderer while my mother slept in the next room. I was afraid of nothing. I had a whole new image and place in the Latin Kings, and everybody knew I'd shoot them dead for any reason, even another King."

"No wonder you were in the leadership by the time you were twenty."

"Straight up. Man, I knew I was going to hell. Only thing I felt bad about was my *madre* took the blame. She knew who I was and what I was, and she cried and prayed and pleaded and said it was all her fault. I don't know how many times I told her it wasn't and that this was all on me, but you know moms."

Boone nodded.

"You know what my favorite story was back then, the one I used to keep everybody in line?"

Boone shook his head.

"Carlos Robles. You know that story?"

"Sure. The guy who got ground up and served in the meat loaf at Stateville back in '83. How much of it is true?"

"All of it. He wasn't loyal, so a hit was put out on him right there in prison. Couple of our guys got a guard to let them use a downstairs room for a party. They was gonna celebrate his release in a couple of days. He was happy to go, you know? They get him down there, kill him, cut his head off, chop him up, and smuggle bags of him to the prison kitchen, where he becomes part of the main course. That was a pretty recent story by the time I joined, and back then I thought it was beautiful. You know they had to bury his skull, 'cause that wouldn't process."

"They dug that up in '95, I think," Boone said.

"There you go. And Stateville? They couldn't find him anywhere, so until they found that skull, they thought he had escaped — two days before he was supposed to get out! Tell you something, man, a story like that will keep guys in line."

"So you become a big deal, one of the most feared guys in Chicago."

"Yeah, but I get a little too famous. I'm living the high life. All the money and women and toys I want. I wouldn't have had to do any of the dirty work myself ever again. I had thousands of lieutenants who would do anything I said. But I loved being in the middle of all of it. I had a feeling I was being bugged and watched and followed, all that. But I got invited to a meeting with the head of the Chicago Outfit and went anyway. Talk about somebody bein' watched. The feds, everybody had to be on his tail for years. How stupid was I?"

"Where'd you meet with him? You couldn't have gone into his neighborhood."

"No, man, those guys are smart. 'Least they think they are. They keep their business from their families. You don't go to their houses. They have places. But I demanded neutral ground. I didn't know what this guy wanted, but I sure wanted to find out. Anything to make the Kings bigger, you know? We met in one of the forest preserves."

"And who was there?"

"Graziano Jacopo himself and a bunch of his guys. I went alone to show 'im I wasn't scared of nothing. It worked. He looked scared the whole time, like I was gonna pull a blade on him or something. He says to me, 'Coming by yourself is very impressive. Very risky but also impressive.'

"I said, 'Risky? You think my people don't know where I am or who I'm with? They know where you live, Grazzy, and they know where your associates live. They also know your grandkids' names and where they go to school.'

"He said, 'There's no need to be rattling our sabers,' and I said, 'Just give me one reason.' "

"You called him Grazzy, really?"

"You bet I did. I wasn't afraid of an old Italian. I probably shoulda been, but you got to understand gangbangers to know I didn't fear nothin'."

"Grazzy rhymes with Jazzy."

That stopped the big man. He squinted and held Boone's gaze. "So?"

"We've got to talk about him, you know."

"What do you know about him?"

"Plenty, but we'll get to him. Stick with Grazzy for now."

It seemed to Boone that it took PC a few moments to collect himself and get back on track.

"Well, uh, anyway, you know he tells me he wants to farm out a couple of hits, that the feds and the Crime Commission are all over him and he can't let 'em trace his enemies' deaths back to him. I tell him to just tell me who and where to find them and how much it's worth to him. He gives me a figure. I triple it. He says no. I stand to go. He caves and agrees. We got it done for him."

Boone stood and leaned against a counter, glancing at his watch. "That was before my time, but the department still talks about how puzzling those hits were. Organized Crime figured out pretty quick that it wasn't some gang against the Outfit but rather the Outfit against itself and using you. But CPD couldn't pin it on anyone."

"You know why?" Candelario said.

"Too many of you, all with the same MO?"

"That's only part of it. Thing is, even I don't know who did it. We — me and Jazzy — bring in our best guys, tell them what their part of the take will be when the deal gets done, and the next morning I see dead guys on the front page of the *Trib.* I pay the lieutenants, they pay the guys, and even I don't know who did it. The paper says Mob guys get killed but that it looks more like the work of gangbangers than Mafia hit men. We had a good laugh over that one."

"So you were pretty much at the top or close to it, weren't you, Pascual?"

"Till I got sloppy; what can I tell you? I don't know if they had me meeting with Jacopo and his guys or not, but somehow they were hotter on my tail than ever. I muscled the wrong guys, got busted, and was sent up."

"Stateville didn't slow you down, though, did it?"

"You know, at first it did. I had a lot of friends in there, but the gangs were hurting each other. It didn't make sense to me. And when I heard about other gang co-ops around the country, it just seemed like a good idea."

"So you did this just to be smart."

Pascual nodded. "I didn't know all of what forming the DiLoKi Brotherhood would mean, but man, it was like a new place overnight. Everybody was welcome, and it was going to be us against the man instead of against each other all the time."

"And it pretty much worked out that way."

Pascual nodded, looking distracted. "Safe to walk outside here?"

"Sure, unless you're afraid of my guys. You think they want anything to happen to you?"

PC laughed. "I need some air."

"Frigid."

"Only for somebody with no insulation, like you."

"I'll be fine," Boone said, zipping his coat.

It was even colder than he expected. Boone thrust his hands deep into his pockets, and as he and Candelario moved in and out of the shadows of the parking lot light

369

fixtures, they were bathed in their own breath vapors.

"So what happened to you, PC?"

The big man stopped under a light. "You know, Boone, it was the strangest thing. . . ."

He paused as if looking for words. Were they going to forge a relationship after all, even a friendship? Boone let the silence stand until his phone chirped. He peeked to see a text from Jack.

UR out of sight. OK? Respond immediately.

"Your guys worried about you?" Pascual said.

"Yeah, till you just said that. You were saying . . ."

"Well, it's a funny thing, man. My mom had me where she wanted me, stuck in one place for five years. She wrote me all the time, and I mean all the time. And she came to see me every time she was allowed. Every letter told me I needed to get right with God, get saved, turn to Jesus, all that. It was kinda sweet, really, but for a long time it didn't get through at all. I kept telling her I believed in God and sometimes I told her I knew I was going to hell. I know it really hurt her when I said that, and even more when I said I didn't care. The thing was, it was true. I did not care, man. I knew who I was and what I was, and I wasn't scared of anything. I mean, I guess if I had thought about it, I wouldn't choose flames for eternity, but if there was one thing my life had done to me, it left me without emotions. At least that's what I thought."

"You learned differently?

"Well, I used to get excited about stuff. Hurting people. Killing people. Getting more money. But every time — and I mean every time — whatever it made me feel faded fast. Sometimes, like when I would add a million dollars to my net worth, it excited me for like ten minutes. But what finally got to me, I think, was that my *madre* told me she prayed for me every day. And not just once a day. Most of every day. Can you imagine?"

"So prayer worked?"

"You know, I never thought of it that way — that the prayer itself worked. I mean, I know it did, now that I look back on it, but at the time it was just that she was doing it. You know what I'm saying? See the difference?"

"I guess, sure."

"I started having trouble sleeping, and that was new for me, even after all the stuff

371

I had done, all the people I hurt, killed, everything. But now, because my mom is praying for me, I can't sleep. Even my cellmate asked me what was wrong. I told him to mind his own business, but not quite with those words."

Pascual fell silent again. Boone watched him expectantly. "So who do you talk to? What do you do?"

Pascual pulled out his phone. "Better turn this on," he said. "I've been out of reach too long. Yeah, see, all kinds of messages from the Wolf."

"The Wolf?"

"Don't you know any Spanish, man? What do you think *lobo* means? Let's get headed back. I gotta call him anyway."

Pascual assured Villalobos that he was all right and would be back soon, but he used such foul language that Boone was surprised. When Pascual clapped the phone shut, he said, "Sorry about that. I hate it, but I got to keep up the image or all this falls apart. I start talkin' like a civilian overnight and everybody's gonna know something's up."

"So you've kept him completely in the dark?"

"You kiddin'? One thing in our world, bro, is that we show no sign of weakness, you know? This would be the ultimate. I would be history."

"I want to hear the rest of your story, PC," Boone said as they got back into the car. "But I need to show you the phones they put together for this operation."

"We got plenty of time for that," Candelario said. "This thing I'm planning is still a ways off."

"How long?"

"I'm looking at January 6."

"Kings' Holy Day," Boone said.

"*Bueno.* You've done your homework, *hombre.* Nobody gonna suspect anything going down on a day that's sacred to the Latin Kings. 'Specially Jazzy. I think I can get all the top guys together with the Outfit guys. That's when I need your fancy phone."

After dropping Pascual Candelario off near where he picked him up, Boone headed back home, careful to be sure he wasn't being tailed. Jack called as soon as PC was out of the car.

"You want me to debrief you guys tonight?" Boone said. "While it's fresh?"

"No. We got it all down. Get some rest. Come in about one tomorrow afternoon and we can talk then."

Boone also found three texts from Haeley,

the last one saying that she had to finally get to bed but pleading with him to leave her a message that everything went all right. He texted her back, *Heading home. See you this afternoon.*

Boone slept like a stone and awoke with an eagerness to see Candelario again. He didn't feel he had really connected with the man yet, but he had been impressed by his intellect and how forthcoming he was. Mostly, Boone wanted to hear the rest of his spiritual journey, but when he had tried to arrange a time to do that, Pascual had put him off the way he had about the phones.

"I'll let *you* know when, Detective Drake," he had said before sliding out of the car, making Boone wonder why he had become formal all of a sudden. "And next time it'll be on my turf."

"Fair enough, but not here, I hope."

Pascual had laughed. "Neither of us is that stupid, *amigo.*"

At the office that afternoon, Haeley gave him a look he could only interpret as relief that he was all right. "Where we going tomorrow night?" she said.

"It's a surprise."

"I like surprises."

"Oh, it's nothing that special," he said. "Just a new place that looks great."

Jack and Pete seemed encouraged by what they'd heard the night before, but Fletcher Galloway was clearly not. "I heard the highlights," he said as the four met in his office. "Your assessment is that the guy has no hidden agenda? We could just bust him as a felon in possession of a deadly weapon and be done with it. He'd be back in Stateville for a long time. That would get one big menace off the streets again."

Boone shot him a double take. "He also told me he had once added a million dollars to his net worth. Should we check and see whether he reported that on his return and bust him for income tax evasion?"

"Are you being smart with me, Detective?"

"No, sir, Chief. I just hope you were thinking out loud, because I think we want to play this out, don't we, for the chance to take down the bosses of all the big crime outfits?"

"Of course. But he could have been leading you on. And I can't say I was amused by your weapons standoff."

"I didn't know how else to play that. I sure didn't want to show weakness."

"I thought you did the right thing," Pete

Wade said, "if my opinion means anything. But what I was left with at the end of the thing was that we may be taking entirely the wrong angle on this. I've been going on the notion that we're going to record him with all these guys, then protect him until he can spill it all before a grand jury, backing it up with the tapes."

"Tapes?" Boone said.

"Microchips, whatever. I'll always call them tapes. But now, if he's sure he can get them all together in one place at the same time, what stops us from just taking them all in at once?"

Galloway was slowly shaking his head. "The potential for a bloodbath, that's what. Any meeting like that would have a security force from every faction. And as soon as we make ourselves known, they start shooting, and not just at us. Everybody will suspect everybody else, and they'll target each other. Candelario gets killed in the process and then where are we? None of those guys will rat the others out."

"You're right," Pete Wade said.

Jack said, "Yeah, let's just carry this out the way we planned. I'm not wild about his getting everybody together at the same place at the same time, but it ought to make for a mountain of evidence. We keep our distance, make sure Candelario survives it and gets out of there, and then we prep him for grand jury testimony based on everything we get."

"It's not like the old days," Fletcher Galloway said. "Back in the day, we would call the shots, tell him how it was going to go down. I don't like his putting it off, setting the date, telling you when he's going to get back to you. I've got to share this stuff with the FBI, the Crime Commission, and the U.S. Attorney, and I can just imagine how it's all going to go over with them."

"I don't see that we have a choice," Boone said. "But I'm willing to be corrected. You want me to push Candelario for another rendezvous, or . . . ?"

"No," Galloway said. "Let's play the cards we're dealt for now. If he stalls you too long, maybe you make a contact. But let's not look too eager. I wouldn't waste so much time on his coming-to-Jesus story, though, Drake. We don't care how he came to this point, as long as he's here."

"I respectfully disagree, Chief. I understand him on this, and it helps me get to know him better. Plus it assures me he's not playing. I'm pretty confident he's for real here, but I'll know for sure when I hear the rest of the story."

"You buying his line about keeping Villalobos out of this?"

"I am. I don't see how he could make it work otherwise."

"Well, suit yourself, but keep the endgame in mind."

Boone and Haeley enjoyed a quiet dinner early Saturday night at a small bistro on the Near North Side that had gotten a glowing review in the previous weekend's paper.

"If it wasn't the dead of winter, I'd suggest walking the beach," Boone said.

"If it wasn't the dead of winter, I'd accept," she said. "Michigan Avenue might be a fun stroll for as long as we can stand the wind."

Boone hesitated, and Haeley said, "What? You don't like the Magnificent Mile?"

"I used to," he said. "Painful memories. Sorry."

"I understand. Anywhere else you'd like to walk?"

"Chicago Avenue?"

She smiled. "Sounds exciting. McDonald's and the Y are favorite landmarks of mine."

"You're mean," he said.

She laughed. "It's just that I've never heard of anyone walking Chicago Avenue

for any reason other than to just get somewhere. Have you?"

"I just want to be with you," he said.

"That's sweet. Let's do it. And you know
what we should talk about?"

"I'll bite," he said.

"Painful memories. I have some too, you
know. Maybe it would be therapeutic or
cathartic or whatever they call it to just get
'em on the table?"

"You think?"

"You look dubious."

"I am," Boone said. "Doesn't sound that
appealing."

"It was just a thought. I figure our pasts
are always going to be something between
us and that they'll have to come out sometime. But it's your call."

"You *want* to talk about this guy who
broke your heart?"

She cocked her head. "I've been so mad
at him for so long that I don't think I put it
in those terms anymore. I disappointed
myself for not seeing through him from day
one. Everything about the relationship was
wrong, and I kept justifying it. I was stupid
and made a horrible mistake."

"And you want to *talk* about that?"

"Look what came of it, Boone. I don't
deserve Max, and of course neither does his

father — which is good, because if I have anything to say about it, he'll never see him. But Max is like living balm to me. Proof that God forgave me and made something beautiful out of the mess I had created."

"You said his dad doesn't want to see him anyway."

"True. But I'm a big girl. I know how things go, how they can change. What if, for no understandable reason, he decides he wants to be part of Max's life? I'd spend everything I own to keep that from happening."

Boone paid and they bundled up, heading out toward Chicago Avenue. He enjoyed listening to her talk, and if she really wanted to talk about a part of her life she regretted so much, he guessed that was all right. She was going to expect him to do the same, though, and he wasn't sure he was ready. When he thought about Nikki, he knew he idealized her and might dwell on how much he loved her. Would that be fair to Haeley? Would she really want to hear that?

Haeley tucked her arm into the crook of his elbow, and they walked close to stay warm. They had just crossed Rush Street heading west when his phone came alive. "Don't answer it," she said. "You're off duty."

"I'm never off duty; you know that. Just a sec. Promise."

They stopped and he stepped away.

"Boone?"

"Yeah."

"PC."

"Hey, what's up?"

"I was going to wait awhile, man, but I want to talk to you tonight."

"Oh, man, does it have to be tonight?"

"What, you got a date?"

"What if I do?"

"You decide what's most important, *gringo.* I'm gettin' spooked by the Wolf, so I may be running out of time. Your call."

"Well, of course, PC."

"I'll pick you up. Just tell me where."

19
THE PLAN

Haeley could apparently tell from Boone's look that the evening was over. "I told you not to take it," she said.

"You know there are only about four people in the world I would have taken a call from tonight," he said as they hurried back to the parking lot.

"You didn't want to talk to me tonight anyway," she said, not unkindly. "Lucky you." He could tell she was teasing.

"We can finish this tomorrow after church," he said.

"I'd like that, at least until Max gets too squirrelly. You sure you're ready to talk?"

"That isn't the point," he said. "I'll talk all you want if it gives me more time with you. Question is, are you sure you want to hear it?"

"Why wouldn't I? If we're going to be friends, I want to know you. Need to know you. Your wife and son had to be the most important things in the world to you. If you can't talk to me about them, then what — ?"

"It's not easy."

"I wouldn't expect it to be. You worried about becoming emotional in front of me?"

"A little."

"Heaven forbid you should show a little humanity. What, you think I think you're a one-dimensional, macho cop?"

"Is that a bad image?"

She shrugged. "It wouldn't hold my interest for long."

"Well, then I'll come prepared to start the waterworks. Whatever it takes to hold your interest."

Boone walked her to her door and they embraced. "Leave me a message that you got home safe, 'kay?" she said.

Boone nodded and waited until she was inside, then greeted the sitter and made sure the girl was in her car before he left. He had arranged with Pascual Candelario to be picked up on the street about seven blocks north of Boone's apartment.

Boone called Jack Keller at home.

"I don't like it," Jack said. "Did he give you any idea where you're going?"

"North is all he said."

"Within the city?"

"No idea."

"Not good. We like to be where we have jurisdiction and at least some control. We should be able to hear you wherever you are, but we have to know where that is as soon as you can determine it. What's spooked him, anyway? Didn't expect to hear from him for a while. Didn't he say something about having plenty of time before January 6?"

"Yeah, I don't know. He just sounded bored to me, like he wanted to get out and do something."

"Great. So now you're his current distraction from DiLoKi leadership?"

"Something like that."

"I don't even know where Wade is this weekend. If he's away, I'm going to have to see who I can rustle up. I don't like you hanging out there by yourself with this guy."

"We have to take what we can get, don't we, Jack? PC is putting his whole life on the line for us. We don't want to scare him off or offend him."

"Make sure you don't wind up in some basement where we lose the signal."

Boone didn't take the time to change clothes, and Candelario noticed as he slid into the front seat of Pascual's late-model Benz coupe. "So I did interrupt a date, didn't I, bro?" he said.

"Matter of fact, you did."

"Sorry. At least I gave you the chance to show her who's boss, huh?"

"There's no question who's in charge with this girl, PC. I'm way out of my league."

Pascual showed a meaty palm and Boone smacked it. "You go, boy!" the big Mexican said. "Good for you."

"Where we going?" Boone said.

"Who's asking?"

Pascual was smiling, but Boone was not in the mood. "You know who's asking. I can't go far without my people knowing exactly where I am."

"Evanston. There's a lighthouse on the shore —"

"Made of stone. There'll be no signal in there."

"I'm talking about the little frame building next to it, so no problem."

"Yeah, but my guys will have to connect with the Evanston PD and —"

"You want me to make it easy on 'em? This is not easy for me, man. It's not like I can have any of my people looking out for me, you know."

"Don't worry. They're on it already."

"You bring your popgun again, Boone?"

"You know cops are armed 24-7. You?"

"It's in the trunk."

"So why Evanston? Why does this deal have to be so complicated?"

"It's where I want to have the meeting next month, so I thought you'd want to check it out. You look surprised."

"You really expect gangbangers in their tricked-out Benzes and Bimmers and the Outfit in their big Town Cars to somehow sneak into Evanston?"

"Wait till you see this place, man. Once we get off the Edens, we hardly go through any neighborhoods. Everything is tree-lined and dark until it feeds into the little lane that leads to the lighthouse. Give me some credit for planning, dude. I'm the one who's got the most to lose here."

"We'll see. What's got you nervous about Jazzy?"

PC shrugged. "Just a feeling, you know? This place, he wouldn't even dream of it. It's a place I know about, but he doesn't."

"Then why worry?"

"It's my job, man."

"Well, meanwhile, finish your story, will ya?"

"Yeah," Candelario said, "where was I?"

"It was starting to get to you that your mother didn't give up on you."

It impressed Boone that Pascual seemed

to have learned how to drive a fancy car without drawing attention to himself. Not too fast, not too slow, just moving with the traffic without excessive lane changing.

"You got to remember what kinda person I was, Boone. Gangbangers, lifers, never learned to think about our feelings, and we sure never talked about 'em. Everything was instinct. Now when I watch those nature shows on TV — and I have to hide that too, of course — I see the birds that strut and show their feathers, the snakes that puff up and look bigger, the wolves and wild dogs that bare their teeth — that was us; that was me.

"I didn't talk about stuff. I didn't think or feel. I just reacted. Every day when I woke up, I had stuff to do. First I had to make sure everybody knew I was still the boss, you know? I had to look mad and bad. Everybody, friends and enemies, had to fear me. And finally I wanted to make money every day. The more we brought in, the more I wanted. That was success. If we made half a million dollars one day, I wanted to make more the next. I stayed off dope myself because I never saw a gangster worth anything who was high.

"And if I woke up next to a beautiful woman — hopefully a different one every day — I figured my life was full. That was it. If there was any thinking, it was business. How can we make more, get bigger, intimidate more people? That's what it was all about.

"When I got in the joint, there were sacrifices. No women. Money, but not the same amount. I was still running things, inside and out, and I was still boiling with rage, so nobody ever dared try a thing with me. But see, all it was was just the same kind of life in a different place."

Boone's mind was reeling. "You never even had normal conversations then, not even with Villalobos?"

"Exactly. There was no talking about the news or asking about somebody's family. We didn't care, and so we didn't even know how to talk that way. I was suspicious of anybody who asked me anything. I tried to give the vibe that I didn't want to be talked to, and believe me, everybody got the message.

"I was violent, a killer, and everybody knew it. Life was about eating everything and everybody. It was about how much you could get and how little you had to give."

"How'd you get hooked up with Jazzy in the first place?"

"It was when he was in charge, man."

"I know, but now he works for you."

"Yeah, well, he had his eye on me for a long time. My stories spread fast. I was ruthless. Once he came to one of my assignments just 'cause he had heard so much, you know?"

"Assignments?"

"I was enforcing back then. Some white dude who saw himself like a chef when he was only a short-order cook bought a little place on the edge of our turf and attracted a kind of a rich crowd. We didn't know if he was making a lot of money, but it looked like he was, and so we wanted it. We offered him protection, and word was that the Outfit offered him garbage service."

"Actual garbage pickup service?"

"Yeah! They're big in that, but you gotta use one of their companies. He told 'em to forget it and they asked us to put the squeeze on him."

Boone squinted. "They even outsourced extortion."

"Absolutely. That's where us young guys got a lot of our training. Anyway, Jazzy went over there with me and we sat at a table by the door for lunch. The waiters and waitresses kept staring at us. You can imagine we didn't look like their regular customers. Finally we ordered big meals and then asked to talk to the chef. They told us he was too busy. I told the waiter, 'You tell that blankety-blank that if he don't come to my table, he's gonna wish he had.'

"So finally the guy comes storming out of the kitchen, ready to tell us off. I saw the fear in his eyes, but I gotta say, he didn't back down. He leaned over the table and whispered that he appreciated our business but that he didn't appreciate being ordered around. I got up and went straight back into the kitchen, Jazzy right behind me, giggling.

"That owner followed us, telling us to get out of his kitchen and all that. I grabbed him and dragged him out the back door to the alley. I told him, 'Man, you don't know who you're dealing with.' I pointed to the garbage bin with the wrong company's name on it and told him he would not be asked again to switch companies. And then I told him how much our protection was going to cost him.

"He told me what I could do to myself. I pulled out my gat, man, and I pressed it into his forehead, right in the middle. I pushed him back against the wall and then pushed the barrel of that gun so hard, with both hands, that it gave him a bruise in the shape of a circle and drove the back of his head into the bricks. I said, 'If you want to see another day, you'll swear on your mother's life you will do what I said.'

"He nodded, and he was our best customer for years. But the thing was, Jazzy was so impressed, he couldn't quit talking about it. He told everybody that I did it so cool and with so little emotion that he knew I would have dropped that guy right where he stood if he didn't agree. And a few months later he saw me kill a dude, same scenario, different answer. I could tell from the look in Villalobos's eyes that he would work for me someday. And now he does."

Boone shook his head. "Guys like you are why I'm a cop today."

"I hear you, man. I don't like that story as much as I used to either."

"So back to your mom."

Pascual nodded. "That's what I'm getting at. All of a sudden I'm starting to feel something for somebody else, and I don't know what to do with it." He dug out his wallet, carefully steering with the heel of his hand while pulling out a tightly folded sheet of paper. "Read this, man."

Boone took it and reached for the overhead light. "No, no," Candelario said. "Use the glove box light. We don't need suburbanites seeing me, do we?"

Boone had to laugh, imagining another

driver catching a glimpse of the massive bald head of the man behind the wheel. He opened the glove compartment and unfolded the sheet under the tiny light. "Oh, man!" he said. "What, are you kidding me? I know a few words, but I don't read Spanish."

"Oh yeah, my bad. Well, I got it memorized anyway. Here's the important part. She says, *'Muchacho'* — that means *boy,* and a lot of times she still calls me *little boy* — 'will you think about this? Imagine me, your *madre,* being terrorized or wounded or even killed by someone like you. I know you wouldn't hurt your own mother, but you know you've hurt, or worse, someone else's child.'

"She went on to tell me to come to God for forgiveness and how to be saved and all that, but mostly she wanted me to start thinking about my life, something I'd never really done. Twenty-three, Boone. Twenty-three people before I ever got to Stateville. I had a reason for every one of them, and each one just added to my reputation. Now my mother, who had never hurt a soul in her life, was trying to get me to just think about it.

"At first I got mad. I started thinking of all the things these people had done to deserve what I did to them. And then it hit me. I was only thinking of the ones I had personally murdered. How many more — hundreds, thousands, of murders — had I ordered? I couldn't keep thinking about that because I could never count that high or remember them all anyway. And remembering how people had disrespected me or stole from me or underestimated me or threatened me, I could have written my mother a long letter about each one and why they deserved to die and why I would never apologize for doing it.

"But what finally got to me was her wanting me to think about somebody doing something to her. Can you imagine what I thought about that?"

"Someone else you'd be happy to kill."

"I got itchy just thinking about it. I decided how I would catch them, how I would make them feel, how I would make them beg, and what kind of weapon I'd use. Did I feel guilty about having killed other mothers' sons? I didn't, at least not then. These were bad dudes, as bad or worse than me. They chose their lifestyle; they knew the risks. So trying that angle with me — trying to make me feel guilty about robbing some family of their boy — that didn't work.

"What worked was makin' me think about

something happening to my own mother. I wasn't the type to stay upset about stuff. If somebody ticked me off, I killed 'em or had 'em killed; that's all. Now I was agitated thinking about something happening to my mother, and she wasn't even in danger. It made a mess of me for weeks."

Pascual left the Edens and pulled almost immediately into a woodsy area that took them toward Lake Michigan. PC had assured Boone it would work for the fateful meeting, and Boone was surprised that an inner-city guy would be aware of such a spot. A few minutes later PC wheeled in between the lighthouse and the side building, doused the lights, and stayed in the car.

Boone's phone vibrated and he peeked to see a text from Jack Keller.

In position. No tails. Safe.

"Your guys happy?" Pascual said, smiling.

"Yeah."

"Big ol' Mexican's not so stupid after all, hey?"

"Believe me, PC, nobody ever mistook you for stupid. Now how did you get from obsessing over your mother to, you know . . . ?"

"Coming all the way to Jesus? Took a

while. But it never would have happened if she hadn't just got me thinking different than I ever did before. Remember, she kept coming to Stateville to see me all the time too."

"Yeah, how'd that go?"

"She could tell I wasn't sleeping, and she asked me what was I doing that would cost me my sleep. I told her it was the noise. That was hard to argue with. No place louder'n a prison. But then she admitted it. She told me she was praying I wouldn't sleep until I got right with God. That was it, man. That worked. I was miserable for days."

"But you *were* thinking differently."

"Was I ever. The longer I went exhausted like that, the more emotional I got. That was so new to me, I didn't know what to do with it. I started saving all my mother's letters, reading them over and over every day."

"And she had the gospel in every one."

Pascual nodded. "What she called the whole plan of salvation. I got the message, believe me. But first I had to see myself for who I was. You have no idea how hard that was. After about a month of misery, I was different, man. I was still playing the game, acting like the boss, scaring people, but inside I was a mess. I started praying for the first time. I was begging God to let me sleep, to give me a break. It was like he was telling me I already knew what would give me peace. And I did.

"I started thinking about every bad thing I had ever done. We're talking crime every day for years, and it was all coming back to me. Lies, theft, assault, murder. And I started feeling horrible. Some nights I would just lie there wondering if there had ever been a worse person in the history of the world. Finally I just listened to be sure my cellmate was snoring, and right after the guards came by for one of their routine checks, I rolled out of bed and knelt on the floor. I begged God to forgive me and change me, but even more than that, I . . ."

Pascual had grown emotional and couldn't continue. Boone felt overcome too. Keller texted him to be careful and not sit out in the open too long. "Show me this building, PC," Boone said.

The big man grabbed a flashlight from the glove compartment and led Boone to the darkened enclave, where even the outdoor lights were off. He unlocked the door and they stepped in. Pascual shined the light in the corners and along the back wall. "See what I like about this place? Only one way in and out."

"Totally out of code."

"Perfect for my meeting. I mean, I don't expect anybody to want to escape, but if something goes wrong, you guys want to know where everybody's heading."

"Yep. Our people will love this."

Candelario turned off the light and leaned back against the wall. Boone could barely make out his form. There was no heat in the place, and while they were out of the wind, they had been a lot warmer in the car. But Boone wanted to hear the end of this story, and if this was where Pascual was most comfortable, this was right where Boone wanted him.

"Well," he said, "I didn't leave anything out. I don't know if I used the right language or even if I do now, three years later, but I knew he was listening."

"Uh, PC, you said you asked God for more than just forgiving you and changing you."

Candelario paused a long time before answering, and Boone just waited him out.

"You know, since that night, I've heard and read about other people going through this. Some of them have deep feelings. Other people don't feel anything and kind of grow into it. I felt free, man. I *knew* something happened to me. I went from being the baddest dude in the place to being a guy who wished he could jump and sing and laugh and cry and tell everybody that Jesus was real, that he could forgive their sins. You got no idea, man, how hard it was to hold all that in.

"And I told God I wanted to make up for everything — and I meant everything. I knew it would have to be a miracle because I didn't know if I could live long enough to do that. I didn't even know the names of most of the people I had murdered, so how do you make that right? Something told me God would have to give me some special idea, and he did."

"Making DiLoKi something positive."

"Yes, the Brotherhood. Because we would cut down on all the violence, and it gave me a way to look like I was still in charge without having anything to do with more killing. And then it would give me the chance to take down all the gang leadership in Chicago at once, even the Outfit."

"Now all you've got to do is keep playing the game and see if you can stay alive long enough to pull this off."

"You got that right."

"You're lucky only the CPD figured out that somebody was firing blanks at your last big shoot-'em-up."

Candelario shot Boone a double take.

"What, you think we wouldn't detect that?"

"That was one crazy scene, man. How did anybody get onto that?"

"Crime Scene Investigation is pretty sophisticated these days."

"Man, that gets out, and Jazzy would never leave it alone. He wouldn't quit till he traced it to me."

"We're sitting on it, of course."

"Press doesn't know?"

Boone shook his head.

PC seemed in his own world for a moment. Then, "I got to take you somewhere and introduce you to somebody that hardly anybody even knows about 'cept my own mother."

"Who's that?"

"I'll show you, but you got to turn off the phone first." Almost immediately, Boone's phone vibrated and PC laughed. "You're gonna have to negotiate this one, aren't you?"

Jack's text said, *Call me now.*

Boone held up a finger and called. "No way," Jack said. "We lose all control."

"You don't have control now, Jack. Let's come up with a way to make this work."

"Send me a signal every five minutes or

we move in. And to make sure it's you doing the signaling, do it numerically. Start with ten and go to zero, then back up and back down. Got it?"

"Got it."

"Don't hang up," Pascual said. "There's something else he needs to know."

"Hold on, Jack. One more condition."

"No more conditions!" Jack hissed.

"Hold on." Boone covered the phone. "What?"

"We're going into my neighborhood, but I want them to back off where you picked me up the other night. I'm taking you to a place between six and seven blocks from there, but I don't want them knowing where. We won't be long, and then I'll get you back to where I picked you up."

Boone told Jack. Jack said, "No."

"No?"

"Absolutely not. You think I could live with myself if this goes sour?"

"It's not going to go sour, Jack. You just heard everything I heard and you don't trust this guy?"

"I don't trust the neighborhood. You weren't going to go undercover or infiltrate. You've got to be in and out of that area, not visiting someone."

"Let me talk to him," Pascual said.

"No," Jack said.

Boone shook his head and the big man turned and left the building, leading Boone into the dim light.

Pascual scowled and pursed his lips. "Let's call this whole thing off."

"The visit?" Boone said.

"Everything. I'll figure out another way to make amends. I'm not asking for much with everything I've got on the line. Now I mean it, Boone. Tell him to trust me or this is all over."

"You heard him, Jack."

"Who you working for, Boones?"

"You don't have to remind me. It's your call, Jack."

"All right, put me on speaker."

Boone hit the button.

"Mr. Candelario?"

"I'm here, and I'm not happy. All I'm asking —"

"I'm up to speed. Now, listen, we're all in uncharted territory. Can you assure me that this is not going to become common practice? We're not prepared to have our guy out of touch on a regular basis."

"This will be the only time."

"If I have your word on that and Drake can signal me every few minutes, I'm inclined to allow this."

"Either that or I'm out," Candelario said. "No need to posture for me, sir."

"You think I'm posturing? Try me. You think Boone's not safe? Nobody's in worse danger than me. Once this all goes down, I'm as good as dead and we all know it."

"I'm going to show you some respect here, Mr. Candelario. And I look forward to meeting you one of these days, probably the middle of next month."

"Me too. Thanks."

Pascual locked up the building and cruised back down into the city to the Northwest Side. Boone was puzzled beyond words and eager to meet whoever it was the DiLoKi king wanted to introduce him to.

Moments later, Candelario pulled up in front of a ramshackle apartment building, drawing the attention of street people on two corners. Everybody in the neighborhood knew his car, of course, and heads were turning. Pascual jumped out and pulled his Ithaca 37 Stakeout from the trunk, tucking it in his waistband at the side. At that, everyone within a block found reasons to look or move the other way. Pascual nodded to Boone to follow, and they entered a graffiti-marred lobby.

They rode a cramped, dank elevator six

floors, and when they emerged, Boone was overwhelmed with the odor of poverty. Food, garbage, alcohol, urine, mold, even animal smells. Wallpaper was peeling, paint was chipped, and graffiti had found its way even to these hallways. The moans of drunks, the shouts of lovers arguing, and the cries of babies filled the place.

Boone had not seen Pascual move so quickly. He followed him to the end of the hall, where the big man knocked quietly at a door and unlocked it. They were met by a Mexican woman who looked to be in her fifties. He kissed her and greeted her in Spanish.

"Hey, *querido,*" she said. "Who's this?"

Pascual introduced Boone and said, "My *madre* and my son's grandmother."

"Your son?"

Pascual motioned Boone to follow. As they headed toward a back bedroom, Boone was struck by the difference between this flat and the rest of the building. First, it was quiet. He could hear nothing outside, telling him that the apartment had extra insulation. It was also clean and bright and stylishly appointed with nice furniture. Pascual had spared no expense to turn this into an oasis in the middle of an otherwise-horrible building.

"I don't want to wake him," Pascual said, "but I want you to see Jose. No other way to say it: his mother is a crack whore doing ten to twenty at Hopkins Park. Tell you the truth, I hardly knew her. In fact, I've probably talked to her three times. She's got kids all over town. One of those who promises she's using protection and then uses the kids to get welfare checks. I should have known."

"And you didn't use protection?"

"Gangbangers? Never, man. It's beneath us. We're geniuses, aren't we?"

Pascual Candelario seemed to melt when he cracked open the bedroom door and caught sight of his son in the light from the hall. "Just turned six," he said. "Come look."

The boy was a luminescent shade of light chocolate with generous lips and long dark hair. "Ah, Jose," Pascual breathed, and he bent low to kiss the boy's cheek.

Jose stirred and squinted in the darkness. "Hi, Daddy," he said, reaching with both hands.

Pascual shielded the boy's view of Boone and said, "Back to sleep, big boy. Church tomorrow."

Jose rolled over and went back to sleep as the men backed out of the room. "His mother's never going to be part of his life?"

Boone said.

Pascual shook his head. "Not if I have anything to do with it. She was a one-night stand and sent up just after he was born. Basically I paid her off, got her to give me full custody. The money's waiting for her when she gets out. I don't know what I'd do without my mother's help."

Boone had been texting numbers to Jack every few minutes to assure him he was okay. Now Pascual put an arm around him and drew him close. "I don't want anybody knowing about Jose. You got it, *compadre?*"

Boone nodded.

"I know he's beautiful and it's a great story, but you got to honor me in this, man. Nobody."

"I promise."

"See, if something happens to me — and let's be real, I'm gonna have the biggest price on my head of any rat in history — I don't want anybody knowing I had a son. I'll set it up to make sure he grows up safe. And you got to promise me you'll protect my family from Villalobos."

Boone had to think about that. Could that be part of the plan? Was PC's son the CPD's responsibility?

"If you even have a question about it, I'm out of this."

" 'Course. We'll have to do that for you."

"I need a guarantee."

"I'm not the one who can guarantee it, but I can't imagine —"

"Somebody's gonna guarantee it, and soon. I mean before I go one more step on this deal."

"I gotcha," Boone said. "If this is a hurdle, the brass will let me know, and I'll let you know."

"It's a nonnegotiable, Boone."

"I heard you. Now did I hear you tell him he had church tomorrow? Where do you go?"

"I can't go. You know that. Mama takes him. Come on, I'll take you back."

Leaving the cozy beauty of the flat Pascual provided for his son and his mother and heading back into the squalor of the rest of the building gave Boone a chill that stayed with him for the ride back to the rendezvous spot. He also felt renewed rage and a deep resentment he couldn't yet understand.

"What's your plan, PC? How are you going to get all the principals together to pull this thing off next month?"

"It's not gonna look like something I dreamed up. Graziano sent me a message when he knew I was getting out of Stateville and said we had to get together as soon as I could do it. I saw him two days after I got out. He told me the Outfit had stayed out of the drug business for too long, and he wanted in. I told him no, that we had a monopoly on it in the city and that there was plenty of stuff for him and his people to be involved with that we didn't want to touch — like the rackets and the unions.

"He said, 'What if I told you that I have direct contact with a new South American cartel that wants to work through us?' I told him I was listening. He said these guys from South America had everything in place — a way to get cocaine in, get it processed and packaged, and get it delivered to him. All he needed was a market, and he knew we had that. Graziano wanted to know how much cocaine he should order, how many drop-offs we could handle, and how much junk in each. When I told him, his eyes got huge. He started swearin' and carrying on and asking if I was pulling his chain. I told him I wasn't. He could see the gigantic dollar signs, man."

"How much money are we talking about, PC?"

"Tens of millions a year. Right away he starts figuring it up and telling me how there's way more than enough in this for everybody, and I tell him, 'Just hold on and slow down, chief.' He hates when I call him names, but I can tell it reminds him I'm not scared of him and he can quit his little intimidation games. I'll be the one calling the shots."

"So what'd you tell him?"

"That it would take time and that I would have to talk to the rest of the leadership. I told him they would want to meet him, see if they could trust him, spell out all the details. I said we had to make sure we had the right security, enough muscle, enough mules, and that the market could really handle what I thought it could. He could hardly stand still. I think the Outfit has fallen on really hard times, and he sees this as a way of getting back to what it used to be."

"No doubt. So where does it stand now?"

"He's callin' me every day, bro. I keep telling him we're close, so he should keep the cartel warm, and that once we have everything organized, we'll all get together and get acquainted and settle on the details. Now you gotta tell me something, Boone. If I do get all these guys together and get them talking about who does what in this big new drug wave for Chicago, is that enough to put them all away?"

"It's conspiracy to commit a felony, sure. And with the numbers you're talking about, if you can get them to say this while we're monitoring it and then you're prepared to testify to it all, it's a slam dunk."

"I can do better than that," Pascual said. "I can testify to conversations I've had with every person who'll be there that day — conversations where we talked about killing people. It'll make this new South American thing look like nothing."

"The more the better," Boone said. "And if you can get something on Jazzy Villalobos, that would help too."

"I got so much on him, he'll never see another day of freedom. But it's got to be the right place and time."

"What does he know about this deal with the other heads and Graziano?"

"He loves the idea. I told him he would be in charge of the DiLoKi while I'm away at the meeting and out of contact."

"But he doesn't know where?"

PC shook his head. "I told him I didn't even know, that I was meeting Graziano somewhere and going with him."

"Perfect."

20
PREPARATION

Boone tossed and turned all night, angry that a person like Pascual Candelario got to have a beautiful son. How did he deserve a healthy child? PC had become a father at least three years before coming to faith and just before he was sent to Stateville. The murderer of twenty-three people and a top leader in one of the most violent gangs in the country was something Boone only used to be — a father. What kind of sense did that make?

It agitated him so that he couldn't pray, couldn't read, couldn't sleep, couldn't do anything. Worse, it made him forget something important. He realized what it was when he showed up bleary-eyed at North Beach Fellowship in the morning. Max was his usual charming self, making Boone feel special but also making him miss Josh all the more.

Haeley, however, was distant and cold,

barely cordial. Fortunately Boone found a few minutes in which to talk before the service, and he went on the offensive. "Obviously something is wrong, so talk to me."

"You don't owe me anything, Boone. I don't know why I expect anything."

"Don't make me guess. I'm not a game player, and I don't think you are. Get it on the table so I can deal with it."

"I was worried about you," she said. "Okay? Was it too much to ask that I would at least find a message this morning telling me you got home safe last night?"

Boone smacked himself in the forehead. "No excuse," he said. "It was a stressful night; that's all I can say."

"I left you a message. You couldn't respond so I wouldn't be tempted to call Jack this morning?"

"Please tell me you didn't, Haeley! It's one thing that you know what's going on because of what you're exposed to in the office. But there was no way you would have any knowledge of last night unless I told you."

"I didn't call him, Boone. I'm just saying . . ."

"I didn't even check my phone this morning. I was running late and —"

"Is that smart with all that's going on?"

"I have a boss, Haeley. I don't need you in that role too."

Boone had never been good at apologizing, and now he had not only fallen way short of that, but he had also stopped her cold. He could see the resignation on her face when she sat with Max in her lap. Boone sat next to her but felt the ice and wished he had taken the hint and just sat somewhere else.

Boone looked forward to relief from the awkwardness when she would leave with the kids. But after the singing, Max ran off with the others, and there Boone and Haeley sat. He felt conspicuous and wrong as he realized this was Haeley's Sunday off from both singing and working with the youngsters.

Being so sleep deprived had made him even more emotional during the singing, so he was close to weeping again when the pastor began to speak. And what should he choose as his subject, of all things? If God is good and all-powerful, why is there evil and suffering in the world? The only comfort Boone got from the message was that this guy seemed to agree entirely with Francisco Sosa's take on the subject.

He pointed out that the question had been

posed long before the birth of Christ by both the Greek philosopher Epicurus and the Old Testament's Job. Jonah and Jeremiah had raised the same question, as had David and Habakkuk.

The most compelling — though not necessarily satisfactory, especially to those who had suffered most personally — answer from God himself was found in Job, according to the pastor. There, God, in essence, asks the suffering and complaining and questioning Job where he was when God was creating the universe.

The message jarred Boone from his funk over evil prospering while he suffered. Not only should he not begrudge Pascual Candelario his son Jose, the one tiny light in an admittedly self-inflicted dungeon of a life, but Boone decided he should also actually be happy for him. Yes, the man had chosen that life and made a horror of it, but now that he had turned to Christ, shouldn't he also be encouraged and nurtured in his faith?

The fact was, Boone was evil too, and he knew it all too well. In a strange way, though that day's sermon was on anything but the topic of forgiveness, Boone sat miserable, knowing he owed Haeley an unequivocal apology not only for having left her to worry after promising to check in but also for his snide comment about not needing another boss.

When the service was over, Haeley immediately stood and began greeting people. Boone waited his turn and then took both of her hands in his. She was still stiff and looked like she didn't want to do this here and now.

"When you're right, you're right," he said. "And when I'm wrong, I'm wrong. I was wrong."

He felt her soften. "Don't worry about it," she said, starting to pull away. "I have to keep an eye out for Max."

"That's not forgiveness," he said. "I need to know whether I can keep coming to this church or if you're going to have me excommunicated."

She laughed. "I can't stay mad at you," she said. "But don't press your luck."

"That's not forgiveness either."

"All right, all right! You're forgiven!"

Max came running, arms outstretched. "Pizza!"

Haeley rolled her eyes. "I'm a little tired of pizza."

"We can go somewhere else."

"Nah," she said. "If the boy wants pizza, he can have pizza. Anyway, there are other things on the menu."

Though Boone was exhausted, lunch that day with Haeley and Max was the most fun he'd had in a long time. He and Haeley set a regular Saturday date night and also discussed that both would be away visiting their families over the holidays. Boone thought it was too early to say it, but he was intrigued by the possibility that they would start missing each other at a time like that, and it would be a good harbinger for the future of the relationship.

The following week was filled with strategizing and preparation for January 6. One day, just before a briefing session, Garrett Fox poked his head into Boone's office. The newspapers and TV news shows had been full of his release from the department after months of hearings, continuances, a countersuit, and appeals. Boone couldn't hide his surprise at seeing him.

"Just wanted to be sure we were all right — personally, I mean," Fox said, accepting the offer of a chair.

"I don't know what to say, Garrett. You stood up for me, like we all want to do for each other. But you know I didn't ask you to lie."

"Turns out it wasn't a lie after all, though, right?"

"Well, you were right in what you guessed happened. But you have to admit, you didn't believe me, and you didn't see what happened."

"I sleep at night, Drake. That's all I'll say. I hope you do."

Boone hesitated. "Shouldn't I?"

"You could have stood up for me is all I'm saying."

"And said what? That you should be exonerated because even though it was proven on camera that you were lying, you meant well and were right and I appreciated it?"

"Something like that."

"That's crazy and you know it, but if it makes you feel any better, I do feel bad you lost your job. What're you going to do?"

"What we all do when we get off the street: look for something in security or consulting or private detective work. I don't know. I'll land on my feet."

"Of that I have no doubt," Boone said.

"You know, don't you, that if this had gone the other way — if you had been canned like everybody knew would happen if Freddy hadn't had an attack of conscience — this would be my office now, right?"

Boone tried to hide his shock, apparently unsuccessfully.

"You didn't know. Well, ask Keller. I hadn't left OCD under the best of terms, but after you, I was the one he knew could hit the ground running here."

"He was probably right about that," Boone muttered, still trying to process it all.

Fox stood. "Well, do me proud, partner. And don't become a stranger."

Boone shook his hand and walked him out, noticing that no one else in the office even acknowledged his presence when he passed, though Fox slowed and clearly tried to make himself noticed. *How awful it must be to be shunned,* Boone thought.

All three men above Boone in the chain of command didn't like that the big meeting of the gang leaders had been set so far in the future. Though the days would move quickly, they all warned him that things like this had a way of falling apart when too much time was involved.

On the one hand, Boone wanted to get on with it too. The FBI, the Chicago Crime Commission, and the U.S. Attorney's office were all brought in at this point, and day-long strategy sessions became the norm.

417

Jack Keller and Pete Wade reminded them that they all had to stay in the background, at least as it related to Candelario, because a deal was a deal. He would work directly with the Chicago Police Department, and specifically Boone Drake, whom he had apparently accepted and learned to trust.

That, however, meant anything other than their staying out of the planning. Boone got from the brass Candelario's guarantee of protection for his family, and he was assured by PC that none of the principals yet knew where their meeting was going to be. "I told 'em I haven't decided yet," Candelario said, "that I want to keep it fluid. If I don't know where we're meeting, it won't leak to the wrong people; know what I mean?"

Boone pressed him for promises that no one would be nosing around that building on certain days when the CPD had to get SWAT sniper positions and camera angles determined. When Pascual balked, Boone said, "Look, this is for your benefit. We need photos to prove these guys were there. You'll testify as to whose voices we get on the recordings. And our snipers will be in position only to protect your life. If something goes bad and you're in danger, that's going to be the only defense you've got."

"I know, *amigo.* I just don't want anybody

gettin' itchy fingers, you know?"

Boone wasn't in a hurry to see his new friend and brother risk his life for such a huge operation. Part of him still resented that the man was blessed with a son when all Boone had were melancholy memories. But he also felt compassion for the boy. What kind of a future did little Jose Candelario really have? If his father survived this, they would likely have to move out of the United States. And if something did happen to Pascual, the boy would be raised in the ghetto by his grandmother. Either way, it wasn't much of an outlook.

Just before Christmas, Boone finally made an appointment to see Pastor Sosa. To his great delight and relief, Francisco was warm and seemed genuinely thrilled to see him and encouraged by his growth. "I guess it's too much to hope we'll see Boone Drake back at Community Life someday."

"I've learned to quit predicting," Boone said.

He told Sosa about Haeley, and the pastor said, "That answers my question. Keep up with your reading and praying and studying. You'll be spiritually healthy, or at least healthier, in no time. As long as you're going to church somewhere . . ."

Boone told him he wanted to discuss the potential of the pastor's meeting with a notorious gangbanger. He shared generally Pascual's story without enough detail to give away whom he was talking about, but he did mention PC's ethnicity. "I think he would be comfortable with you, because you'd understand him."

Sosa looked thoughtful. "And he can't attend church anywhere right now?"

Boone shook his head. "Has to play the game a little longer. I worry that he's not growing, though."

"I'm willing," Sosa said. "But if he resists for any reason, *you* need to do this, Boone. You know as well as anyone the importance of the nourishment of the spiritual life. If he trusts you, he'll take it from you, and in discipling him, you'll learn more than you can imagine. It'd be great for both of you."

Boone immediately regretted telling Sosa enough to make him curious about Candelario because he had to tell him that he could divulge nothing else.

"How long are you downstate for the holidays?"

"Just three days."

Sosa shrugged. "This is the busiest time of the year for me. I think you should take on this task yourself. Get him grounded in the Bible and thinking about God all the time."

Boone said, "I have to remember not to get too close. My relationship with him is not to be personal."

"It's too late for that. I can see it all over you. You care about this man."

Boone couldn't deny it.

21
RECONNOITERING

Boone drove down to central Illinois for Christmas with all the plans for January 6 rattling in his brain. Though he, Fletcher Galloway, Jack Keller, and Pete Wade had spent countless hours with FBI agents, members of the Chicago Crime Commission, and the U.S. Attorney and his people, Boone kept silently running through every detail to be sure they hadn't missed anything.

Pascual told him that in the few meetings like this he'd had before, the principals agreed to come to the table unarmed and thus free to talk. There would be all kinds of security sweeps by each leader's people, checking the area for interlopers, scanning the building for bugs, and of course ensuring no one had been tailed to the rendezvous point. Nothing would be left to chance.

That was why the SWAT team and the feds were already in the area, building blinds in high trees that would give their snipers and photographers clear angles. Boone had been assured that no one would be able to detect a thing with the naked eye.

The best development, according to the FBI, was that they had determined that one window in the building had no drape or shade, and if they could be assured it would stay that way, they thought they could aim a video camera into the room from high in a tree eighty yards away. That way, in a nondescript van the CPD would park a few blocks from the site, Boone and his superiors would be able to monitor the meeting both visually and through the phone's audio signal.

The more Boone had talked to Pascual, the more encouraged he was by the man's ability to strategize. Candelario had all kinds of ideas on how to best sting his former compatriots. "I never thought I'd ever be a rat," he'd said, "but I know this is the right thing and the only way to even start making amends." He added that the best way he knew to keep people from suspecting anything was to distract them with accusations. "If I make 'em think I'm suspicious that *they're* trying to pull something on me, it makes them concentrate on convincing me they're not. That keeps 'em from suspecting me."

The only glitch so far was that Pascual had begun to think that it made the most sense to keep the meeting as small as possible. The FBI, who knew all the negotiating had to go through Boone, urged him to agree that it should be kept reasonable but to not let Candelario cut it to where it was just him representing all the gangbangers and Graziano Jacopo representing the Outfit.

"While that would be the cleanest and easiest," the lead agent said, "it makes the U.S. Attorney's job that much harder on the other end. The more guys we can get in there, on picture and on record, the easier it will be to indict them."

Boone and Pascual finally agreed on getting the heads of the three biggest gangs there, plus Graziano and his top lieutenant, because they had all personally worked with Candelario on hits. Besides getting them to somehow acknowledge those on the record, Pascual would get them all to commit to agreeing on the new drug deal.

Boone put on his best face for the reunion with his family. It was good to see his brothers and their families, but it was also hard.

This was the first time he had been home since the tragedy, and while he appreciated the Christmas Eve service at church, he hated the rueful looks he got from old friends. Toughest was when his irrepressible mother insisted they call Nikki's parents to wish them a merry Christmas.

The McNickles sounded awful, naturally, lamenting a third such holiday without their only child.

When it was finally time to leave, Boone endured the obligatory embraces and promises to stay in touch. Then his mother hung back by his car when everyone else hurried in out of the cold. Over the three days, Boone had made every effort to make his promotion to detective and the work in his new unit sound as routine and boring as possible. And he had informed his family that he had found a little storefront church, explaining that the memories at Community Life were just too painful.

That seemed to satisfy everyone except his mother. She always seemed to have something on her mind, something she wanted to say. And now she had her opportunity. Boone had slid into the car and started the engine, and there she stood, without even a coat, leaning into his window and shivering.

"You know, Boone, how long it's been. I don't think anyone would fault you if you started getting back into the swing of things. Socially, you know."

"Meaning what?"

"Meaning you have the right to be happy again. To start seeing people."

"I see people every day at the office. And I'm back into a decent routine."

"You know what I mean, honey. I wish you'd have stayed at that big church where there have to be a lot of young single women. . . ."

"Mom, please."

"Maybe there's someone in the new place."

"I'll keep my eyes open."

"You don't sound like you mean it. You know, in our church there are three or four girls from your past who wished they'd had their chance —"

"Mom! Stop. I'll know when I'm ready, all right?"

"Just don't close yourself off from possibilities is all I'm saying. You know I'm only looking out for you."

And it was true. He knew that. But it was way too early to even mention Haeley and any possibilities there. For one thing, Boone had no idea what the future held. He thought Haeley was as open as he was to seeing how the relationship developed. But the whole thing was embryonic. Besides, if and when the time came that he needed to introduce her to his family, he worried about their reaction to her having had a child out of wedlock.

His childhood church preached forgiveness and acceptance, especially toward people who were repentant. But that didn't always translate to biblical charity when it came to actually living it out — especially for Boone's mother. Well, if the future included Haeley and Max, the boy would melt his mother's heart. She would have to accept or get used to Haeley's situation.

Boone and Haeley had agreed not to talk to each other while each was at home for Christmas, just to avoid misunderstanding from their families. But now, as he was driving back to Chicago and knew she and Max would be on the road too, Boone couldn't wait to talk to her. He had planned to make fun of his own experience and tell her how glad he was to be headed back home, but her giddy tone stopped him.

"I had *such* a good time," she said. "It was great to see everybody, and of course Max is the perfect age to keep everybody entertained. He was the center of attention."

"Let me talk to him."

"Oh, he's dead to the world. He got so much stimulation, I don't know how I'll keep him entertained when we get back. But he missed his naps, wore himself out, and loved every minute of it. He's been sleeping since we pulled out of the driveway."

"So your family has forgiven you for . . . you know . . ."

"Living in sin? They were pretty good about it all along, Boone. They were disappointed, sure, and they reminded me — which I knew all too well — that I was raised better. But last Christmas was when I visited them as the ashamed prodigal. They're thrilled I've come back to the Lord, am active in church, gainfully employed, all that. They just hate that I'm not with Max most of every day, and that tears me up too, but I can't change it."

Maybe someday, Boone thought.

"We still on for Saturday?" he said. "First one of the new year."

"I was hoping you'd ask. I didn't know if you wanted to make that a regular thing for the whole year or not."

"What do you mean?"

"Well, I didn't want to be presumptuous. Single mom with a crazy schedule. I don't want you to feel obligated. I mean, there are fifty-two Saturdays again this year."

Boone was silent for a moment. Then, "I hope you're just being polite, Haeley."

"I'm giving you an out, you big goof."

"Do *you* want an out?"

"I don't need an out. I can just tell you I'm done. But I'm the one with the kid, and you're too nice to break my heart. So I'm just saying, you have an out if you want it."

"All right," he said, "I'm thoroughly confused. Are you trying to tell me something?"

"Yes."

When Haeley didn't elaborate, Boone feared the worst. "And that is?"

"That I would love to spend time with you every Saturday this year, as long as you can put up with me."

"And what about Sunday lunches with both of you? Those still on too?"

"I have a meeting scheduled with Max where that's one of the items on the agenda," she said. "Oh, wait, I make his decisions for him. Yes."

"I have a Christmas gift for you," he said.

"That makes two of us. We'll have our Christmas after New Year's, then."

"I'll save Max's till the next day," Boone said.

"You didn't have to do that."

"It's nothing. But it's only fair. We don't want him feeling left out."

"Are you kidding? He thinks I'm interfering with his relationship with you as it is."

Saturday Boone and Haeley waited more than an hour for a table at Giordano's on Rush, which they discovered had been each other's favorite pizza place since long before they met. Boone gave her a thin gold necklace with a dazzling sapphire.

"Oh no," she said. "It's too much."

"Really? Sorry. It wasn't exorbitant."

"No, no, I love it. I just mean, my gift for you is more of a novelty, so now I feel bad."

"Anything from you will be cool."

And it was. She'd had a key ring made with a fob that contained a tiny picture of her and Max on one side and lettering on the other that read, "Pizza!"

"Perfect," Boone said. "Really." And he began switching his keys to it immediately.

"But yours was serious and mine was silly."

"Not to me," Boone said.

Haeley laughed. "You're seriously going to cherish that," she said. "I can tell."

He raised his brows and nodded.

The next day after church he presented

Max with a Nerf football, then had to take him out in the parking lot when the boy wouldn't quit trying to throw it inside the restaurant.

"You've created a monster," Haeley said as Boone ducked between and under cars to keep fetching the thing in a frigid wind. "I'm going to have to tape down all my lamps at home."

At work Monday she reported that Max insisted on sleeping with the football.

D-day was just two days away, and Boone found himself spending alternate hours between Pascual Candelario and the task force that had been camping out in the Organized Crime Division offices. His and Pascual's clandestine meeting places kept changing so no one would catch on. Boone was intrigued that his new friend seemed to be growing more excited by the day.

Though there was also trouble and worry behind those dark eyes, PC kept saying, "I can't wait, dude. I know I'm doing the right thing. For me, for Jose, for Chicago, for God."

Boone mentioned Pastor Sosa and the idea that someday Pascual would have to get serious about his faith.

"You know how I'm doin' it now, man?

On the Internet. I downloaded a couple of Bibles — one of 'em was a modern translation in Spanish. I can understand it good. And there's all kinds of stuff you can study on there. But yeah, I'd like to talk to somebody too. I just don't know when I could ever do that. You and I both know that once this thing goes down and those guys get arrested, I'm gonna have to be held somewhere until I testify. Nobody's gonna want to come where I am. And the prosecutor's not going to want to risk revealing where I am. That would be the end for sure."

"I'll come."

"You're going to do this? Teach me? Bring me along?"

"If you want."

" 'Course I do! That would be great, before I get sent away."

Even the prospect of that, though Boone knew it was coming, made him feel horrible. He knew there was no choice. A man as big and recognizable and notorious as Pascual Candelario would be signing his own death warrant if he tried to stay anywhere in the United States. He and his mother and his son would all have to go to Mexico or South America, and after the cartel was exposed by his testimony, South America would likely be out of the question too.

The FBI was working with the State Department on that eventuality. Boone could pray only that wherever he landed, Pascual would find a nice spot, a good church, and a set of supportive friends. Boone wondered how extensive plastic surgery would have to be to eliminate all of Candelario's tats and perhaps even change the structure of his face. But even with that, he might be left looking like a giant Mexican with a traumatized face, and who would that fool?

The night before D-day the task force techies picked up the Chicago PD personnel most closely connected with the operation and drove them to a warehouse on the Southeast Side. There sat a plain beige van, looking like some trades-man's dilapidated vehicle. It had mismatched tires, random dents and scrapes, an ancient broken radio antenna, and was windowless behind the front seat.

As Galloway, Keller, Wade, and Boone climbed in the back, however, it was as though they had entered a new world. Not only had the technicians loaded the vehicle with every gadget necessary, someone had designed it in such a way that all four men were able to sit comfortably and look over the shoulder of the middle-aged woman named Courtney who ran the controls.

"So we'll be able to see the video feed when we're close enough tomorrow?" Boone said.

"You can see it now," Courtney said. "If the signal can reach us from 33.8 miles away, which is where we are now, it will easily reach a quarter mile tomorrow." She hit a button and said through her headset, "SWAT and photo, are you in position? Task force is in place."

Immediately on the screen appeared a clear view through the window of the building in Evanston. "Looking good," she said. "And it'll be light enough early tomorrow afternoon to give us good images, correct?"

"Affirmative," came the reply.

"What kind of sound will we be able to get out of that building?" Boone said.

"Unless there's some unusual interference we don't know about, it should be close to what you're about to hear. The photographer about eighty yards from the building and maybe a hundred feet off the ground has a phone just like the one you were issued." She pressed her earphone closer and flipped another switch. "Mark, I'm putting you on speaker here. Can you give me a level?"

Mark said, "One, two, three, four, no gangbangers anymore."

Besides making everyone smile, it sounded as if the man was in the van.

"Of course," Courtney said, "your man will be on the ground, sea level. But the signal bounces off a satellite anyway, so I'm guessing you're going to hear your meeting tomorrow as well as you just heard Mark."

"Works for me," Chief Galloway said. "Everybody back here at ten in the morning and we'll head to our prearranged spot."

"If it's this clear," Boone said, "why don't we just monitor it from here?"

Galloway gave him a look. "You have my permission to camp out here, Detective Drake. I happen to have a team in place that could mean the end of organized crime in Chicago as we know it. I'd like to be close by when it goes down. How about you?"

"Ready to go at ten, sir."

22
D-DAY

"If you have any trouble sleeping tonight," Haeley told Boone at the end of the day Tuesday, "call me and I'll bore you to death."

"That'll be the day. But I might take you up on that."

"Anytime before midnight."

Boone wanted to avoid having to bother her, so he vigorously went through his routine, including a hard run in the early evening, despite the cold. Settling in bed after eleven, he felt anything but drowsy. He dialed Haeley.

"Can't sleep?" she said.

"That and I just wanted to hear your voice."

"Sweet. What do you want to hear me say?"

"There's a loaded question. How about that you'll remember me fondly if this thing blows up tomorrow?"

"Not funny. You guys couldn't be more prepared. It'll go like clockwork. How does clockwork go, anyway?"

"We're ready," Boone said.

"You've been ready for weeks. How's your man doing?"

"Funny thing. He's been living a lie for quite a while now. He's not going to miss that. But he knows his life will never be the same."

"He's doing a special thing."

"Yeah, but you know how he'll be thought of in his own community."

"That's no community, Boone. That's a war zone. He has to know what he's doing is right."

"He does. It's the only motivation he has. A lot of people he has known forever are going to go down in this."

"And rightfully so," she said. "Well, love, just know I will be thinking of you and praying for you. Past that, I don't know what else will help you sleep."

"What did you call me?"

"Sorry?" she said.

"You heard me. What did you call me?"

"You heard me, too, Boone. Good night."

That didn't allow Boone to sleep any easier, but it did give him something to think about other than what had monopolized his thinking for longer than he could remember.

By 10:05 the next morning the OCD quartet was in the back of the van, on their way to Evanston, and discussing how they were to explain a vehicle sitting at the curb for up to a couple of hours if anyone grew suspicious. Both the driver and a cop in the passenger seat were wearing painters' garb. "Their story will be that their foreman told them where to wait for him, and he would lead them to the job," Galloway said. "Anybody gets pushy, we can move a few blocks and set up again."

Boone's secure cell beeped. "It's Candelario," he said.

"Put him on speaker," Galloway said.

Courtney hit a button, and they could all hear him. To Boone he sounded more enthusiastic than ever.

"Mornin', *muchacho!* You and your people ready?"

"We are. How about you?"

"I'm ready, but we gotta change the meeting place. Jacopo got cold feet at the last minute."

Galloway shook his head and dragged a finger across his throat. Boone said, "PC, you said you were waiting till the last minute so he wouldn't have time to make a change like this."

"I did, but listen, man, I tried to force him into Evanston by telling him first that I wanted him and his guy to come to the Northwest Side. He said he wouldn't be caught dead there. So then I do my switch and tell him I might be able to get my friend to let me use his place on the North Shore, you know? At first he said okay, and then he just called and said he had a better place."

"You have got to be kidding."

"I am, *amigo!* Can't you take a joke?"

"You dog."

Pascual was cackling as Boone's bosses sat shaking their heads. "Boone, you need to tell your people everything's off and we're goin' somewhere else! C'mon, they'll love it!"

"I work with a different breed of cat than you do, PC. So, seriously, everybody's in?"

"They're in, bro. I did use that line about meeting in my neighborhood first, though. I thought Grazzy's head was gonna fly off. He says, 'I come to you with the biggest deal you've ever had and you want me to come into DiLoKi land?' I pushed him and pushed him and promised I would protect him, but he wasn't buying. I sounded real reluctant about Evanston, telling him that getting my people to go up there was like asking him to come here. That he bought."

"You going to be okay, Pascual? You can play this game to the end and pull it off?"

"Me? Oh yeah, man. C'mon. I made my living doing this. I know these guys. You're gonna enjoy this. They'll all posture and threaten, and I'll give it right back to them. When we leave Evanston, they're going to think they just made the best deal of their lives."

"Ask him about the weapons," Keller whispered.

"Hey, PC, what did you guys agree to about guns?"

"Everybody's leavin' their straps in their cars. Jacopo's lieutenant will be frisking everybody; then I'll frisk him and Jacopo."

"So everybody in that room will be unarmed."

"Right."

"That changes everything," Boone said.

"Now you're kiddin' me, right, *hombre?*"

"No, listen. We were going to let these guys get back into the city before rounding them up, and we were thinking we might take you along with them to make it look good until they figure it out."

"Yeah, that's got to still be the plan, man. That'll work. What are *you* thinking?"

"We want to do this when we can guarantee nobody gets hurt. We don't want you guys shooting each other or us, and we sure don't want to have to shoot anybody we'd rather indict. Understand?"

"Yeah, but —"

"Once we have recorded everything we need in order to bust all these guys, we'll move in and arrest you all, making sure nobody can get to his car. You follow?"

"They're gonna know — and I mean as soon as you show up — that it was me."

"Maybe, if they're smart. But we're going to cover for you as long as we can. We'll tell the press we're booking each of you in solitary to keep all the principals isolated. The plan is that everybody will think you're in the joint until it comes time for you to testify."

"You better get a picture of me bein' processed in somewhere. Make it look real. Face it. It won't be long before it gets out."

Boone looked to Pete Wade, who consulted with the others and nodded.

"We think we can do that, PC, and we'll make it look as good as we can."

There was a long silence while Pascual was obviously processing this. "I guess that's okay," he said. "But you want to have a little more fun?"

"*Fun* is your word for this, PC, not mine."

"Yeah, but this will be good. There's a guy coming who's as bad or worse than I ever was, and you know that's saying something. Name's Skeeter Robinson. You know him."

" 'Course we know him. His roots go way back before your time. Bad dude."

"Maybe in the middle of the bust, you just thank him."

"PC, you're not right." He was cackling again.

"He's gonna get what's coming to him anyway, but if even for a split second everybody in that room thinks he's the snitch, it would be too sweet."

"PC . . ."

"Yeah?"

"You really that lighthearted about all this? You see what's going to happen here, right? You realize the ramifications."

A long pause. "Yeah, I know. I'm just representin', pretending it's going to be something else. My *madre* doesn't even know what's happening today."

"You want us to call her when it's over?"

"Nah, I'll do that. I'll be able to, right?"

"Sure."

"And you still can't tell me where I'll be holed up before testifying?"

"If you don't know, that guarantees no

one else will know."

Pete Wade slipped Boone a note.

"Okay, it's official," Boone said. "We'll invite the press to central booking, where we'll process you; then when they're gone, we'll sneak you out of there. Now, everything else aside, Pascual, you set to go?"

"Locked and loaded."

Boone snorted. "I was hoping it would be you who used that cliché and not us. How about unlocked and unarmed?"

"That too."

"See you on the other end. And on behalf of the citizens of Chicago, thanks."

"You got it, man."

"And on behalf of me personally, know I'll be praying for you, Pascual."

"Now you're talkin', *amigo.*"

If Boone had ever wondered how Fletcher Galloway reached his exalted position, he had no doubt after watching the man in action over the next ninety or so minutes. The chief was in constant contact with SWAT and central command, arranging for the location of teams and the cues that would send them into action. He seemed to think of every exigency.

"The one thing we'll want to watch for," he told the SWAT leader, "is whether any

443

of these guys — and I would expect Jacopo to be the most likely — will have some compatriots following at a distance and looking for CPD personnel to be staging somewhere, ready for a takedown. Somebody gets that word to Jacopo by some code, and all of a sudden half those guys are out of there and on their way to their cars and their weapons."

The van was positioned three streets over from the route the gang kingpins would have to take to get to the lighthouse side building, and one of the cameras in the trees was focused on the road so Courtney and the Organized Crime Division personnel would know when they were coming.

Boone had a list of the principals and their most likely vehicles. As specified, Pascual was the first to arrive, and he was alone. He parked in the shade of a grove of trees, unlocked the building, and set plastic folding chairs around a cheap particleboard table inside.

"Can you hear me, Boone?"

"Affirmative."

"Grazzy's gonna hate this, man. It'll be the dumpiest place he's had a meeting in forty years."

Galloway gave Boone the scissors sign with his fingers, and Boone told Pascual,

"Consider me off the air now, PC. We've got you covered. Don't risk talking directly to me."

"Suspect vehicle," Courtney announced, and the men leaned forward to see Skeeter Robinson and a young associate pull into view. A few minutes later, when Robinson's tricked-out BMW slid in next to PC's car, Pascual emerged from the building and greeted the two as long-lost friends.

All three of them were vile and profane, as was the custom among these types. Skeeter would be the oldest of the gang-bangers, in his fifties. As for the Outfit, Jacopo was in his seventies and his lieutenant in his late sixties.

Skeeter said, "Where's Jazzy, man? I know he's hip-deep in this."

"Mindin' the store, Skeet. What you think, I leave there with nobody in charge?"

"Not unless you wanna be robbed blind!"

"You got that right."

Skeeter's associate, whom PC greeted as Ray-Ray, would be the youngest at not yet twenty-five. "Glad you could come, bro," Pascual said as the two newcomers entered the building and began checking it for security.

"Wouldn't miss it, man," Ray-Ray said. "I'm in charge of the markets for us now, you know."

"I know, I know! Haven't seen you since you offed that business owner's wife, the one on South State?"

Boone was furiously scribbling notes.

"Shot her face off, man. That takes care of her ID'ing anybody on her deathbed, don't it?"

"She was way gone before they even put her in the ambulance, wasn't she?"

"Before she hit the ground, PC. Buckshot done mixed with brain, baby."

"Man, you're ahead of my pace, and I thought I was doin' good. How many is that for you now?"

"Seven."

"Get out of here!"

"It's true! Tell 'im, Skeeter!"

"I don't care who tells me," Candelario said. "You ain't got no seven kills at your age."

"He does," Skeeter said, apparently not even sniffing the trap, while pulling out his phone. "His first three was all at once."

"Three at once? Where?"

"You remember that," Ray-Ray said. "Over by Chicago Vocational, those football players. Made the papers and TV news, here in the city and everywhere else."

"I didn't know that was you."

"Nobody knew it was me, man. That's the beauty of how I work. I change methods. All the experts think they got a handle on you if you do 'em all the same way. Those three I gut-shot in the kidneys, then capped in their brains in case they bled out too slow."

"A masterpiece."

Ray-Ray nodded.

Keller said, "I hope PC's smart enough to know we've got plenty on Ray-Ray now. He gets him to recite all seven, and Skeeter's going to smell something."

As if on cue, PC turned his attention to the older man. "You weren't that young when you broke your maiden, were you?"

"Close," Skeeter said, studying something in his phone. "I'm gonna say I had three by the time I was twenty-one."

"Man, you guys start young! I mean, I was a teenager, but I was crazy. You were all sophisticated and stuff by twenty-one, weren't you, Skeeter?"

"We all were. Not thugs like so many today. But we were the first to use AK-47s."

"I 'member that," PC said. "At least I heard it by the time I was coming up. How many did you do with a '47?"

"Just my first. We knew the cops knew we were strappin' 'em, so we didn't want to leave an easy trail."

"Your first was a woman too, wasn't it?"

Boone knew that PC knew better. The CPD had never been able to prove it, but they believed Robinson had nearly cut a superstore night watchman in half with an AK-47. PC had confirmed it for Boone, and now he was about to get Robinson to say it for the camera.

"Nah! I never did no woman. My first was that guard at that big store, tried to run us off from sneakin' in the back after hours."

Bingo.

Skeeter was still playing with his phone. "You're not fixin' to call somebody, are you?" Candelario said. "Nobody can know where we are."

"You think you're talking to a rookie, PC? I wouldn't talk to nobody you didn't want knowin' where we are."

"Then who?"

"I thought I was gonna see Jazzy is all. Got to check in with my man."

"Yeah, listen, he didn't want to know where we were meeting and I didn't want to tell him. That way, you know, nobody could get it out of him."

"Good thinkin', dude! You think he's gonna track me with GPS if I call him?"

"Don't call him! ;'Course he can track

where you are. You've got the same technology the rest of us do."

"I'm just bustin' your chops, PC," Skeeter said, slapping his phone shut. "Chill now."

"Hey, you guys leave your gats in the car?" Pascual said. "You know the rules for this meeting."

"You want to search us?" Skeet said coldly.

"Nah, Jacopo's guy's gonna do that."

The techie in the van held up a hand. "Robinson said he wasn't calling Villalobos, but he hit the Call button. He's signaling somebody."

"We've got to know who," Boone said.

"If it's the DiLoKi, we'll know," Galloway said. "We've got Villalobos and the rest of the leadership staked out."

Within minutes two more cars pulled in, one a Hummer and the other an Escalade. The five bangers now shared handshakes and embraces and the two who had just arrived did their sweep for bugs inside. PC brilliantly informed them that he had decided that Skeeter and Ray-Ray had been the baddest dudes of everybody he knew, at least when they were starting out. The other two immediately took the bait and began bragging about how violent their early kills were and how young they had been.

Only once did PC strain credulity by asking for one detail too many. Boone could tell he was just trying to ensure CPD had enough detail, and he wished he could communicate to Pascual that they had plenty. Skeeter gave Pascual a long, hard look and said, "What're you doin', bro? Writin' a book?"

PC laughed a little too hard and said, "That's a good idea, man! Hey, the senior citizens are here."

It was obvious from the moment Jacopo and his lieutenant emerged from their Town Car that the old-timers and the gangbangers neither liked nor respected nor trusted each other. "You all know Tommie Z, right?" Jacopo said as Tommie checked out the room.

They all nodded and mumbled some greeting, formally shaking both men's hands.

In the van, Galloway took a call on his personal cell. "Terrific," he muttered. "Got it. Don't let 'em get anywhere near here, and if there's a way to jam their phone signals, do it now. I don't want anyone here knowing they're coming. And listen, if we can get this done before they get here, don't — do not — apprehend them. That would not end well. What we're doing here will be way more effective in the long run than rounding up those guys now."

He slapped his phone shut and swore. "The DiLoKi, Jazzy in the lead, are loading up and heading this way. Robinson and Villalobos must be closer than Candelario knows."

Boone leaned forward. "Do I need to tip off PC, get this thing moving?"

"I wouldn't risk it," Keller said.

"Me neither," Galloway and Wade said in unison. Galloway added, "Our guys'll keep an eye out for company."

23
THE BUST

In the room next to the lighthouse, Jacopo said, "This is your idea of a meeting place?"

"What'sa matter, Grazzy," PC said, "you didn't take your happy pills today, or what? Come on. It's not a palace like you guys are used to, but it's secluded. Can't beat that."

"Got to agree with you there. Nobody must come here except on purpose. Now, did you inform everybody of the rules? Tommie will frisk all of you, and you will frisk him and me. Let's get on with it."

Once all were satisfied that no one was carrying, they sat. Jacopo and Tommie sat next to each other, and the gangbangers spread out. Though at times it was difficult to see individual faces, anytime the camera caught Jacopo, he looked in a foul mood. He pulled out a file folder, and PC produced a small pad of paper.

Pascual suddenly turned formal. "Well, Mr. Jacopo and Mr. Z, I haven't seen you two since we accommodated you on the unfortunate disappearance of your former associate. What was his name?"

There was a long silence. "That's the difference between us and you," Graziano Jacopo said finally. "You guys like to run your mouths. You think it's smart to talk about this stuff? I always go by the rule that every place is bugged, so I never make a mistake."

"Yeah, you gotta watch out for this place, Grazzy. Like I told Skeeter here, I'm writin' a book."

"And quit calling me that. That's disrespectful. I'll call you anything you ask, so extend me the same courtesy."

"Well, okay, as long as you speak right into the radiator."

Everybody laughed, including Jacopo, but he was also the first to grow serious again. "Speaking of that, is there no heat in this godforsaken dump?"

"Not much, so we got to hurry," PC said.

In the van the techie said, "That's good, because I think Robinson is still transmitting. Wouldn't surprise me if Villalobos is listening in."

Ray-Ray raised his hand.

"What're we, in school?" Jacopo said. "What do you want?"

"Just wanted you to know it was me who

did your boy. My number seven. PC's guys said it had to look like our work and not yours."

"And you did fine. We paid for it and we appreciate it. Now can we get on with the reason for this meeting?"

"*I* didn't even know it was you, Ray-Ray," Pascual said. "All I heard was that it got done, right there in the entrance to that travel agency. I passed the payoff on down the line. Good work, *amigo*."

"Thanks, but that wasn't the travel agency. You're thinking of that accountant who found out we were skimmin' their books. The one for the Outfit was the guy who turned on 'em. We took him out in the parking lot at Midway."

"Oh yeah!"

Galloway reached for the radio. "This guy ought to get an Academy Award. Brilliant. You coach him, Drake?"

"A little, but I can't take credit. Got a lot of input from Jack and Pete — even some from Garrett Fox, who used to be with you guys. But then Candelario is just something special on his own."

Galloway held up a hand and spoke into the mike. "Stand by. We've got more than enough on every one of them already, but I want to get as much on this cartel as I can;

then we move."

Jacopo was riffling papers and breathing so heavily through his nose that Boone could hear it through the speakers. "If you thugs are finished comparing gun-barrel sizes, I'd like to get down to business."

"No sense getting disrespectful, gramps," Ray-Ray said.

"And calling me that is respectful? I owned Chicago before you were born."

"Yeah," PC said. "Let's hear the man out and see what we can do together. You know the numbers are off the charts, so let's hear all about it."

Jacopo sounded like a college professor, carefully laying out how the cartel had come to him through former associates who had fled the country and then put in a good word for him in South America. "As you know, we have never been in the drug business, but this is too plump to pass up, and I'll show you why."

The old man began laying sheets of paper on the table and turning them so everyone could see. He outlined how much cocaine was available to be shipped, how it would come into the country, where it was to be processed, and how he foresaw getting it to the street gangs for delivery. Then he asked for an idea of how much business they thought they could do with him.

"We've been talking about this," Pascual said, referring to his own notes. "And here's what we think we can do. 'Course we'll want the option to adjust this as we go, in case we're way off in our estimates, good or bad."

Jacopo's mood began to shift, and he became much friendlier and more animated. "You can see there's way more than enough here for everyone, wouldn't you agree? How about you, Mr. Ray-Ray?"

The young man threw his head back and laughed. "Never been called that before, *Mister* Jacopo, but it sounds good. And yeah, I do agree. My piece of this alone will set me up nice."

Galloway barked into the mike, "Now."

He instructed the driver of the van to head through the woods to the lighthouse, and in the meantime, everybody inside watched the bust unfold on the monitors.

Boone was impressed that the SWAT team, in full heavy gear and looking like black-clad RoboCops, was somehow able to surround the building, putting sentries at the entrance and windows, without being detected at first. One, brandishing a massive submachine gun, was posted by the cars that contained all the perps' weapons.

Just before the SWAT team leader kicked

456

open the door, Skeeter Robinson must have seen something. He leaped to his feet, his chair sliding across the floor, squealing a string of curses that caused the others to rise and reach in vain for their weapons.

The door resounded with the leader's kick, then seemed to explode again when it slammed against the wall. Everyone responded at once except Graziano Jacopo, who remained seated, slowly shaking his head and not even watching the proceedings. It was as if he understood immediately that he had been set up.

The gangbangers, Candelario included, backed away, but from deep inside his boot Skeeter produced a switchblade. He yanked it out, the blade snapping open as he raised it, but he was immediately driven back with a blow to the chest by the butt end of a SWAT semiautomatic. As Skeeter hit the ground, the SWAT team member said, "Oh, sorry, Skeeter. I forgot you were the one who called this in. I should have pulled my punch, eh?"

The others glared at Skeeter, who looked stricken. "Whatcha talkin' 'bout, man? I never called nothing in! It wasn't me!"

While the others were each subdued by two team members and cuffed at the ankles and behind their backs, Jacopo finally stood slowly and turned to face the SWAT team leader. "May I reach into my pocket for my lawyer's card?"

"Of course," the leader said, his weapon leveled at Graziano's chest. He pocketed the card and nodded to a subordinate to cuff the old man. "Just the wrists," he said. "This old boy ain't runnin'."

"That's for sure," Jacopo said, and as they were led out, he seemed to look wistfully at the car full of weapons.

The SWAT team member standing guard smiled at him. "Eat your heart out."

By the time the van pulled in, SWAT was loading the suspects into a paddy wagon and tethering them to steel loops in the wall.

All were swearing and blaming each other, and Jacopo was fuming about Candelario "thinking this place was so perfect. If you're behind this, fat man, believe me, you're going down."

Boone stayed in the van to protect his own identity, but he watched on the monitor as Jacopo turned to one of the cops. "Officer, I was just here to listen. If you find my prints on those documents, it's only because I was being kind enough to read them over. I had no intention of engaging in any illegal activity whatsoever. I will say nothing further without legal counsel."

Meanwhile the report came in from unmarked squads on the Edens that all five cars that had left DiLoKi headquarters exited the same ramp, crossed the highway, and headed back the other way in a single line. "Must have heard the whole thing go down on Skeeter's phone," Galloway said. He turned on the mike and reminded the officers, "Let 'em go. We'll have them soon enough."

It took the rest of the day for the Bureau of Investigative Services to comb the crime scene, impound the cars, and confiscate the weapons. The videoing and recording of the meeting had gone without a hitch and gave the U.S. Attorney's office a mother lode of incriminating evidence that would make this the most massive sting of organized crime in the history of Chicago.

As promised, Pascual Candelario was processed at central booking in front of a press pool that disseminated the pictures all over the country. PC was then spirited via unmarked van to the garage of a luxury condo tower downtown, where he was transported via service elevators to a penthouse. There he would enjoy a phalanx of round-the-clock security until he was due to testify before the grand jury.

Within two days it became obvious and widely reported that Pascual was the turncoat, and his mother and child were also put into protective custody. The story became the biggest in Chicago in decades, and the priority of the Chicago Police Department, primarily the Organized Crime Division, became to protect Pascual at all costs.

Because of the police activity in and out of the high-rise, it soon became obvious where he was ensconced, and tenants complained of the interference. Day after day inside, the U.S. Attorney's office walked Candelario through recollecting hundreds more names of notorious gangbangers and members of the Outfit he had worked with. Arrests were made nearly hourly as the media circus continued.

Boone spent much of his day and also many of his off-duty hours with Pascual. When off the clock, he and the former gang leader would study the Bible and pray together. Pascual told Boone, "I feel a huge weight off me, man. I can't wait till this is all over and my mother and son are with me somewhere far away."

"It won't be long, brother," Boone said. In truth, he too longed for that day so he could get back to relaxed times with Haeley and Max. Their Saturday dates had become impossible after it came out in the press that the officer who had lost his family was the principal detective in the sting operation.

Boone and Haeley still saw each other at church, but to get any time together they had to order in at one or the other of their apartments. These times were more awkward than they might have been because Haeley expressed such fear about Boone's safety, and he was so distracted planning for the day Pascual would be transferred to court to begin his testimony.

That move alone was being planned with military efficiency. There would be fake starts and stops, decoys, and — of course — no notification of the press. Still, members of the media knew how to sniff out information, and somehow, someway, someone was likely to stumble onto the actual transfer date and time.

Rumor had it that Jazzy Villalobos and the rest of the DiLoKi leadership were in concert with the Outfit and had already selected a suicide killer who would get Candelario, knowing full well it would cost him his own life in the process.

"Some things you can control," Boone told Haeley. "Some things you cannot."

"Do you have to be there when he's transferred?"

"I wouldn't have it any other way. He's my guy. I'll be there for him."

"And if someone comes after him?"

"I'll do whatever I have to to protect him."

24
OFFICER DOWN

Fletcher Galloway, working with the U.S. Attorney in planning to move Pascual Candelario to the court where he would testify in secret before the grand jury, decided that the safest way would be to do it in the middle of the night without fanfare. Test runs were made via typical exit routes from the penthouse through the bowels of the high-rise, but when the time came, Boone Drake and four undercover cops merely went directly to PC's door and ushered him out.

At two in the morning, they took a service elevator to the basement garage, then, just to be sure, backtracked and went through a first-floor banquet kitchen. Finally they made their way to the garage from another direction and headed for the unmarked van.

As they passed a lone security guard, one of dozens Boone had seen over several days at the condo tower, he gave the man a quick once-over to be certain he was armed only with a nightstick, handcuffs, a flashlight, and a can of Mace.

But something caught Boone's eye. Tucked up under his uniform cap were cornrow curls. Boone squinted, thinking. The rest of the security guards in uniform seemed to have a dress and hair code similar to the Chicago PD's.

As the group passed the guard and approached the van, Boone felt compelled to glance back to where Cornrows had seemed to lazily watch them. The man was in full crouch and reaching behind his back. Taking no chances, Boone bellowed, "Gun!" before he even saw it, and moved between the phony guard and Candelario.

His instinct was right. The man produced what looked like a .45-caliber Glock and squeezed off one deafening round from about fifteen feet away. The slug hammered into Boone just below his left clavicle and knocked him to the concrete floor. He could feel something shatter — whether it was bone or bullet he did not know — and immediately felt his left lung collapse. As he lay there sucking wind, he realized what he had just seen.

Before the impostor could get off even a second shot, two of the officers had wheeled around and emptied their service revolvers into him while the other two hustled Pascual into the van. One officer screamed at the driver, telling him where to take PC and to call for an ambulance.

The other was on his radio, shouting, "Ten-one! Ten-one! Ten-one!" and reporting their position. Within seconds, dozens of squads screeched onto the scene.

Boone lay there knowing Pascual was safe and that every Chicago cop in the vicinity would respond to a 10-1, one of the few number codes the department used. 10-4 served its universal purpose. 10-1 was a distress call asking for all available manpower.

Had bone or bullet fragments done more than nick a lung? Boone tried to control his breathing, but he felt his pulse racing and was aware of a widening pool of blood beneath him. The shooter was clearly dead, and as the officers bent over Boone, trying to reassure him and keep him comfortable, one was tearing off his own shirt to press it into the gaping wound. The other paled looking at Boone's injury.

Boone felt himself go woozy and fought not to lose consciousness. He was afraid of going into shock before the ambulance arrived. "Suicide shooter?" he rasped, trying to keep his mind on the issue at hand.

"Shut up and stay with me, Drake," one officer said.

"Had to be an inside job," Boone said. "Who would have known what route we were gonna take?"

And he felt himself drifting, drifting.

Boone saw a kaleidoscope of images over the next several minutes. Jack Keller and Pete Wade pushing the others aside and talking to him. He could not respond, did not understand. Now emergency medical technicians probing, testing, feeling. An injection. Floating. Now roughly transferred to a gurney and slid into the back of the ambulance.

Moving from the warmth of the vehicle seemingly seconds later to the frigid air on the way into the emergency room at John H. Stroger Jr. Hospital of Cook County. Lights flying by overhead. In triage, doctors and nurses working feverishly, trying to talk to him, using his name. "Breathing trouble. Collapsed lung. Other damage? Surgery . . ."

Being bathed for an operation, anesthetic drip, the sweet relief of unconsciousness.

EPILOGUE

Boone awoke midmorning, oxygen in his nostrils, the back of his throat ravaged by what must have been forced down it for surgery, screaming pain in the shoulder. He was exhausted and achy all over, and his mouth felt cottony.

At least he had lost the panicky, no-breath sensation. As he squinted against the sun, Boone slowly pieced together what had happened. He tried to talk and produced only a gurgle of gibberish.

"He's waking up."

"Nurse!"

"Get Keller in here. He wanted to know when —"

Keller and a nurse arrived at the same time. "You comfortable, Mr. Drake?" she said.

Boone shrugged and winced at what that did to his shoulder.

"We can increase that drip. Chief Keller,

467

he should be able to hear you."

Jack leaned close as she moved out of the way and finagled with the tubes and machines. "You got questions?"

Boone nodded. "PC," he managed.

"Safe. And very grateful to you."

Boone lifted his right hand and waved off the compliment. "Everybody else?"

"Nobody else hurt. And you're going to be fine. Lucky. Bullet fragments reached but didn't damage your heart. That shoulder's gonna have to be rebuilt."

"We got a traitor?"

Jack whispered, "That or a real smart gangbanger. He either got lucky or he was tipped off. Could have been a lot worse. We'll talk more later. Your pastor friend is coming this afternoon. But they tell me rest is best. That morphine kicking in?"

Boone nodded, eyes heavy.

When Boone awoke again, it was after noon, and while he heard voices in the hall and a painful turn of the head told him officers crowded the area, the room was empty. "Hungry," he said, but his eyes fell shut again before he could make himself heard.

Boone had no idea how much later it was when he felt a cold washcloth bathing his face. Then a small sponge full of ice water spun over his tongue, refreshing his mouth. He forced his eyes open to tell the nurse he needed food, but the face before him was no nurse's.

"Haeley," he said. "My breath must be horrible."

"Not anymore," she said, clearly forcing what looked like a brave smile. Her eyes were red. "Boone, what have you done to yourself?"

"Well, I didn't do it. Everybody agree it was an inside job?"

He could tell from her look that they did. But she said, "You just worry about getting better."

He nodded. "Hungry."

"I'll bet you are. I'll tell the nurse, but first I want to give you some incentive."

"Incent — ?"

"To get better."

She took his good hand in hers and gripped it warmly, then leaned close to his face. "Come back to me, love," she said.

"What'd you call me?" he mumbled.

"You heard me," she said, then kissed him on the mouth.